KATE ELLIS

Watching the Ghosts

PIATKUS

First published in Great Britain and the US in 2012 by Crème de la Crime,
An imprint of Severn House Publishers Ltd
This paperback edition published in Great Britain in 2024 by Piatkus

1 3 5 7 9 10 8 6 4 2

A CIP catalogue record for this book
is available from the British Library.

ISBN 978-0-349-44095-8

Typeset by Palimpsest Book Production Ltd., Falkirk, Stirlingshire, Scotland
Printed and bound in Great Britain by Clays Ltd, Elcograf S.p.A.

Papers used by Piatkus are from well-managed forests
and other responsible sources.

Piatkus
An imprint of
Little, Brown Book Group
Carmelite House
50 Victoria Embankment
London EC4Y 0DZ

An Hachette UK Company
www.hachette.co.uk

www.littlebrown.co.uk

ONE

Tick tock. The thing had eyes. And it was watching her. It stood in the corner, taller than a man, and its deep insistent voice boomed out across the silent room – tick tock. The painted eyes swivelled from side to side as it beat away the time. Tick tock, tick tock.

It had a face, round and pallid, and its smiling lips were half parted to reveal a painted planetary scene which changed with the phases of the moon. But the strangest thing was those moving eyes that watched her and rejoiced in her fear.

Lydia's limbs were paralysed and she knew there was no escape from the horror to come. Tick tock, tick tock, tick tock. She could smell him now; a strange hospital smell, clean and threatening. She knew he would take her by the hand and lead her from the room and she knew the hand that held hers would be cold and clammy like a dead man's. Then she would glide down the stairs like a phantom towards that open door, towards the rectangle of bright light. And the clock with its tall, dark, oak case would follow her. Tick tock, tick tock. He was coming . . . and he was coming for her.

Now he had vanished but there was no way she could stop herself moving towards the door. She anticipated the horror she would witness when she passed beyond the light and she tried to scream. But no noise emerged. Tick tock, tick tock. The clock was still there watching as she inhaled the whiff of burning flesh and the metallic scent of blood.

Suddenly her eyes opened and she could see the grey dawn light seeping in through the blinds. But for a few moments she lay sweat soaked and shaking, hovering between nightmare and reality.

She forced herself upright and flicked on the bedside light, taking deep, calming breaths. It was only a dream but it had been disturbing her sleep every night since she'd moved into the new flat, leaving her jittery and exhausted.

And she knew that if it didn't stop soon, she'd have to do something about it.

Daisy loved the small park in the centre of Pickby so it was the least Melanie could do to take her there on the way home from school on the last day of term, the one day she'd managed to leave work early.

She'd told everyone in the office she was taking work home but that had been a half-truth; she hadn't told them that she'd felt a sudden urge to see Daisy so she'd rung the child minder to say she'd take care of school gate duty that day. The child minder had sounded surprised, which she thought said a lot. But why shouldn't she spend a little quality time – how she hated that term – with her daughter?

Daisy dumped her school bag at Melanie's feet and ran towards the swings with a six year old's enviable energy. Her fair curls bobbed as she ran, splashing in small puddles left over from yesterday's showers, while Melanie followed her, tottering on office high heels. The other mothers sitting around the fringe of the playground were wearing a summer uniform of jeans and T-shirts and Melanie felt out of place in her dark business suit and crisp white blouse. A couple of the women shot her suspicious glances as they gossiped on the wooden benches, and she felt like an intruder on their territory.

She picked up the bag, walked over to the swing and stood awkwardly as Daisy climbed on to the seat. The other mothers looked so at home there as they sat chatting, unaware of her need for some social contact, however slight. A smile, a comment on the improving weather. Anything would have been welcome.

'Push me, mummy.' Daisy was sitting on the swing, jiggling her legs impatiently and Melanie forced out a *mummy* smile – the kind she had always imagined she'd give her children in the days when motherhood had been a vague future notion.

But as she positioned herself behind the swing her mobile phone rang. 'Just a minute, darling,' she said in saccharine tones.

But children have an instinct for when they're being fobbed off. As Melanie answered the call Daisy slipped off the swing and ran off in the direction of the climbing frame – a large contraption of wood and ropes that, if she hadn't been so preoccupied, Melanie would have considered too challenging for a slightly built six year old like Daisy. But it was a call from one of her senior partners so Melanie had no choice but to answer and watch helplessly as her daughter ascended the ladder and vanished into the house-like structure six feet off the rubber-matted ground. She held her breath, her mind half on the phone call and half on Daisy. She was out of sight now but the senior partner – a pompous man who loved the sound of his own voice – was droning on about some meeting scheduled for the next day. Melanie attempted to make intelligent and professional-sounding interjections, trying to suppress the mother and bring the solicitor to the fore, but all the time her eyes were searching for Daisy, wishing she wasn't wearing the dull, navy-blue uniform that made her so hard to spot in the shadows.

She walked round to the other side of the climbing frame, hoping for a glimpse of her daughter, aware that her replies to the senior partner's questions were becoming more absent-minded.

But it was all right. Daisy was there, smiling and waving from the unglazed window of the play house and Melanie felt as if a weight had been lifted from her heart as she waved back. When the little face disappeared from the window, she turned her back. Daisy was safe and it was time she concentrated on work.

Holding the phone tight to her ear, she stared out across the park. It was filling up now as people on their way home from work mingled with those strolling at a more leisurely pace with children, lovers or dogs in tow. At last the senior partner was saying goodbye and it was with considerable relief that Melanie pressed the key to end the call.

She slipped the phone back in her handbag and when she turned she saw a man walking purposefully towards her, his eyes fixed on hers. She looked round, searching for Daisy. But there was no sign of her.

He was a few yards away now, just outside the playground, his dog straining on the leash as though it was anxious to reach her. It was a big dog – a Boxer possibly, although she didn't know much about dog breeds – but it looked reasonably friendly.

'I see you've knocked off work early,' he called across to her, his thick lips curling up in a smile. He was short and wiry but there was a suggestion of strength in his tattooed arms. He wore shorts, revealing a pair of pale and hirsute legs and a sleeveless T-shirt of the kind she had once heard referred to as a 'wife beater'. She wondered if he had a wife to beat – but then she realized she knew very little about Chris Torridge apart from what he'd told her during their meetings in her office.

'Have you made any progress?' he asked and it struck Melanie, not for the first time, that his deep and cultured voice belied his appearance. 'You do remember, don't you? Dorothy Watts?'

Melanie walked over to him. This wasn't the sort of conversation you could hold from a distance. She resented the note of reproach in his voice, as though he was accusing her of neglecting her duties. She remembered, all right. Discovering what had become of Dorothy Watts was one of her more interesting cases – an intriguing change from the usual round of wills and conveyancing – and she had put a good deal of effort into finding witnesses and uncovering the truth. 'Of course I remember, Mr Torridge. I've made some progress since our last meeting. In fact I think I've made a breakthrough. If you'd like to make an appointment . . .'

'Can't you tell me now?'

'The file's back at the office. Sorry.' She turned her head to look for Daisy but again, she was nowhere to be seen. 'Look, I've got to go. I'll speak to you soon.'

She saw him hesitate and when the dog began to bark she felt like thanking the creature for coming to her rescue. Without another word Torridge walked away, tugged by the dog, and she stood for a few moments, watching as he vanished into the trees that separated the park from the suburban gardens beyond.

She looked at her watch. It was time she got home. She picked up the school bag which she'd dumped on the ground when she answered the phone and went in search of her daughter.

She hurried to the heart of the playground, calling Daisy's name softly, one eye on the group of gossiping mothers who seemed to be absorbed in their own affairs. She couldn't see Daisy on the climbing frame or on the swings and as her search became more frantic panic began to well up inside her, making her heart thud and her legs feel like jelly. After a while, all dignity and reticence abandoned, she rushed up to the group of mothers who looked up at her as if they resented her intrusion into their conversation.

'Have you seen a little girl? Six years old, fair curly hair, wearing a navy-blue school uniform?'

The mothers all shook their heads but a couple of them, suddenly sympathetic, offered to help her look and they shouted questions across to their own children who answered with bored shrugs. One of the women assured her that they'd seen no lone males inside the playground in the last half hour or so. These days any lone male in the vicinity of a playground without a child in tow triggered all sorts of alarm bells in the maternal head.

The thought that Daisy might have wandered off while she'd been talking on the phone or being questioned by Chris Torridge brought on pangs of guilt. How could she have turned her back like that and left the confines of the playground? How could she have let her precious Daisy out of her sight?

The mothers quickly organized themselves into some sort of search party and, while some stayed to keep a close eye on their own offspring, they fanned out, calling Daisy's name and accosting passers-by to ask if they'd seen a child matching her description while Melanie stood by the climbing frame, paralysed and feeling strangely detached from the situation. She felt as though she was a spectator watching a scene of immense horror and all she could do was stand there and stare ahead, useless and powerless, scanning the faces of any children in view in the hope that one of them would be Daisy. She couldn't pray and she couldn't cry as the numbness took hold. Daisy. All she wanted was to see her running across the grass towards her.

When she spotted a fair-haired child of around Daisy's height, her hopes were raised for a second. But despair took hold as soon as she realized the resemblance was slight. Daisy was nowhere to be seen.

Warm tears of frustration trickled down her cheeks as one of the park bench mothers, a plump woman with cropped hair, put a comforting arm around her shoulders and led her to the bench. 'You're in shock, love. If we don't find her in the next few minutes we'll call the police. Try not to worry, eh.' Her last words didn't sound convincing. She could hear the anxiety in the woman's voice.

Melanie nodded and as mucous began to drip from her nose she fumbled in her bag for a tissue. As soon as the bag was open her phone rang, loud and insistent. She stared at it, unable to move.

'You should answer it,' her new ally said. 'It might be news. She might have found her way back home.'

Melanie's hand was shaking as she pressed the key and held the phone to her ear. She could hardly utter the word 'hello' but it didn't matter because Jack didn't wait for her to speak.

'I've had a call,' he said. 'Someone's got Daisy.'

'I only took my eyes off her for a few seconds. I . . .'

'Shut up and listen.' Jack sounded angry. More than angry . . . furious. 'They want money or they say we'll never see her again. They say they're going to call later.'

Melanie's hands, suddenly clumsy, refused to obey her panicked brain and she dropped the phone, sending it clattering down to the cold, unforgiving ground.

TWO

Perhaps it was a good thing that Eborby's Tourist Office was always busy. When you're busy you don't have time to think and brood and although the nightmare had broken her sleep, Lydia hadn't felt too bad at work.

She enjoyed working in the elegant eighteenth-century building near the cathedral and she'd managed to fix a smile to her face as she'd handed out the glossy leaflets advertising Eborby's many tourist attractions and looked up the times of sightseeing buses and river cruises. But when she'd visited the little staff cloakroom and looked in the mirror above the sink, she'd seen dark smudges of blue-black beneath her eyes.

Even in her busiest moments she could never quite banish the memory of that clock with its watchful, swivelling eyes. She'd had that same dream so many times that she'd begun to wonder whether it was some sort of warning. Or perhaps some terrible suppressed memory – she'd read about such things in magazines but had never quite believed them.

At five thirty the working day was over and Lydia headed towards Boothgate, passing the Eborby Playhouse, an old theatre with a recently added glass frontage. The red and black posters outside announced that the latest production was called simply *Mary*. It had received good reviews and she'd read in the publicity leaflets in the rack at the Tourist Information Centre that the play had been inspired by the building now known as Boothgate House – the building where she lived – so maybe one day she'd make the effort to see it . . . even though the subject matter didn't really appeal.

The July evening was too warm for the cardigan she'd stuffed into her bag that morning – just in case – and she felt somehow lighter and more optimistic as she made her way home. She passed the shops and pubs at the city end of the street and soon she reached Boothgate's rows of elegant Georgian houses, many now converted into offices. She paused to look in an estate agent's window, purely out of habit, before waiting at the pedestrian crossing for the lights to change and interrupt the stream of cars flowing out of the city down the straight Roman road at the end of the working day.

Then she carried on walking and soon Boothgate House came into view. It was an impressive eighteenth-century building of elegant proportions set well back from the main road behind an expanse of lawn and from the street it had the look of some urban stately home. Perhaps that's why she'd found it so attractive when she'd come to view the new apartment with its bright modern kitchen, its high ceilings, its long sash windows and its reasonable price tag. But now she knew that the place had a different, grimmer, history.

At one time it had been known as Havenby Hall and there had been a forbidding seven-foot wall around the grounds, now reduced to half that height by the developers. Once its stone had been blackened by Eborby's myriad smoking chimneys but now the wall and the building had been sandblasted to an unthreatening pale gold. Havenby Hall had begun life as a charitable foundation, an asylum for lunatics and the mentally disordered, renowned in the nineteenth century for its enlightened and experimental treatments in an age when such patients were rarely treated with understanding or kindness.

Later in its history it had been taken over by a private trust as a hospital for the treatment of various mental conditions, chronic and acute. Then in the 1960s one section had been set aside as a secure unit for the more serious cases, the cases judged a danger to the patient – or others – and, as a consequence, in its last days Havenby Hall had acquired a fearful reputation in the town. The hospital had closed in 1981 and had been derelict for years before the developer, Patrick Creeny, had gutted and renovated it beyond recognition. Only one wing round the back lay untouched now. But she had been assured that it was only a matter of time before that too was transformed from ruined utility to twenty-first-century luxury.

Lydia slipped down the side road and through the decorative iron gate that had replaced its secure and solid predecessor before making for the grand front door.

She let herself in and passed the grand central staircase, the sort that might conjure childhood fantasies of being a princess – Cinderella at the ball maybe. But she was just past thirty-two – far too old for such things.

When the door of her flat came into view she readied her key for the lock. It was a handsome mahogany door, one of the originals. The developer had made a great thing of retaining some of the more attractive original features. To date only half the flats had been finished and, of them, only half had been sold. She assumed it was something to do with the recession. But there were times when she wondered whether it was something else. Maybe it was the building's past history and the accompanying taint of madness that put potential buyers off.

She was about to open the door when the sound of a voice saying hello made her swing round. The woman who stood there was large but solidly built rather than fat. She wore a red T-shirt with faint sweat patches under the arms and a flared floral skirt which emphasized the dimensions of her hips. Her long hair was mousy and pulled back into a pony tail and although her chin merged into her neck, her skin was clear and flawless. It was difficult to guess her age, which could have been anything between thirty-five and fifty.

'Lovely day.' The woman smiled, showing a row of perfect teeth.

Lydia responded with a bland remark about the weather. It was good to have a friendly neighbour and Beverley was more than happy to take in parcels and keep a spare key in case of emergencies.

'How's your mum?' she asked. Beverley had moved up to Eborby from the Midlands with her frail, elderly mother a few months ago. Both of them had visited Eborby and liked it so they'd made the decision to sell up and relocate when Beverley gave up her job in her local council offices to care for her mother full time. Lydia considered this a noble sacrifice, and one that she didn't think she herself would be capable of making.

'She has her good days and her bad days. You know how it is,' she said. Her voice was high pitched, almost girlish.

Lydia nodded sympathetically and turned to put her key in the lock.

'I had a visitor before.' The way Beverley said the words, as though she was harbouring some delicious secret, made Lydia turn back. She sensed gossip. And, knowing her empty flat was waiting for her on the other side of that door, a bit of gossip was just what she felt like at that moment. Besides, she felt that Beverley must be lonely so she'd also be doing a service to a fellow human being.

'A man called. He left his card with me. Hang on a moment.' Beverley disappeared through her flat door which she'd left ajar. Lydia had always been struck by the way she moved so gracefully for someone of her build. She returned after a few seconds and handed Lydia a small white business card.

Lydia studied it. 'Dr Karl Dremmer. Eborby University, Department of Psychology. Researcher in Parapsychology and Paranormal Phenomena.'

'He asked me if I'd noticed anything strange about this building,' said Beverley.

'What did you tell him?'

'I told him that, apart from that problem with the drains when we first moved in everything's been fine.'

Suddenly Lydia was grateful for Beverley's lack of imagination. But their conversation had given her a small, nagging feeling that something wasn't right; that her dream had somehow been triggered by something in this place that was impossible to explain.

'He said one of the builders contacted him. Said things had been happening.'

'What sort of things?'

'I don't know.' Beverley's open face suddenly clouded. 'I'd better get back to Mother.'

As Lydia let herself into her flat and made for the kitchen, she found the news that she wasn't the only one who'd sensed something amiss in that place strangely comforting.

'When did he say he'd call back?'

'He didn't specify a time. I don't even know whether it was

a he. The voice was put through one of those machines . . . sounded like a robot.'

The words sent a shudder through Melanie's heart as she paced the polished wooden floorboards. The prospect of sitting down on the soft leather sofa seemed unbearable. To sit would seem as if she was admitting defeat . . . as if she was doing nothing. She stopped moving and looked Jack in the face. He appeared to be mildly concerned but not worried like she was. Not frantic, primitive worried. But Daisy wasn't his own flesh and blood. She was the child of Melanie's first, ill-advised marriage and Jack had had to accept her as part of the package.

She kept replaying the scene at the park in her head. The way she'd lied to the other mothers when she'd told them that Daisy had found her way home. But if they had scented the truth, they'd have insisted on calling the police immediately. And the last thing she'd wanted was a patrol car turning up, sirens blazing and making whoever had Daisy panic. A frightened criminal is a dangerous criminal and under no circumstances was she going to gamble with Daisy's safety.

She tried desperately to recall every detail of the scene, cursing that call from the senior partner, cursing Chris Torridge and his presumption that he could take up her private time with what was really a work matter, although she did find the case intriguing. If she hadn't been distracted, if she'd been watching Daisy as she should have been, this nightmare wouldn't be happening. The mothers had been quite adamant that no lone man had approached the playground – in the current climate of suspicion they would have noticed – which left the possibility that the abductor was a woman; someone whose presence created no suspicion. Jack had thought that the caller might have been a woman. But kidnapping didn't seem like a woman's crime somehow. Unless the woman was the accomplice. Unless Daisy had been taken by two abductors.

Melanie stared at the phone on the sideboard, willing it to ring. She needed to know Daisy was safe. She needed to know what she had to do to get her back.

Suddenly she felt out of her depth. She needed help. She needed someone to tell her what to do . . . and her instincts told her that Jack was hardly going to be a tower of strength.

'We can't cope with this on our own.' She hesitated. 'I've been considering all our options and I think we have to tell the police.'

'They told us not to. I'm surprised you'd even think of risking Daisy's life.'

His words annoyed her . . . the implication that she didn't care. 'I wasn't thinking of calling nine nine nine. We need to go about it discreetly. I know someone who might be able to help . . . someone I can approach unofficially. She'll know what to do. She'll be used to dealing with things like this.'

'They knew where Daisy would be when they took her so they're probably watching us. We mustn't take any risks.'

'But I need some advice . . . some support.'

Jack put a tentative arm around her shoulder but she shook it off. She saw the look of annoyance on his face but she didn't care; she wanted to hit out at someone – to make someone suffer the way she was suffering. His sin was to argue with her reasoning . . . and she felt a strong desire to punish him for it.

The moment was broken by the insistent bleating of the telephone and the shock of the sudden noise breaking through the awkward silence made Melanie jump.

'Do you want me to answer it?'

She nodded. She knew she was in no state to deal with anything resembling a negotiation. She knew she would just scream and plead like a hysterical child. Jack picked up the receiver and said hello, casually, as though he was expecting to talk to a friend or colleague.

He appeared to be listening for what seemed like an age and Melanie watched him, hands clenched and heartbeat rapid, lurching between hope and despair, fighting the urge to grab the phone. She heard him asking when. Then he asked where. Then she heard him say OK before he put the receiver down.

'What did they say?' She clawed at the sleeve of his striped shirt, scrabbling for information.

'She's fine. They want ten grand in cash and they're going to call tomorrow to tell us where to leave it. They say Daisy will be returned as soon as they've got the money.'

'How? How are they going to bring her back?' She tightened her grip on his arm and he winced.

'They didn't say. Look, we've got to get hold of the cash first. I'll arrange it first thing in the morning.'

'Can't you do it sooner?'

'They won't call back till tomorrow.'

'Did they let you talk to her?'

'No but . . .'

She fought an impulse to punch him, to shake him out of his complacency. 'Then how do we know she's OK?'

'They said she was.'

'You should have insisted on speaking to her. If I'd answered I would have . . .'

'Well you can speak to them next time then.' He almost spat out the words as if he was getting fed up with the whole situation.

But Melanie didn't care how he felt. She wanted Daisy back. 'I'll have to tell Paul,' she said.

'You always said he was a waste of space. What was it you called him . . . a doped-up drop out? I think the fewer people we involve the better.'

'He's her father. He's got a right to know.'

'He'll be stoned. He can't be trusted.'

But she wasn't listening. 'Why did they pick on us? We're not millionaires. Why Daisy?'

Jack gave a shrug. 'It could be someone who knows us.' He paused. 'One of your clients maybe.'

She shook her head, fighting back tears and a vague, guilty feeling that maybe he could be right. 'No way. I don't deal with criminals. Why are you trying to shift the blame on to me?' She could feel herself losing what little self-control she had left.

'I'm not. It's just that architects don't usually encounter the criminal classes in the course of their work. Solicitors do.'

'You're always saying that some of the developers you deal with are pretty dodgy.'

'They might cut corners but . . .' Jack hesitated. 'Are you sure there's nobody you can think of who . . .?'

'Of course I'm sure.' She barked the words. She wasn't

going to let him off the hook. She wasn't going to be the guilty one. 'What about the bloke behind the Boothgate House development? Patrick Creeny.'

'Patrick's all right.'

'You said he was in financial difficulties.'

'Just cash-flow problems, that's all. Half the flats are unsold and he's waiting for funds to start the second phase of the development. When things pick up . . . Anyway, it's one thing to delay payments to creditors, but kidnapping . . .' He walked over to the cupboard in the corner and opened the door. 'I need a drink,' he said as he took a bottle of single malt and a glass from the depths of the cupboard. 'Want one?'

Melanie didn't reply. She needed to keep a clear head. She watched as he poured the golden liquid into the glass and took a long sip. He was staring at the model on top of the cupboard. It had originally been in his office at the other end of the house but he'd moved it to the drawing room when he'd invited Patrick Creeny round for a celebratory drink and it had remained there ever since. On that occasion the decision had been made to change the name of the development from 'Havenby Hall' to 'Boothgate House'. Jack, as a native of Eborby had managed to persuade Creeny that any mention of Havenby Hall would remind people of the building's original function as an asylum for the insane. They needed, he said, to blot out the past. The politicians called it spin but it was really just a matter of perception.

Melanie went to the phone and dialled 1471 but the electronic voice told her that the caller had withheld their number. This was what she'd expected but she'd convinced herself that, in the drama of the moment, there was a chance that the kidnapper would have forgotten. She stood with the receiver in her hand for a while before making a decision.

'I'm calling Paul,' she said. 'He has a right to know.'

Before Jack could raise any further objection, she'd pressed the keys. Jack sat there watching and she could sense his hostility as the phone rang out at the other end.

THREE

When Jack felt he couldn't stand the strain any longer, he'd retreated to his office with the single malt. Melanie was glad of the solitude for once. She needed to think.

Emily Thwaite had been on her mind since it had happened. She'd met her a few times at PTA meetings and school functions and, if it weren't for this tentative acquaintance, she'd have obeyed the kidnapper's orders about not contacting the police without question. But she needed to confide in someone. She had to know the right thing to do. She couldn't afford to make mistakes.

She knew Emily was a Detective Chief Inspector. When she'd found out about her job she'd been rather surprised because she seemed the motherly type, a little overweight with wavy fair hair and freckles. She had three children at the school and she looked remarkably ordinary for a woman who spent her working days investigating murder and robbery. She also looked the type of woman who could be trusted to be discreet when dealing with a sensitive matter like a kidnapping.

She made a search of the phone directory before picking up the telephone.

They called him The Builder.

Emily knew how the press loved to invent names for criminals whose work followed any sort of pattern. In her opinion, this only encouraged them by giving their sordid crimes a spurious glamour. And she saw nothing glamorous about breaking into lone women's houses and barricading the front door with piles of furniture before pinching cash and their most intimate items of underwear and escaping through a back door or window.

She looked up and saw that DI Joe Plantagenet had just

returned to the office. He'd been interviewing The Builder's latest victim and he looked serious, as if he'd found the experience disturbing. When she'd first arrived in Eborby, she'd been struck by his black hair, blue eyes and pale, freckled complexion inherited from his Irish mother. Since that time a few grey hairs had appeared at his temples; with the cases they'd had to deal with over the past couple of years, she was surprised that he didn't have more. He was good looking and from time to time Jeff had made tentative jokes about him when she was working late, almost as if he was seeking some kind of reassurance that Joe wasn't after her slightly overweight body. At first she'd blushed and protested too much but now she didn't even bother to comment. Joe was a colleague, that's all, and she had no time to bother about Jeff's insecurities.

She stood up, curious to know whether he'd discovered anything useful, anything that might help bring the bastard to justice. But as she moved towards the door the phone on her desk began to ring so she retraced her steps and picked up the receiver.

The woman on the other end of the line introduced herself as Melanie Hawkes and when she said they'd met at her children's school it took Emily a few moments to place her. Then she remembered: a smartly dressed woman of medium height, slim to the point of emaciation with shoulder-length brown hair and a slightly receding chin. She also recalled Melanie's husband, who occasionally came to meetings with her; he was in his forties with a permanent tan, well-cut hair and expensively casual clothes, the type who emanated smooth prosperity from every pore. Melanie Hawkes was nothing more than a passing acquaintance but the urgency in her voice intrigued her. So much so that she agreed to meet her the next day.

The Builder had been watching the house. He always watched before he acted.

It was only a day since his last intrusion but he saw no reason to wait. Not when it was all going so well. Everything was planned down to the last detail as usual. He'd toyed with the idea of changing his method but he knew that would take courage. Courage to do it while they were at home; courage to trap them there inside their safe refuge so they couldn't escape him.

Often at night he lay awake, imagining what it would be like to have them at his mercy, to look into their pleading eyes and feel the power he'd have over their life . . . and maybe their death.

Perhaps one day he'd find out. One day very soon.

FOUR

Sunlight was streaming through the thin blinds at the bedroom window and Joe opened his eyes to look at the clock on the bedside table. It was time to get up but he closed his eyes again. He hadn't managed to drop off to sleep until the early hours of the morning because the old bullet wound in his shoulder had started throbbing. It sometimes happened when he felt under pressure at work and, with The Builder stepping up his activities, he knew they had to catch the man fast before things escalated and somebody got hurt.

He showered and dressed in record time and grabbed a slice of toast before setting off for work.

Walking down Gallowgate, he saw a young man slumped against the doorway of a discount shop, mousy haired and pale as a ghost with a mongrel lying loyally by his side. Joe stopped and squatted down in front of the lad who watched him with wary eyes as the dog stood up, ears pricked, suddenly alert.

'You OK, mate?' Joe asked. He could see the boy's eyes were sunken and dark rimmed.

'Have you got a quid for a cup of tea?' he said in a low whine.

Joe delved in his pocket and pulled out a ten pound note. The boy's eyes lit up.

'There's a shelter in Tarngate . . . near the superstore. Promise me you'll go down there. They'll give you a bed and a hot meal.'

The boy nodded and stretched out his hand eagerly for the money. Joe handed it over, knowing he was taking a gamble: it might be used for food and shelter but on the other hand it might buy drugs or booze. But he couldn't pass by and do nothing. Recently he'd been toying with the possibility of helping out occasionally at the shelter run by the cathedral. Work had got in the way as usual but a voice inside him insisted that he should make more effort. Maybe one day.

He left the boy, glancing over his shoulder to see that he hadn't shifted, and as he walked away down the street his phone rang.

It was the station. A woman had returned home earlier that morning after spending the night with a friend, only to find that her front door was blocked with furniture.

The Builder had paid another house call.

Lydia had heard crying in the night. Distant heartbreaking sobs. She knew Beverley's mother often became distressed in the night. But when she'd passed Beverley in the corridor, she made no mention of it as they exchanged the usual empty pleasantries. She probably found the subject embarrassing and the truth was that she herself found the thought of the confused and frightened old lady in mental distress uncomfortable.

Last night she'd met her old friend Amy for a drink. Amy worked in the box office at the Playhouse and Lydia had asked about the latest play, *Mary*. According to Amy it was by a new writer and concerned the eponymous young woman who had been locked up in a mental hospital in the 1950s purely for offending against the morals of the day. From Amy's description, it didn't sound the sort of thing she'd be able to recommend to visiting tourists as a fun night out.

The sun was already burning through the high white clouds as she walked to work down the wide street towards Boothgate Bar, the old city gate which stood like a truncated castle, guarding Eborby's ancient centre as it had done for centuries. She passed beneath the gate, glancing upwards at the massive slots where a wooden portcullis had once been suspended to keep the city safe from the attentions of hostile armies. She had plenty of time so she decided to take a quick detour down one of the shopping streets that lay beyond the city walls.

It was only eight forty-five in the morning so the shops were still shut and window shopping was her only option. When she reached the small side street off Pottergate where the antique shops congregated, she moved from one shop to the next, checking her watch at regular intervals, putting her face close to the windows and shielding her eyes so that she could see inside. There were a few small items to tempt her into a return visit in her lunch hour: a small nineteenth century bedside cupboard – she'd been looking for one for ages; a pretty bracelet which she could buy with her birthday money; and a cheerful floral jug made by a Clarice Cliff wannabe. Some friends who favoured the more modern look turned their noses up at her treasures. But her father had been an antique dealer and she liked to think she had a good eye for such things.

She reached the last shop in the row, a small establishment with dusty windows. Inside she could see bare, splintery floor-boards and dusty furniture piled in inaccessible heaps. Then she spotted it standing at the back of the shop, half hidden by a massive oak corner cupboard.

As she peered through the glass she could make out its painted eyes and its round, pallid face. She could even see the mouth half open to reveal something inside that she knew would be a group of painted planets.

It was the clock of her nightmares. She'd found it at last.

Melanie called into work to say she'd be late but she wasn't sure whether she'd be in any fit state to go at all. She hadn't eaten anything that morning, not even her usual single slice of toast topped with a smear of honey. The very silence of the place was a constant reminder of Daisy's absence. And she blamed herself for what had happened. If she hadn't been distracted. If she hadn't turned her back to concentrate on her phone call. At that moment her world was full of regrets.

When she'd called Emily Thwaite the night before she hadn't mentioned why she wanted to meet her and the woman had sounded a little impatient, as though she felt Melanie was wasting her precious time. Then, as she'd lain awake that night in the spare room, she'd kept visualizing Daisy, frightened and sobbing in some dank cellar and she wondered whether she'd done the right thing. Would they know she'd met Emily? Was she risking Daisy's safety?

Emily had agreed to meet her at half twelve at the National Trust tea rooms near the cathedral, well away from Eborby Police Headquarters where she worked. She'd suggested this as it felt like neutral ground and she was grateful that Emily hadn't questioned the arrangement.

Melanie sat at the breakfast table in their large square kitchen with its hand-painted units and glossy granite worktops, playing absent-mindedly with her untouched toast while Jack opened the morning post: bills as usual; it always seemed to be bills these days. He looked over at her and she could sense his irritation. He had enough problems without all this.

'What time are you getting the money?'

'It's all in hand. If they call just keep calm and write down any instructions they give you.'

'I will.' The words were said as solemnly as a marriage vow.

'I've got to make a call.'

She half stood, her eyes anxious. 'About . . .?'

He didn't answer. He disappeared into his office and when he returned to the kitchen she was still sitting there, staring at her untouched breakfast.

'You'd better get dressed,' he said. 'We've got to be ready for anything.'

'What do you mean?' she asked, trying to control the panic rising inside her.

'If they let Daisy go we'll have to be prepared to pick her up right away.'

Her eyes widened, bright with panic. 'They will give her back once they've got the money, won't they?'

'Why shouldn't they? They want the cash and I'm going to get it for them. I'd better go. I won't be long.' He walked over to her and gave her a half-hearted kiss on the top of the head, a kiss more out of habit than affection.

She didn't respond. All she could think of was Daisy and a wave of panic shot through her like a knife twisted in her heart.

In spite of the fine weather outside it wasn't a good day. Last night's reported burglary had followed precisely the same pattern as the others – as if the perpetrator was working to a set of unbreakable rules – and DCI Emily Thwaite was still no nearer identifying the man who had so far put five women through that frightening ordeal. She had come into the office early that morning to re-examine the case but, no matter how many times she read through the files, inspiration refused to come. She sat in her office hidden behind the paperwork on her desk and wished she was home enjoying the sunshine with Jeff and the children – sometimes she envied Jeff his teachers' holidays – but she knew she'd probably be stuck there in the stuffy CID office until dusk.

She looked at the watch Jeff had given her for her last birthday and saw that it was almost time to keep her appointment with Melanie Hawkes. She hardly knew Melanie and she'd been more than a little puzzled by her phone call. Why should a woman she'd only encountered before in passing at PTA events at her children's school want to meet her for lunch? She was hardly under the delusion that the woman was a friend so it had to be something to do with her work; something she'd probably have to direct to the appropriate department – tactfully, of course. She'd toyed with the idea of calling her and making some excuse to avoid their appointment but, after the morning she'd had, she needed to get away from the office for a while.

She stood up, opened the office door and looked around before walking over to Joe Plantagenet's desk. It was more untidy than her own – something she hadn't thought possible – heaped with paperwork arranged haphazardly around his flickering computer. He was sitting there, reading through witness statements and he looked up as she approached.

She pulled up a chair and sat down beside him. 'Anything new?' she asked casually, trying to hide the impatience she felt with their lack of progress. It was time they got this man. Joe looked tired, as though he'd slept badly. She was tempted to make some comment but she thought better of it.

Joe shrugged his shoulders. 'This latest burglary's exactly the same as the others. He's not only been careful, he's been lucky. Nobody's ever seen a thing.'

'You'd think someone would hear him shifting all that furniture around but he seems to be able to come and go as he pleases. It's almost as if we're dealing with a ghost.'

'He'll slip up sooner or later,' Joe said with a confidence

that Emily couldn't share. 'Dave's going out for sandwiches later. He's taking orders now if you want one.' He stood up and began to look around the office for the youngest detective constable who'd been volunteered for sandwich duty.

Emily put her hand on Joe's arm. 'Don't bother about me. I'm nipping out at lunchtime. By then I'll be glad of some fresh air. I won't be long.' She wasn't sure why she didn't mention her appointment with Melanie Hawkes. Perhaps it was because she had a bad feeling about it, although she wasn't quite sure why.

The phone had begun to ring at nine thirty precisely and Melanie had waited for a few moments before answering. Her hands were shaking. They'd been shaking ever since she'd found the bank statement.

They both had professional jobs and, as far as she knew, they'd always been solvent. However, in recent months her constant whirl of work and childcare meant that Jack had taken sole charge of all the financial stuff. But now she'd discovered they were overdrawn and small slivers of doubt began to worm their way into her head. Had he got into financial difficulties with his latest project . . . difficulties that had swallowed up her salary as well as Jack's earnings? He'd never mentioned it to her but now the thought flashed across her mind like a warning flare. What if there was no money for the kidnappers? What if she never saw Daisy again?

She'd breathed deeply, telling herself to keep calm, to concentrate. The notepad was there to take down instructions if necessary but when she picked up the pen lying beside it, she was trembling so much that she dropped it on the floor. The phone was still ringing and she knew she couldn't put it off any longer.

'Hello.'

'Am I speaking to Melanie Hawkes?'

'Who's that?' She tried to speak calmly and clearly but the words came out as a nervous squeak.

'I called your office to make an appointment but they said you might not be in today. I need to see you.'

She closed her eyes and tried to concentrate. 'Who is this?'

'Chris Torridge . . . it's about Dorothy Watts.' He suddenly sounded unsure of himself. 'You do remember?'

'How did you get this number?'

'I looked you up in the phone book,' he said as though he was answering a particularly stupid question.

This man had been there when Daisy had disappeared. And now he was phoning her at home, invading her life. 'Look, if you ring the office and make an appointment . . .' she said, trying her best to sound calm and reasonable, trying to keep the panic she felt out of her voice.

'I need to see you as soon as possible. Can we meet today?'

'Not today.'

'I can come to your house.'

'No,' she said quickly. The man knew her number from the phone book so, presumably, he knew her address too. She suddenly felt sick. 'I'll see you tomorrow . . . in the office. First thing in the morning if you like.' She put the phone down and felt hot tears stinging her eyes.

Then the phone rang again and this time it was the call she'd been waiting for. And the voice on the other end of the line told her in a threatening whisper that Daisy was safe but she needed to get the money together at once.

There'd be another call in half an hour. And then she'd receive her instructions.

FIVE

Jack's phone began to ring and when he lifted it to his ear and said hello, he heard Melanie's voice. She sounded breathless, as though she'd been running. Or maybe it was just panic.

'I've got to drop the money off this evening. They're calling back later to say where.'

He told her to take a deep breath and stay calm. He was on his way to get the money.

He walked through Singmass Close, past the small modern houses, built in jagged rows with overhanging windows like their medieval counterparts. It was a nice development in a central location and Jack only wished it had been one of his. The cobbles gave way to tarmac as he passed beneath another archway and walked the fifty yards to the Georgian town house with twin bay trees beside the open glossy black front door and *Creeny and Co.* etched on the glass inner door leading to the hallway. Patrick had always said that, whatever happened, it was vital to keep up the show of unostentatious prosperity. And this place was upmarket all right; tasteful, elegant and understated. It smelled of money and money was the one thing Jack needed at that moment.

He pushed open the glass door and found himself in the familiar open plan office. Here the walls were covered with pastel pictures of Creeny and Co's past developments; all old buildings, all renovated to high specification and in the best possible taste. A sleek PA, tall and slender with dark, glossy hair, looked up from her desk and smiled. 'Well hi. I wondered when you were going to . . .'

'Sorry, Yolanda. Is Patrick in? It's rather urgent.'

She picked up the telephone.

'Don't bother. I'll surprise him. I know the way.' He knew he had to act as though nothing was wrong so he forced himself to give her a knowing wink.

'Fancy a drink after work?' she said in a low voice.

'Sorry, not tonight. We'll fix something up soon, eh.'

Before she could reply he was through the door at the back of the office that led to Patrick Creeny's inner sanctum.

Creeny was sitting at his desk and he looked up as Jack entered, his only sign of surprise being a momentary raising of his eyebrows. He sat back, shielded by the massive bulk of the mahogany desk.

'Jack. I was meaning to get in touch. We've had a few more enquiries about Boothgate House. I reckon things are looking up. What can I do for you?'

Jack had intended to go in, all guns blazing, and demand his money but he knew that Creeny was too valuable as a business contact for him to irk him more than was necessary.

'That money you owe me, Patrick. I'm afraid something's come up and I need some of it as soon as possible.'

Patrick's expression gave nothing away. He was a big man in every way; forty-something with a shaved head and a nose bent in some past battle on the rugby field. Some thought him a gentle giant but during their business dealings Jack had seen another side to him. Patrick Creeny was ruthless when he needed to be. And his creditors usually had a long wait for their money. He felt his heart beating faster while he awaited the reply.

Patrick stood up, dwarfing the desk. He smiled with his mouth but his grey eyes remained cold. 'No problem, Jack. I was going to arrange a transfer this week.'

'I'd prefer cash . . . if that's OK.'

And when he came out fifteen minutes later, he was carrying a Tesco carrier bag stuffed with twenty-pound notes. No problem.

The sight of that clock had given Lydia more of a jolt than she'd expected.

Her instincts told her that she should forget about it. Leave well alone. But when her lunch break arrived at twelve o'clock, her natural curiosity made her forget the growls of hunger in her stomach as she made her way back to the shop through the tourist-packed streets. Lunch would have to wait.

The sign on the dusty door was turned to 'open' and the gloomy interior was illuminated by a single electric bulb dangling from the ceiling. It was hardly the sort of place to lure in the casual shopper. But she could see the clock there at the back, half hidden behind the heavy brown cupboard.

She was trying to summon the courage to go in when she saw a man emerge from a door at the rear of the shop. Somehow she had pictured the owner as some desiccated antique dealer with long white hair and a bow tie, but this man was in his early thirties with cropped fair hair and he wore jeans and a short-sleeved T-shirt which showed strong forearms tattooed with what appeared to be swallows on the wing. He walked over to the far corner of the shop and sat down at a desk blanketed with paperwork. She saw him pick up a ledger but after a few moments he looked up and stared straight at the window. And when he caught her eye she felt the blood rush to her cheeks.

She turned to walk away, to move on, buy some lunch and forget all about the clock. But something made her stop. What would be the harm in asking the question that had been on her mind since that morning? At least then she'd know if she was likely to have seen the thing before . . . if her nightmares arose from some terrible and long-buried memory.

Summoning all her courage, she pushed the door open and a bell jangled somewhere above her head. And when the man stood up to greet her she fought an impulse to make a swift exit.

'Hi,' he said. 'Feel free to look round. Are you interested in anything in particular?'

He was well spoken, probably public school, and he seemed out of place in such dingy surroundings. But his casual friendliness gave her new courage. And beside, there was something attractive about him, something that encouraged confidences.

'I was looking in the window this morning before you opened and I saw a clock.'

'Which particular clock are you interested in? We've got quite a few to choose from as you can see.' The new enthusiasm in the man's green eyes told her that he was anticipating a sale, possibly the first of the day.

She hadn't noticed before that the place was filled with clocks of various shapes, sizes and ages, none of them ticking and all of them veiled in a layer of dust.

'Sorry about the state of the place, by the way. The shop's been closed for a couple of weeks because my uncle's not been well. I just came in to catch up on the paperwork but if I can make a sale on the way . . .' He gave her a dazzling smile, showing a row of perfect teeth that seemed slightly too small for his mouth. 'My uncle's always had a thing about clocks,' he added. 'Quite the expert. Unlike me.'

She had the impression that he expected her to ask about his life but she thought it safer to keep things on a business-like footing. She had a gut feeling that she should keep her distance. But that was something she'd been doing since the break up of her marriage . . . and, besides, the presence of that clock, watching her from its shadowy hiding place with its painted eyes, made her uneasy.

'Sorry, I'm not here to buy,' she said. 'It's just that I'm sure I've seen this particular clock before and I wondered if you could tell me where it came from.'

She half expected his manner to change, for him to lose all interest once he knew he wasn't going to part her from her money. But instead he picked up a large ledger that had been lying on the edge of the cluttered desk. 'Which clock is it?'

She made her way to the back of the shop, keeping those painted eyes in view. Coughing a little with the dust, she pointed to the clock and it stared back at her. At least the eyes were still now, not swivelling from side to side like a living thing as they had in her dreams. 'It's that one, there. The grandfather clock.'

'The long-cased clock,' he corrected gently. 'It's an interesting one. Oak case and painted face. Dated around 1850 and made by Eccles of Eborby . . . quite a well regarded maker. I haven't seen one like it before. But you say you have?'

'I'm not sure. It looks very familiar.' She feared that any talk of dreams would mark her out as strange in this man's eyes so she kept to bald facts. 'That's why I wondered where it came from.'

He opened the ledger and flicked through the pages,

frowning with concentration, while she stood and waited, shifting from foot to foot. She took a peep at her watch. She didn't have long.

'Got it,' he said, tapping his finger on the page. 'It came from a house in Hilton. Why did you say you wanted to know? Do you think it might be a family piece or . . .?'

He looked straight at her, a challenge in his eyes, and she realized that he might have interpreted her curiosity as a desire to claim the clock for herself. But nothing could be further from the truth. 'Like I said, I'm sure I've seen it somewhere before and I wondered where. I don't want it if that's what you're thinking. In fact it gives me the creeps.'

'Why's that then?' he said sharply. 'It's only an old clock.'

She suddenly felt foolish and mumbled something about feeling the eyes were watching her. She realized how feeble it sounded but it hadn't felt feeble in the early hours when the clock had towered there like a predatory creature, its painted eyes boring into her soul.

'Can't say I've noticed,' the man said. 'I'm Seb, by the way. Seb Bentham.'

He suddenly thrust out his hand towards her and she took it. His handshake was firmer than she'd expected and she felt herself wince at the pressure. 'Lydia.'

'Well, Lydia, apart from a clock that gives you the creeps is there anything else here I can interest you in?' He suddenly sounded like a salesman, polished and persuasive.

'Not really . . . I just came to . . .'

'Have you got your own place? Looking for furniture? Or a picture maybe? The shop's full of my uncle's stock but I've been doing a bit of buying myself and I picked up some lovely prints the other day. Come and have a look.' He took a step towards the back of the shop as though he expected her to follow.

She looked at her watch. 'Sorry, I'm on my lunch hour and I should be heading back.'

'Where do you work?'

'The Tourist Information Office.' The answer came out automatically but as soon as the words left her lips she wondered whether she should have parted with the information. She forced out a smile. 'I might come and have a look at those pictures you mentioned when I've got more time. I do need something for the flat. It's looking a bit bare at the moment.'

'Where is it . . . your flat?'

He was probably just being friendly, she told herself, but she felt this was an intrusion too far. 'Near the city centre,' she said, trying to sound casual. 'Have you got that address?'

He returned to the ledger and spun it round so that she could see it. 'There it is. Long-cased clock with face painted to resemble the moon. Bought in April this year from a Mrs Judith Dodds at this address in Hilton.' He smiled, showing his small, white teeth.

She'd got what she'd come for and the hunger pangs in her stomach had suddenly become more urgent. 'Thanks. That's been a great help. I'd better go. I've got to buy something for lunch. Thanks,' she repeated, edging out of the shop.

As soon as she got outside she walked away down the street quickly, almost breaking into a run when she reached the corner.

She recited the address to herself, memorizing it. Oriel House, Hilton Lane. She wondered whether she'd have the courage to act on her new knowledge. But sometimes you have to face a demon if you're going to conquer it forever.

Emily had decided not to tell Joe where she was going. After all, she wasn't sure whether her appointment was connected with work or her children's school. But whatever it was, she was glad of the break.

As she left the police headquarters the early cloud had burned back, leaving the sky a cloudless blue but the chilly breeze whipping down the road made her wish she'd put her jacket on. She quickened her pace, keeping the towers of the cathedral in view. As she neared the great gothic building the streets were thick with meandering tourists, stopping to take photographs and getting in her way. She nipped across the road, narrowly avoiding being mowed down by an open-topped tour bus, and dodged through the throng until she had passed the cathedral's south door and reached the open expanse of lawn that was

Vicars Green. There were tourists here too, lounging at the foot of a tall Roman column protruding from the centre of the grass and staring in awe at the surrounding medieval buildings. She could see the National Trust café on the corner and she hoped Melanie Hawkes had arrived first and bagged a table.

But when she pushed the door open and went in, she was nowhere to be seen.

Melanie stood in the archway on Gallowgate that led to Singmass Close, almost opposite the café. When she saw Emily she stepped back into the shadows. At least she'd come – that was something. Now it was a case of thinking up the right words to say. She'd blown hot and cold about the meeting all morning, one moment longing for someone else to assume the burden, the next having terrifying visions of what would happen if Daisy's abductor discovered her duplicity.

She was glad Emily didn't look round. If she'd seen her, she'd have had no choice but to keep the appointment. But as it was, she still had time to decide. She could see Emily at a table by the café window, looking around. Eventually she stood up to queue by the counter and Melanie could see something on the tray she'd collected from the side. A sandwich . . . and a large cake. Whether she kept the appointment or not, Emily Thwaite intended to enjoy her lunch.

She'd sat down again and Melanie watched as she stuffed her face with a large slice of chocolate cake. She seemed so intent on her task that she didn't look up, which Melanie took as a sign. Perhaps she'd been too hasty to involve the police. Jack had called to say he'd managed to get the money so they might be able to get Daisy back without alerting the authorities and putting her life in jeopardy.

There were other ways. Better ways.

SIX

When Lydia arrived home at six o'clock she met a man in the entrance hall. He was dressed entirely in black and he stared at her as she passed which made her a little uneasy.

She was sure that she hadn't seen him before. She would have remembered the rather prominent eyes and the slicked-back dark hair. His short-sleeved black shirt was open at the neck to reveal a string of wooden beads and she wondered what or who had brought him there. There were three flats occupied in her wing of the building; her own, Beverley's and Alan Proud's – a taciturn man who kept himself very much to himself. The man in black hardly seemed Beverley's sort so, by process of elimination, she concluded Proud had been entertaining a rare visitor. But it was really none of her business. And besides, she found the way Proud looked at her unsettling so she hardly wanted to encourage any of his associates.

When she reached the corridor she heard a voice behind her. A male voice, slightly high pitched, saying 'excuse me'. She swung round, almost dropping her canvas bag full of emergency shopping. The man in black was behind her, coming nearer and she was surprised she hadn't heard him retracing his steps.

'Sorry if I startled you. I take it you live here?'

'Yes.'

'I was looking for your neighbour, Beverley Newson, but there's no answer.'

'How did you get into the building?'

'Someone from one of the other flats buzzed me in.'

Lydia felt annoyed that one of her fellow residents had been so cavalier with their security. 'If you knew Beverley wasn't in, why did you . . .?'

The man raised his hands, a gesture of appeasement. 'No,

no, you don't understand. My name's Dr Karl Dremmer and I'm from Eborby University, department of Psychology. I've already spoken to Beverley. Maybe she's mentioned it to you.'

She began to relax. This was the man Beverley had spoken of in glowing terms. He held out his hand and Lydia did likewise. 'Lydia Brookes. I'm in flat three.'

'Would you mind if I talked to you?'

'What about?'

'This building.'

If Beverley hadn't provided the man's credentials, she would have exercised caution but, as it was, she was merely curious. And besides, she had nothing else arranged that evening. 'OK. Come in. I'll put the kettle on.'

She put her key in the lock, glancing behind her at the man who was standing there patiently. Once she'd turned the key he picked up her shopping bag for her and as she pushed at the door nothing happened. She pushed again. The door had opened an inch or so but there was something behind it, blocking the way. She turned to Dremmer who was watching her with dispassionate interest, like a scientist observing an experiment.

'Something the matter?'

'I can't get the door open.'

He put the bag down and pushed the door. The blockage seemed to shift a little but not enough.

Lydia began to panic. She'd read about the burglaries in the local paper, the barriers of furniture built to block the front door before the burglar searched the premises and escaped through a back door or window. His victims were always women who lived alone and the thought that she'd been targeted made her feel nauseous. He had known she lived alone and violated her home, her refuge.

'I think I can shift it.'

Dremmer was only average height but he was wiry, probably stronger than he looked. He pushed, breathless with the effort, and after a while the door had opened wide enough for him to squeeze around the barrier of furniture.

'Stay there,' he said, raising a warning hand. 'I'll make sure everything's all right.'

He vanished into the flat, leaving Lydia chewing her finger nails, something she'd sworn to herself she'd never do again. She could hear her heart pounding and her hands felt numb. Perhaps this was just another nightmare. Perhaps she'd wake up soon and her state of helpless semi-paralysis would disappear.

But she heard a voice, all too real. Karl Dremmer's voice, calm and matter of fact. 'We'd better call the police,' he said. 'I don't think we should touch anything in here so have you got your mobile?'

When she opened her bag there seemed to be no feeling in her fingers and, as she fumbled for her phone, the contents spilled out on to the floor.

Emily was annoyed. Annoyed with herself for eating an extra large slice of chocolate cake and annoyed with Melanie Hawkes for standing her up. She'd called her as soon as she returned to the office, ready to tell her that wasting police time was a serious offence. Then she'd reminded herself that their appointment had been a private matter, a request made to a social contact rather than anything official, but this didn't make her feel any better. She'd been quite short with Melanie when she apologized, saying she'd been unavoidably delayed. And no, she'd sorted the matter out herself, thank you very much.

She'd given no hint as to what 'the matter' might have been. In fact she'd sounded cagey – guilty even – and Emily couldn't help being curious, it was in her nature. But she had other things to worry about.

It was six thirty – the time most people were heading home. But a call had just come in; a young woman living in a flat on Boothgate had just returned home to find she'd been burgled and this one fitted the same pattern as the others. It was The Builder all right and she was his sixth victim.

So far nobody had disturbed the burglar as he went about his work, but sooner or later that situation would change. And if he was cornered, Emily had a nagging fear that things could turn nasty.

She'd driven there right away with Joe in an unmarked car and now they were standing side by side at the front entrance to Boothgate House. It was an impressive building, built of mellow stone with white-framed sash windows at a time when taste and good proportion ruled. Joe had told her it had been built two hundred and fifty years ago as an asylum for the insane and the small overgrown graveyard to the left of the building with its crooked, blackened headstones, hinted at this darker history. Joe also told her that there used to be a high wall around the perimeter of the grounds so the people of Eborby couldn't see what was going on inside. But the developers had lowered it. No secrets now.

'How does he know they're female and live on their own?' Joe said as he pressed the key with Lydia Brookes's name beside it.

'He probably follows them . . . stalks them,' Emily replied.

'That's worrying,' said Joe. 'I'm just afraid that maybe one day he'll take it into his head to do more than pinch their cash and knickers.'

Emily felt a cold shudder pass through her body. She felt hungry again now but eating would have to wait.

She heard the buzzer and pushed one of the arched glass front doors open. The double doors, etched with the words 'Boothgate House', lent a modern look to the building. Inside was a spacious hall with a checkerboard floor and an elegant staircase sweeping up to the first floor. It looked more like a stately home than a hospital. The Georgians just couldn't help themselves when it came to interior design.

Joe turned right, following the signs to Flat Three, while Emily held back a little, looking around. There was a new smell about the place which had obviously been gutted and refurbished to a high standard. Pity, she thought, that they hadn't concentrated more on security.

She followed Joe down a wide corridor which reminded her of an expensive hotel, and as she rounded the corner she saw a constable standing awkwardly by the door to one of the flats, shifting from foot to foot. When he spotted them he pulled himself up to his full and considerable height, trying to look efficient.

He cleared his throat. 'Sir, ma'am. It's exactly the same as the others.'

She looked around. There were two more doors on the corridor, both shut. 'Have you spoken to the neighbours? Did anyone see anything?'

'I couldn't get a reply from either of them. Must be out. Actually, there's something you should see.'

'What's that?' Joe said. She thought that his slight Liverpool accent made him sound impatient.

'This time he's left a note.' He handed a plastic bag to Joe who studied it before passing it on to Emily.

'Oh shit,' she muttered as she read the words.

I'LL SEE YOU NEXT TIME I CALL. BE READY.

Melanie had been gone for a long time.

The call had come at nine o'clock and she'd driven off to the drop at the Museum Gardens' car park with the holdall filled with money. She'd taken her mobile and after two hours had elapsed Jack had tried to call her but there'd been no answer. He'd left a message on her voicemail. Where are you? What's happening? But she hadn't called back.

He had tried to call Paul, her ex, to eliminate the unlikely scenario that Melanie had taken a newly released Daisy to see her father, but there'd been no reply.

Even though he knew he should keep a clear head in case he needed to drive, he helped himself to a scotch, trying to banish the bad feeling he was getting about the whole affair.

SEVEN

Karl Dremmer knew that he should have obtained permission from the developer but when he'd met Patrick Creeny he hadn't liked the man. His instincts told him he wouldn't be sympathetic to his research. He'd caught a strong whiff of cynicism, maybe even disapproval. Creeny had been quite adamant that he didn't want Boothgate House to be associated with madness and death. And certainly not with spooks and all that nonsense. The apartments were hard enough to shift without that sort of thing. Karl hadn't mentioned the electrician who'd spoken to him about the strange experiences he'd had when he'd been working alone in the building because he hadn't wanted to get the man into any sort of trouble.

He'd persuaded the woman in flat two to let him down into the basement. Like many women of her age, Beverley Newson was susceptible to a bit of flattery. She had taken early retirement to look after her ageing mother and he'd singled her out because he reckoned she'd make a useful ally, one who would seize any sliver of vicarious excitement on offer. And he'd been right.

For a while he'd feared that the burglary at the flat next door to Beverley's and the resulting police presence might put paid to his plans, but instead it had proved a welcome distraction. Nobody had noticed when he'd returned to the building at nine thirty that evening and Beverley had released the door to admit him. By then the place had been quiet; the police had gone and Lydia, the burglary victim from Flat Three, had left to stay the night with a friend. Nobody had seen when Beverley met him in the hall and helped him carry his equipment down into the basement, bubbling with excitement at being involved. She'd brought down hot chocolate and biscuits at ten thirty and when he'd told her he didn't want to be disturbed for the rest of the night she'd looked disappointed. But he'd had no choice. This was a serious scientific investigation and it was something he had to do alone.

The equipment was set up. Cameras, digital recorders, the latest gear. He had placed his camp bed and sleeping bag in the corner of the dank underground room with its brick walls, painted a shade of dull cream, and mysterious wooden bunkers ranged along one wall. From there he had a good view of the flickering red light on top of the night vision camera and he found that pinpoint of warmth rather comforting.

As the dawn light crept in through the barred and dirt-veiled window at the top of the wall, casting a sickly grey glow around the room, he squinted at his watch in the gloom and saw it was just past seven o'clock. Time to return to the university and examine the results of his vigil. He had to make sure he hadn't imagined the events of the night.

Melanie hadn't come home and she wasn't answering her phone. She had disappeared. So had Daisy. And so had his money.

During the wakeful early hours, it had crossed Jack's mind that Melanie might have set the whole thing up as a trick, a way to get her hands on the money. After all, he'd sunk everything they had, including everything she'd earned as a solicitor over the years, into his business ventures so perhaps this was her way of recouping what she thought he owed her. He thought back, examining in his mind every nuance of his marriage to Melanie, from the time he'd met her at a drinks party and decided to abandon his wife and children to be with her to the recent cooling of their relationship. She had begun to annoy him in so many ways, and Daisy's presence hadn't helped. Things had been difficult lately, especially once he'd become involved in the Boothgate House development. And of course there was Yolanda, although he didn't think Melanie had any suspicions in that direction.

He knew how much she begrudged his relationship with his children by his first wife. According to her, Daisy should have taken priority. But Daisy wasn't his own flesh and blood – not like his own kids. He'd done his best to act the good stepfather but he wasn't sure whether the act had been convincing. But was their marriage in such a parlous state that she would pull a stunt like this? And wouldn't she have demanded more than ten grand?

He had risen early after a night of fitful sleep and now he was in the kitchen sipping a strong coffee. After half an hour sitting there with the phone in his hand, trying her number every few minute, he rang Paul's again but got no reply.

Then, as he stared helplessly at the phone, he began to wonder whether he should call another number, one that Melanie had rung yesterday. She hadn't kept the appointment with Emily Thwaite but at least the woman might be able to give him some guidance.

But while he was still contemplating his options his phone began to ring. His heart pounded as he pressed the key with trembling fingers.

It was a mechanized, robot voice, the voice he'd heard before. 'Your wife didn't turn up. But I'll give you one more chance. I'll call later with further instructions and if you pull another stunt like that you won't see Daisy again.'

Jack opened his mouth to explain. But the caller rang off before he could get the words out.

Joe didn't live far from Boothgate House. When he'd moved back to Eborby twelve years ago, he'd known the place simply as Havenby Hall, a derelict place of fear hidden behind high, soot-blackened walls. Most people in Eborby knew of it second-hand; the place where family members who were considered strange, over-nervous or downright antisocial vanished from sight, only to be spoken of in loud whispers by tactless aunts. In less enlightened times, but still within living memory, girls who transgressed the moral codes of the day had disappeared into the forbidding edifice, only to see the light of day again as pale elderly women, released blinking into the light of a brash modern day world where their supposed sins had become the norm.

When he'd gone there to investigate the burglary last night he'd sensed an atmosphere of deep melancholy in the place in spite of its recent transformation. Or perhaps it had been his imagination. There had certainly been no hint of its former function as he'd walked into the entrance hall and stood admiring the twinkling central chandelier and the tasteful decor.

It had been ten o'clock before he'd arrived home and there had been a message from Maddy waiting on his answering machine. She had asked how he was and for a few seconds he'd felt rather gratified that she still cared. He resolved to call her back . . . when he had the time.

There'd also been a message from his sister reminding him of their mother's imminent birthday – she'd sounded distant, almost businesslike, but things had never been the same with her since he'd abandoned his vocation for Kaitlin, a woman his family considered alien because they came from different worlds. The days when they'd looked to him for some sort of guidance had long gone. He'd left the fold, taken a different path.

He'd settled down to eat his microwaved spaghetti bolognese and switched the TV on, more for company than entertainment. There were times when he envied Emily her hectic family life and this was one of them. If Kaitlin had lived . . . if they'd had children . . . if Maddy hadn't chosen to go to London . . . His life was full of ifs. He opened a bottle of Old Peculier to wash down his food and sat back listening to the forced laughter of the comedy show that had just replaced the news. It almost seemed as if they were laughing at him.

The following morning he left the flat and went straight to Boothgate House to interview Lydia Brookes's immediate neighbours in the hope that someone had seen something relevant at the time of the break in. The officers conducting the door-to-door enquiries hadn't been able to get hold of them the previous night and he wondered whether they'd been trying to avoid the police for some reason. But his job had given him a suspicious mind.

He'd already spoken to the man who'd been with Lydia when she'd discovered the break-in. He was an academic from the university, a researcher in paranormal phenomena, and Joe had found his presence there intriguing. From what he knew of Havenby Hall's history, it was likely he'd find lots of material there: memories of grief and distress; agitated ghosts in mental pain. Some didn't believe in such things but Joe kept an open mind. He knew the power of the unseen and unprovable. He was only too aware that he would have made a lousy priest but some things had never left him.

His first port of call was Flat Two, which belonged to a Beverley Newson who, according to Lydia, lived there with her elderly mother. Beverley was a large, strongly built woman and most would have called her plain, but her greeting was almost gushing and he refused her offer of coffee as tactfully as he could, staying at the door, ready to make a quick exit. If he'd settled in Beverley's living room with coffee and biscuits, he knew he'd find it hard to get away; he knew her type.

She explained that she'd seen nothing yesterday because she'd been out taking Mother to the hospital for a routine appointment. They'd stopped for something to eat in a café on the way back and hadn't arrived home till eight. The police had left by then but one of the other residents had told her what had happened. It was awful for poor Lydia, she said. Such a nice girl. Then she asked whether much had been taken.

Joe gave non-committal answers and after five minutes he managed to make his escape. It looked as though the thief had only taken items of underwear and a ten-pound note that had been lying on the hall table and he suspected that the underwear had been important and the cash had just been a bonus. But it was that note that made him uneasy. *I'll see you next time I call. Be ready.* This was a new departure. An escalation. He had seen the fear in Lydia's eyes and he'd felt for her.

In spite of her eagerness to help, Beverley hadn't seen or heard anything. But there was another neighbour on the corridor and this one interested Joe far more. Flat One was occupied by an Alan Proud and, from the brief check he'd made when he returned to police headquarters the previous night, he knew that Proud had served six months for threatening behaviour when he'd stalked a former girlfriend. If they were looking for a stalker, this one was already there on the premises.

Proud's door was opened by a bleary-eyed man wearing a grubby towelling dressing gown. He was in his forties, Joe guessed, with thinning brown hair, blotchy skin and a body that looked as if it had consumed too much junk food over the years. As Joe held up his warrant card, the man rolled his eyes but he stood aside meekly to let him in.

'You've heard that your neighbour's been burgled?'

'Yeah. Why?' He sounded defensive – like a man with something to hide. Perhaps this one would be easier to clear up than they'd feared.

The hallway was wide so he didn't have to make physical contact with Proud as he passed him, made his way into the living room and sat down uninvited. It was a spacious flat and although the room was neat there were no homely touches; no cushions, no ornaments, nothing unnecessary. The only thing approaching decoration was an array of framed letters, almost filling one wall. Proud stood hovering in the doorway as though he was preparing for a swift getaway.

'I take it you know Ms Brookes?'

'Who?' Proud's mouth was hanging open as he adjusted the belt on his dressing gown.

'Your neighbour in Flat Three. Lydia Brookes . . . the one who's just been burgled.'

'Just to say hello to.'

'You haven't been in her flat?'

'Never been invited.' He sounded disappointed.

'Where were you yesterday afternoon?'

'I was visiting someone. It was to do with work.'

'What do you do?'

The man hesitated, as though he was wondering whether to share a confidence. 'I deal in memorabilia.'

'What sort of memorabilia?' There was something cagey about the man's replies to his questions that aroused Joe's curiosity.

'Crime memorabilia.'

'Do you mean things like Dr Crippen's toupee and Jack the Ripper's false teeth?' Joe couldn't resist lightening the mood.

Proud stared at Joe as if he wasn't sure how to react. 'As far as I know Dr Crippen never wore a toupee. And the Ripper was never identified . . . for certain.'

Joe knew his attempt at humour had fallen on stony ground.

He walked slowly over to the framed letters and peered at them, trying to decipher the spidery handwriting. 'What are these?'

'Letters.'

'I can see that. Who wrote them?'

The secretive smile that played on Proud's thin lips made Joe uneasy. 'Ever heard of Peter Brockmeister?'

Joe caught his breath. 'They're from him?'

He stared at the one of the letters. The handwriting was almost illegible but he could make out a few words. From the little he could read the author seemed to be complaining about the quality of the food and enquiring about someone called Darren. But he didn't know what he'd expected – a detailed confession perhaps or a description of where he'd left other bodies?

'They put him in here, you know, when it was a hospital.'

'From what I've heard he should never have been released from prison.'

'He was transferred here in 1978 after he'd served almost ten years for his alleged crimes. The authorities decided he was mentally ill – mad not bad. He might have spent the rest of his days here if the place hadn't closed down. Mind you, the psychiatrists reckoned he was cured by then so . . . And he died a few weeks after his release so he didn't get to enjoy his freedom.' He sighed, as if the killer's death was a matter of great regret. 'I got these letters from a relative of the man Peter shared a cell with in prison. They kept in touch after Peter was transferred here . . . until Darren got killed in a fight with a fellow inmate. Sad.'

Joe opened his mouth to say something but thought better of it.

'Look, I can't help you. I didn't see anything. And I've got things to do.'

'I'm sure you have, Mr Proud.' He walked to the door and turned round. 'What do you think of Lydia next door? Would you say she's attractive?' He wanted to see the man's reaction.

'Can't say I've noticed.' The reply was quick and Joe didn't believe a word of it.

'I'll need the name of the person you visited. To eliminate you from our enquiries.'

Proud recited a name and address. And from his confidence, Joe guessed that his alibi would stand up. Perhaps this one wouldn't be so easy after all.

'Where's the money? Don't you want Daisy back?'

According to the caller with the robot voice, Melanie hadn't delivered the money he'd given her. Which meant that the ten grand he'd placed carefully in the holdall had vanished into some black hole. He dismissed his earlier nagging suspicion that she'd found out about his relationship with Yolanda and the liberties he'd taken with their bank account and staged Daisy's abduction, absconding with the money as some sort of twisted revenge. He didn't really think that was Melanie's style.

He sat on the sofa and put his head in his hands. He'd had his reservations about involving the police but now he knew that he was out of his depth. And the longer he delayed, the worse it would look. His father had been a policeman and he knew how their minds worked. At the time he'd been glad that Melanie hadn't kept her appointment with Emily Thwaite, but now he just hoped that the woman had a forgiving nature.

EIGHT

Forensic hadn't found anything useful in Lydia Brookes's flat. The man they called The Builder had been careful as usual. Joe reckoned the bastard had been watching too many cop shows – everyone with a TV was an expert in avoiding detection these days.

'I'm worried about that note he left,' Joe said as he and Emily got into the car.

'Yes, it's a departure from his previous MO. And when criminals start branching out, I start getting worried.'

'I might call on Lydia Brookes later to see how she is, give her a bit of reassurance and check her security while I'm at it.'

Emily gave him a knowing wink. 'Yes, she's a good-looking lass.'

'I didn't mean . . .'

'I'm a woman of the world, Joe. I know about these things. It's about time you had a bit of female company.'

He felt a stab of irritation that she felt she had the right to interfere. His private life was none of her business, provided it didn't affect his work. On the other hand he knew she was probably right. He wasn't the type who flourished in isolation. Maybe that's why he felt annoyed. Because the truth hurts.

'Is something the matter?'

He turned to her and saw that she had put her head to one side, waiting for a response. 'No. Why should it be? What did this Jack Hawkes say?' It was safer to return to work matters. Love and sex were things he'd rather not think about at that moment. He'd lost everything when his wife, Kaitlin, had died soon after their wedding so he knew love could be bad news. On the other hand, so could loneliness.

'I'm not sure why I'm rushing there at his beck and call. His wife bloody stood me up yesterday.' It was the third time Emily had mentioned this; Melanie Hawkes' cavalier attitude to her valuable time clearly irked her. 'He said it was urgent but I'm just not sure whether I believe him. I've met him a few times at PTA meetings and he struck me as the sort who's full of himself . . . the sort who likes playing games.'

'What sort of games?'

'Power games.'

Joe didn't answer. Emily had obviously taken a dislike to Jack Hawkes on scant acquaintance and he suspected her animosity wasn't only due to his wife's no-show at their appointment. But he'd wait till he met the man before he decided for himself.

Emily drove through the busy streets, keeping the grey stone city walls to their left and soon they reached Picklegate Bar, one of the four medieval gates that guarded the old city. Centuries ago the heads of traitors were displayed on top of the city gates, Joe thought as he watched it in his rear view mirror. You could still see the spikes there if you looked carefully enough.

They turned on to the main road out to the southern suburbs and travelled in silence until they reached the suburb of Pickby, an affluent area of detached houses, near to the place where criminals had once met their death at the end of the hangman's rope. That particular site was now a racecourse which Joe supposed was progress of a sort. Emily herself lived here, surrounded by Eborby's professional classes.

Jack Hawkes lived in a detached Edwardian villa set in a large, neat garden. It had gables, gleaming paintwork and a glossy oak front door set with elaborate stained-glass windows. A desirable residence. Emily pressed the doorbell and waited.

Hawkes opened the door; he had a worried frown on his tanned face. 'Thanks for coming,' he said humbly as he stood aside to let them in. He checked outside before he closed the door, as though he was making sure nobody was watching.

He led them through to a large drawing room, immaculate in shades of blue with a fancy plaster cornice and a large crystal chandelier hanging from an equally fancy ceiling rose.

Emily sat down heavily on the sofa without waiting to be invited. 'So what's your problem, Mr Hawkes?'

He looked from one to the other, as though he was making a decision. 'My wife's disappeared.'

'She arranged to meet me but she never turned up.'

'I know. She thought it might be a good idea to ask your advice but she changed her mind.'

'Why?'

Hawkes hesitated. 'My stepdaughter's been kidnapped.' He paused to let the words sink in. 'The kidnapper told us not to tell the police so . . .'

'Don't worry, we can do discreet.' Joe had been standing there but now he sat down beside Emily, fearing that this was going to be a long story. 'You'd better start from the beginning.'

Hawkes inhaled deeply. 'My wife picked Daisy up from school yesterday and they went to the playground in the local park on the way home.'

'Is that Lovett Road Park?' asked Emily, the local.

'I think so. She just said the park but . . .'

'What happened?' Emily was leaning forward now with professional interest, all resentment gone.

'Daisy – that's her little girl – was playing on the swings or . . . Anyway, Melanie had a phone call from her boss and turned her back for a minute and . . . and when she turned round Daisy wasn't there. She rushed round asking people if they'd seen her but nobody had. Anyway, while she was out – before she'd even called me to tell me what had happened – I had a phone call from someone who said they had Daisy.'

'Man or woman?' Joe asked.

'I couldn't tell. The voice was disguised through one of those electronic things.'

'Go on.' Joe caught Emily's eye. If this was a case of kidnapping they'd have to hand it over to a specialist team, people more used to delicate negotiations than themselves. There'd be a news blackout to arrange and other things to be set in motion. But first they needed the facts.

'They asked for ten grand in cash.'

'And what happened?'

'I got the money.'

'Where from? Your bank?'

'Er, no. From a business associate who owed me money.'

'Name?' Emily was leaning forward, notebook at the ready.

'Patrick Creeny. He's been working with me on the Boothgate House project.'

'Havenby Hall?'

'Boothgate House. We're hoping people will forget about . . . It's not good for business. Patrick gave me the cash from his safe and when I got home the kidnapper called again and told Melanie to take the money to the car park behind the Museum Gardens. They said she'd receive further instructions when she arrived.'

'She went alone?'

'I . . . we thought it was best if someone waited here. In case . . .'

'And did she receive further instructions?'

'I don't know. After she left I never heard any more. I've been trying to call her but her phone's switched off. I've left messages but . . .'

'I presume she wanted to see me about the kidnapping,' said Emily, more sympathetic now.

'Yes. I didn't think it was a good idea but . . . I didn't want to do anything that might put Daisy in danger but now Melanie's missing too and . . .'

'When did she leave with the money?'

'Yesterday evening. Around eight. There's been no word from her since.'

'We'll need to trace the phone calls you received. And put a trace on any future calls,' said Joe.

Hawkes nodded meekly and looked up. 'There's something else,' he said quietly. 'Something I haven't mentioned.'

'What's that?'

'I had a call from the kidnapper this morning asking why Melanie hadn't turned up.'

Lydia had forgotten when she'd first met Amy but she knew their friendship dated from the time when she used to stay with her grandparents in Eborby during the long school holidays. Amy's own grandparents had been close friends of her grandmother's and, as the two girls had been the same age, Amy had been roped in to play with the friends' lonely little granddaughter. Fortunately the two girls had hit it off back then and they'd stayed in touch ever since . . . even after Lydia had lost her baby; even after her divorce.

Amy had given her a bed for the night after the burglary. She lived with her boyfriend, Steve, in a terraced house in Bearsly, not far from the huge, red-brick chocolate factory that provided so much employment in the town. It was a small house with a dingy yard backing on to the railway line and, in spite of Amy's protestations to the contrary, Lydia couldn't help feeling she was getting in the way. Besides, she'd have to return to Boothgate House sooner or later. Although she found it hard to get that note out of her mind. *I'll see you next time I call. Be ready.*

The detective who'd called – DI Plantagenet – had told her to contact him if she was worried and a crime prevention officer was due to visit later that day, as was someone from Victim Support. She couldn't complain that the authorities weren't taking the violation seriously. She'd kept Joe Plantagenet's card in her wallet with her precious photos and her credit cards and from time to time she took it out and looked at it, deriving comfort from the memory of him. The dark hair, the watchful blue eyes, the mouth that turned up slightly at the corners. A sympathetic face. But she had known faces like that to hide a darker nature. Sometimes appearances deceive.

First thing that morning Amy had gone back with her to Boothgate House to help tidy up. By the time she'd had to leave for her shift at the theatre everything in the flat had been returned to its proper place, dusted and disinfected to blot out all trace of the man who'd intruded on her life. Once Amy had gone, Lydia had opened the windows to let some air in and sat in her living room listening to the faint hum of traffic noise from nearby Boothgate, feeling uneasy and alone. But it was something she knew she'd have to get used to. She'd got used to worse in her time.

She made herself a coffee, wishing she hadn't rung into work to tell them she was taking the day off. The clock on the kitchen wall told her it was only ten thirty and the hours stretched out before her like an empty sea. She needed something to take her mind off her intruder.

The address Seb Bentham had given her was still in her handbag and she took it out carefully and studied it. Seb – she supposed it was short for Sebastian. There'd been something interesting about him, perhaps even something a little dangerous. He reminded her a bit of her ex husband; the man who hadn't been able to bear the grief when they'd lost the baby and had decided to run rather than live with the pain. He'd taught drama to sixth formers and harboured ambitions to write. She'd lost touch with him so she didn't know whether these ambitions had come to anything.

The address Seb had given her wasn't far away, just up the road. And at that moment the prospect of a walk in the fresh air seemed irresistible. She could think about what she was going to say to the clock's former owner on the way.

She slung her bag over her shoulder and left the flat, pushing the door to make doubly sure that it was locked. From now on she knew she was going to be paranoid about security. At least, she thought as she strode across the entrance hall and out into the fresh air, she hadn't dreamt about the clock while she'd been staying at Amy's. She'd been half afraid that she would wake up screaming and bring Amy – or, worse still, Steve – hurrying in to see what was wrong. Perhaps now she'd seen the clock in reality, the nightmares would stop.

She walked down Boothgate, heading out of town. There were no tourists here; they all congregated in the centre like wasps around a jam jar. As she crossed the railway bridge and Boothgate turned into Hilton Road, the Georgian houses gave way to newer properties. This was the Eborby the visitors didn't see; if they were approaching by car or coach down Hilton Road, they'd be scanning the horizon for their first sight of the cathedral towers. This wasn't to say that Hilton wasn't an attractive place with its tall trees and its little green surrounded by Victorian cottages.

Oriel House stood on one of the side roads; stone built, detached and Victorian, all gables and gothic windows. Lydia stood with her hand hovering over the gate latch, suddenly apprehensive. What if the woman didn't want to discuss her sale of the clock with a stranger?

But she told herself firmly that she had nothing to lose and pushed the gate open. Her heart was pounding as she walked up the path between the neat flower beds and rang the doorbell. She was preparing to make a hasty retreat when the door opened a crack and a suspicious female voice said 'Yes?' as if she was expecting some con man or pushy salesman.

'I'm sorry to bother you. I'm looking for Mrs Dodds.'

The door opened a little wider and Lydia saw that the woman had silver-blonde hair cut in a neat bob. Her white trousers and denim blouse flattered her tall, slim figure. She must have been in her early sixties but she'd taken care of herself. 'I'm Judith Dodds.'

Once Lydia had explained the reason for her visit, the woman seemed to relax. She invited her in and led her into a room of understated elegance, all duck-egg blue and cream. When she sat down Mrs Dodds sat opposite, back straight and legs neatly arranged. Lydia noticed that her hands were clasped tightly in front of her like a defensive barrier.

'So you've met Mr Bentham?'

'Seb?'

'Is that his name? Elderly gentleman . . . longish grey hair. Really looked the part.'

'I met his nephew. He's looking after the shop while Mr Bentham senior is ill. I hope you don't mind me coming like this but there's something I'd like to ask you. It's about the grandfather clock you sold.'

Her eyes widened. 'You've bought it?'

'No but I was wondering about its history.' She hesitated, wondering how she was going to explain the inexplicable. Eventually she decided to approach the subject head on. 'I know this might sound strange but when I saw it in the shop I thought I'd seen it before. And I wondered whether that's possible.' She'd decided that any mention of the nightmares might mark her out as disturbed. And she needed this woman to trust her and talk freely.

Mrs Dodds stared at her. 'What did you say your name was?'

'Lydia Brookes. I'm not from Eborby but my grandparents

lived here and I sometimes came to stay with them when I was young. Is that any help?'

'Where did they live?'

'Bacombe.'

Mrs Dodds shook her head. 'The clock belonged to my father and when I inherited the contents of his house I asked Mr Bentham to deal with their disposal.'

'Perhaps my grandparents knew your father. My grandfather was a doctor. His name was Speed. Dr Reginald Speed.'

'My father was a doctor too.'

All sorts of possibilities were passing through Lydia's head. 'My grandfather died in an accident when I was three but perhaps he visited your father sometime and took me along.'

'My father wasn't a sociable man.' Mrs Dodds' expression was hard to read. But Lydia sensed that her memories of her father weren't happy ones. 'My parents divorced when I was a baby and I hardly saw him when I was growing up. My mother never wanted me to have anything to do with him. I didn't know him well but I really can't see him entertaining colleagues and their children.'

Lydia sensed an untold story, a tragedy, maybe, or something more sinister. She was intrigued and she longed to discover the reason behind the estrangement. But good manners made her hold back.

'I certainly don't remember the clock,' Mrs Dodds continued. 'I would have remembered it because it's a horrible thing. I was glad to get it out of the house.'

Lydia wondered whether to mention the nightmares, then she thought better of it. She knew it came from an antisocial doctor in Eborby and, in spite of what Mrs Dodds said, her grandfather could well have visited the man for some reason, social or professional, with his small granddaughter in tow. The clock might have frightened her then and stayed in her subconscious for all those years. Like a dormant seed.

Mrs Dodds suddenly interrupted her thoughts. 'I think he might have brought it from where he worked. He lived in for a while . . . had a flat on the premises.'

'Where did he work?'

When Mrs Dodds told her, Lydia's stomach lurched. This was something she hadn't expected. But it made a kind of horrible sense.

Dr Karl Dremmer sat at his tidy desk in his office at the university, glad for once of the mundane, modern surroundings, of the stark brick walls and the Scandinavian chairs.

He tried to read a departmental memo but he couldn't get the muffled sobs and the half-seen dim shapes out of his mind. He'd almost managed to convince himself that he'd imagined everything; that the atmosphere of the place had altered his perception somehow. He was a man of science and he wouldn't accept such things without solid proof. And so far the proof had eluded him.

Down in that basement the air had seemed thick, like an ice-cold smog with a faint whiff of the grave. And he had felt a pain within him close to grief. It had seemed very real at the time but in the light of morning he'd told himself that the brain could play powerful tricks. But he still didn't feel up to talking about what had happened. The truth was he felt vulnerable and maybe a little foolish.

He abandoned the memo and began to watch the recordings he'd made, hoping they'd prove that some earthly agency was responsible for his night of fear; faulty plumbing maybe, or someone playing a practical joke. But as he watched the computer screen he experienced an unfamiliar feeling of dread.

After a while he tapped his keyboard to bring up his list of email addresses. He'd been in touch with the clergyman who dealt with the diocese's deliverance ministry several times before. Canon George Merryweather was a down-to-earth character. Self-effacing, balding and a little tubby, George seemed like some comfortable country doctor or solicitor rather than a seeker of ghosts. But even so, Karl felt slightly embarrassed about asking for his opinion.

And yet he'd experienced something strange down there in that basement so he sent the email anyway. A chat would do no harm.

NINE

Eborby Rowing Club took their sport very seriously and the two boats were neck and neck as they sped along the glittering surface of the water, the coxes yelling their instructions to the sweaty rowers. The rowers were too preoccupied to notice the onlookers watching lazily from the banks where the Museum Park swept down to the water's edge. Nor were they aware of the corpse caught up in the overhanging branches of a large willow tree until one of the rowers hit it with his oar, letting out a flow of expletives which were drowned out by the cox's amplified orders.

Soon the cox, realizing something was amiss, abandoned his megaphone and peered over the side.

She was floating face down in the shallows, her naked flesh pale against the dark water and her hair spread out like dull gold snakes.

And she was definitely dead.

When Lydia arrived home she made herself a cup of tea, although she was longing for something stronger, and she stood staring out of the window as she sipped the hot liquid from her mug. She could see small white clouds scudding across the blue sky like boats on a river driven by invisible oarsmen, and the thick foliage of the surrounding trees shifted as the breeze disturbed the branches. She could see one corner of the graveyard from her window, the headstones standing at crazy angles, black like rotted teeth. Memorials to the dead; memorials to the mad . . . or the supposedly mad. The plan had been to remove the graves and rebury the occupants elsewhere but recently nothing had been said, probably because of the halt to the renovations. She'd heard that the developers had run out of funds, although she suspected that the existing residents would be the last to learn of any problems.

Now she knew that the clock had actually come from

Havenby Hall, that it had once stood ticking the hours away in the Medical Superintendent's quarters, somehow it made everything worse. Judith Dodds' father, a Dr Pennell, had lived and worked there tending to the physical sicknesses of the inmates, although Mrs Dodds had been keen to point out that he had nothing to do with their psychiatric treatment. But he'd been there and he must have sent some of the inmates on their final journeys to that neglected graveyard. At least now it seemed more likely that her nightmares weren't the result of some suppressed childhood memory. This was a building she'd never have entered back then. Why would she?

The sound of knocking on her front door made her jump, spilling a little of her tea on the wooden floor. The burglary and the discovery about the clock had taken their toll on her nerves. She put her mug down and hurried to the door

She'd hardly had anything to do with Alan Proud, apart from the occasional nod of acknowledgement when they met in the corridor, but now he was towering over her, smiling a smile that made him look vaguely menacing.

'I thought I'd call to see how you were after . . .'

'I'm fine. Thank you.' She prepared to shut the door.

'Would you like to come round for a coffee . . . or something?' The suggestion in the words made her uncomfortable.

'Sorry. I've got lots to sort out. Another time maybe.'

'I've got some letters that might interest you.' His gaze focused on her breasts and she put up a defensive hand to hide the bare flesh revealed by her low cut T-shirt. 'They're from a murderer,' he continued. 'He was in here when it was a hospital.'

Lydia began to close the door, suddenly determined to get rid of him.

He stepped forward, almost crossing the threshold. 'Have you ever heard of Peter Brockmeister?' The question was asked with relish, as though it excited him and there was a hungry gleam in his small eyes.

'No. Now if you'll excuse me . . .' She shut the door and stood in the hallway, aware that only a piece of wood separated her from her neighbour. She'd lied. She had heard of Peter Brockmeister. And she knew what he'd done.

Joe stood on the concrete path which ran alongside the river. The forensic tent had already been erected and when the body had been pulled from the water, it had been taken there to lie on a plastic sheet. As it was being photographed, filmed and examined he felt a little sick. Fish had attacked the dead woman's eyes. He hadn't imaged fish could do that much damage. When the body had been turned over he'd seen that the mouth had been stuffed with flowers, now sodden and brown. Silenced with sweetness.

Emily was already inside the tent, clad, like Joe, in what she always referred to as her 'snowman suit'. It was true, the white crime-scene suit did rather emphasize her bulging waistline but it wasn't the most flattering garment for anybody. Apart from Dr Sally Sharpe, the pathologist, who was one of those fortunate women who looked good in anything. Sally had just become engaged which put paid to his tentative plans to ask her out. He knew now that he should have been more decisive when he'd had the chance.

He took a deep breath and stepped into the tent. Sally was kneeling beside the naked corpse, taking samples while the photographer circled, capturing the scene from every conceivable angle.

'Anything to tell us yet, Sally?' Joe asked.

The doctor looked up at him, her face solemn. 'I won't know for sure until the post-mortem but it looks as if she's been strangled . . . some sort of ligature. She was probably put in the water after death. What does all this flower stuff mean?'

'Do you think the flowers were stuffed in her mouth before she died?'

'Not sure.' Sally shifted one of the limp, pale arms and examined the wrist. 'I think she's been restrained at some point . . . you can just make out faint bruising on both wrists.' She looked up at Joe and he saw a hint of anxiety in her eyes. 'And there are other marks and cuts. I don't know yet whether they were done post-mortem or . . . Do we know who she is yet?'

'She fits the description of a woman from Pickby who was reported missing by her husband,' said Emily. 'Name of Melanie Hawkes.' There was a short pause before she spoke again. 'Her six-year-old daughter's missing too.'

Sally looked up, shocked. Then she swore under her breath.

Jack Hawkes looked stunned. There were no tears but Joe knew only too well that the shock of losing a loved one hit different people in different ways. When he'd lost Kaitlin, he'd been unable to cry at first but once the tears came, he hadn't been able to stop them.

Hawkes kept on shaking his head in disbelief. Who'd want to do that to Melanie? She was a high-street solicitor, for God's sake. She hadn't an enemy in the world.

Melanie's unlocked car had been found in the Museum Gardens' car park. There had been nothing to indicate anything suspicious; just a neatly parked VW Golf, newly valeted and shiny. Her handbag and phone had been found inside which was a tribute to the honesty of the citizens of Eborby . . . or maybe just luck. But there was no sign of any ransom money.

But what had happened to Daisy? That was a question they all needed answered.

After half an hour of gentle questioning and tactful words, Emily caught Joe's eye. They had learned all they could for the time being and they both knew they should leave the bereaved husband in the capable hands of the family liaison officer who'd take him through all the procedures and arrange for him to identify the body.

In a case of murder the spouse is always the first to be eliminated from enquiries, so Jack's statement was being checked and double-checked. His alibi for the previous night had already been confirmed: Patrick Creeny had called round and stayed till after midnight.

In the meantime there were other avenues to explore. There had once been another man in Melanie Hawkes' life – her ex-husband who was also Daisy's biological father, Paul Scorer. They could have sent someone to break the news and conduct an initial interview but Joe and Emily both wanted to see the man for themselves.

Emily sat in the passenger seat as Joe drove out towards the small village of Berrow, a few miles north-west of Eborby. After leaving the city suburbs they reached a rolling landscape of sheep-filled fields and dry stone walls. From time to time they passed clusters of mellow stone cottages, their gardens bursting with bright flowers. If Paul Scorer lived here, Joe thought, he was a lucky man.

Berrow was more of a hamlet than a village, although it did boast a small medieval church with a squat tower. There was no sign of a pub. Scorer's address wasn't easy to find so they had to ask one of the neighbours. From the guarded reaction to his question, Joe sensed that Scorer wasn't Berrow's most popular resident and he wondered why. He followed the directions and found the house at the end of a rutted track.

The place had probably once been a farm labourer's cottage but, unlike many similar dwellings in the area, this one hadn't been modernized to within an inch of its life. The windows were still the originals with flaking paint and layers of grime and part of the roof was covered in thick blue polythene to keep out the rain. Someone had painted a garish orange flower on the front door and there were bright Indian hangings at the windows.

'Reminds me of my student days,' Emily muttered. 'No wonder Melanie didn't want Daisy to come here. Let's see if they're in, shall we.'

Joe followed her as she picked her way across an expanse of naked soil cluttered with rubbish; scraps of wood, old tyres, a couple of redundant fridges and a rusty microwave.

Emily reached the front door first and rapped on the rough wood with her knuckles. When there was no answer she knocked again and eventually the door was opened by a man wearing tattered shorts and a faded T-shirt with a string of wooden beads around his neck. His hair was long and fair and he hadn't shaved for several days. The amused expression on his face vanished as soon as Emily showed him her warrant card.

'What's this about?' He sounded worried now.

'We're looking for Paul Scorer?'

'You've found him. What is it?'

'Can we talk about this inside,' said Emily.

As he stood aside to let them in, Joe caught a faint whiff of cannabis. But what this man did in his spare time didn't bother him. Murder and kidnapping trumped illegal substances any day.

They were invited to sit but as the only available seating was a pair of brightly coloured beanbags, Emily decided to stand to emphasize the serious nature of their visit and Joe did likewise.

'It's not about Daisy is it?' Scorer looked worried. But then, she was his daughter. 'Melanie called to tell me about the kidnap and . . . I've been worried sick. Is there any news?'

'I'm sorry. Not yet.'

Emily spoke. 'I believe Melanie Hawkes is your ex-wife. You're Daisy's father.'

'Me and Melanie met when we were at uni in Leeds; married in haste and repented at leisure.'

Joe noted the bitterness in his voice.

'Look, what are you doing to find Daisy?'

'We've only just been told she's missing,' said Joe, suddenly feeling sorry for the man. 'It's early days but we're doing all we can.'

'So what are you doing here? Why aren't you out looking for her?'

'Because Melanie Hawkes was found dead earlier today,' said Emily bluntly.

Tears began to form in Scorer's eyes and he shook his head in disbelief. Joe watched him carefully. Either the man was a good actor or the news had come as a complete shock.

'We believe she was murdered,' Emily continued.

'How . . .?'

'Her body was found in the river near the Museum Park in Eborby. There are indications that she was strangled.'

'What about Daisy?'

'Sorry. There's no sign of her . . . and nothing to indicate she's come to any harm.'

Paul put his head in his hands.

'When did you last see Melanie?'

He looked up. 'Around Easter. I wanted to see Daisy more

often but Melanie . . . She didn't want me to have anything to do with her. I got a few drug convictions when I was younger and she reckoned I was a bad influence. Not like bloody Jack.'

'So you didn't get on with Melanie and her second husband?'

'Jack thought I was shit and Melanie went along with it.' He looked Joe in the eye. 'Let me tell you about me and Melanie. We were both studying law at Leeds and when she found out she was pregnant we got married – old fashioned, I know, but it seemed like a good idea at the time. I would have stuck it but she made the choice to go it alone soon after Daisy was born 'cause by that time I'd decided to drop out. I ended up living in a squat and that wasn't the kind of lifestyle Melanie wanted at all. She was always a bit of a material girl, whereas me . . .' He gave a shrug. 'Anyway, she took up with Jack who was a successful architect and she married again – he was already married with three kids when they met, by the way. This time it was all very bourgeois. She was very into her career and her posh house in the suburbs and if it hadn't been for Daisy we would have gone our separate ways years ago. Although since Jack came on the scene she hasn't liked me doing the dad bit.'

'You must have resented that,' said Joe.

Another shrug. 'I don't do resentment. I just made sure that Daisy knew who I was. Every couple of months we'd meet in parks and places like that. I've not got the funds for all the estranged-daddy Disneyland stuff so we made our own entertainment and I think Daisy liked that. She'd had all the material stuff off Jack and her mother . . . what she needed was a bit of attention for a change.'

Joe caught Emily's eye. 'You don't think Melanie and Jack gave her much attention?'

'They were busy with their jobs and the poor kid got pushed to the sidelines. I offered to have her more . . . to let her stay at weekends and all that. Una, my partner, was up for it – she loves kids – but Melanie objected . . . or maybe Jack did.'

'Is Una here?'

'She's down in Somerset. Drumming retreat near Glastonbury. Look, my only crime was not wanting to join the rat race and spend every day in a suit dealing with people's divorces and wills. I didn't hate Melanie. If you must know, I felt a bit sorry for her.'

'Why?'

''Cause I don't like Jack. 'Cause I don't trust him. But maybe I'm just prejudiced. Look, I'm really sorry she's dead but I can't help you, I'm afraid. It was obviously some maniac or . . .'

'Or what?'

He hesitated. 'I don't think everything in that particular garden is rosy, let's put it like that.' He stepped forward. 'I'll do anything I can to help find Daisy. You don't think she could have come to any harm?'

'There was a ransom demand. Melanie had the money and was going to deliver it to the kidnappers but it seemed she never turned up.'

Paul thought about this for a few moments. 'So she could have been robbed?'

'It's a possibility,' said Joe, thinking of the mouth stuffed with rotting flowers. 'Or she might have been killed by whoever's got Daisy.'

'Why should they kill her?' Paul asked.

'If she saw them. If she could identify them.'

Paul shook his head, as though he couldn't quite believe it.

'As I said before, we've only just started working on the case. But don't worry, Mr Scorer, we'll find your daughter.'

'You better had.' The words were half hearted, as though there was something else on the man's mind. He stood up, walked over to the window and stared out at a back garden which, in contrast to the front, was well tended and filled with healthy-looking vegetables. 'This is a bloody mess,' he said softly.

'What do you mean?' Joe asked.

'I can't believe Melanie's dead.'

When they announced they were leaving he didn't look round so they left him there with his memories.

'I thought it sounded familiar.'

Joe looked up and saw DS Sunny Porter standing by his desk, his thin, prematurely lined face miserable as usual. From the way he was fidgeting, Joe guessed he was longing for a forbidden cigarette.

'What does?' He knew he sounded impatient but he hadn't got time to decipher Sunny's riddles.

'The MO. Melanie Hawkes. It's identical. Peter Brockmeister. The serial killer.' Sunny looked round as though he was afraid of eavesdroppers.

'He's dead.'

'I know, but maybe someone's decided to copy him. Maybe there's a new keeper of the flame.

TEN

Karl Dremmer had watched the recordings he'd made down in the basement three times . . . just to make sure. A small orb of light moving through the darkness of the basement had been caught on the night vision camera along with a faint, barely audible sound like a muffled sob. And the temperature had definitely dropped; the instruments had recorded it all.

Karl had given in to temptation and shared his findings with research fellow, Dr Tatiana Chenakova, who'd been sceptical. But she hadn't been down there in that atmosphere of cold despair.

As a scientist, Karl knew that he mustn't allow himself to get carried away. Tatiana could well be right about dust particles and equipment malfunction. Science dictated that the experiment needed to be repeated.

George Merryweather had already replied to his email, expressing interest and offering help if needed. George mentioned that a couple of the workmen who'd been carrying out alterations to the building had been in touch with him to report several incidents that had bothered them: things being moved; sudden blasts of cold air; weird noises when they were working after dark; and an inexplicable feeling of deep fear and melancholy. Karl had told him about the electrician who'd contacted him but George had raised the possibility that the workmen knew the history of the building and were being over-imaginative. Or perhaps it was a case of mass hysteria. Such things had been known to happen. George claimed that his job was to eliminate all earthly possibilities before considering any alternatives. He was a canon at the cathedral and a busy man so Karl needed something more definite before he bothered him again.

It was a case of assembling the evidence.

*   *   *

When Sunny said Peter Brockmeister's name, Joe felt himself shudder. His name had come up only yesterday. Lydia Brookes's neighbour, Alan Proud, had a collection of letters the killer had written and, if Sunny was right about the similarity to Melanie Hawkes' murder, this was too great a coincidence to ignore. If they were looking for a weirdo who broke into women's houses and stole their underwear, Proud had to be top of his list to be interviewed. But he knew he shouldn't allow his prejudices to affect his judgement. He'd seen officers leap to conclusions before and find themselves mistaken.

'Sit down, Sunny. Tell me all about it.'

Sunny pulled up a chair and made himself comfortable. 'It was way before your time in Eborby but I remember it from when I was a kiddie.'

Joe nodded. He'd been brought up in Liverpool, not arriving in Eborby, the city of his father, until he was well into his twenties. The Brockmeister case had obviously become part of Eborby folklore, spoken of in hushed voices so the children wouldn't hear. But children catch on quicker than parents think and, from the expression on Sunny's face, it looked as though he had chapter and verse.

'You know the basics, of course?'

'I remember he killed four women back in the late 1960s,' said Joe. 'Wasn't he a lawyer or something?'

'Yes. He was the son of a Yorkshire girl and a German prisoner of war who'd decided to stay on after 1945. Peter Brockmeister was a clever man; he'd studied law at Cambridge but he never qualified and he ended up doing casual work. Then in 1964 he began to burgle houses he'd worked at. He piled stuff against the front door so he could escape through the back if the householder came back.'

'Same as our Builder?'

'Exactly. I pointed it out to the boss but she just said that someone's been reading true-crime books and decided to copy the MO. Anyway, Brockmeister graduated to murder a couple of years later when he broke into a house and the woman who owned it was having a day off work – she had flu and she was in bed. He tied her up and strangled her and she was found naked but she hadn't been sexually assaulted. Her mouth had been stuffed with flowers from a vase in the living room. Carnations. She lived alone and she wasn't found for a few days.'

'Why the flowers?'

Sunny gave a dramatic shrug. 'Who knows? Maybe just because he was mad. After that he didn't bother burgling houses when the occupant was out and he killed three more women. The shrinks reckoned the murders were sexual, although his victims weren't raped. He always picked on women who lived on their own and the killings all followed the same pattern, including the flowers. He was convicted in 1970 and sent to prison. Then in 1978 it was decided that he was insane and I don't know how he wangled it but he was sent to Havenby Hall.'

Joe stood up. 'Why has nobody connected Brockmeister with The Builder?'

'Brockmeister was a long time ago . . . and he's dead. Also, The Builder hasn't killed anyone.'

Joe thought of the note left in Lydia Brookes's flat and experienced a feeling of dread, like icy fingers gripping his heart.

'All this stuff's common knowledge, you know,' said Sunny. 'Apart from the flowers. The police kept quiet about the flowers at the time.'

'You mean it was never made public?'

'It certainly wasn't at the time but . . .'

'True-crime books?'

Sunny nodded. 'There's always some ex-copper or witness ready to fill in the gaps for a free drink or a few quid. Anyway, Brockmeister's dead so it can't be him.'

'Is that certain?'

'He was found in the sea off Scarborough in October 1981 and identified from documents in his pocket. This was a week after he'd been released from Havenby Hall which was in the process of closing down by then. He'd been staying in a B and B on the sea front and his belongings were still in his room. It was him all right. Positive ID from the landlady and all.'

'For the sake of argument, let's imagine he's still alive.'

Sunny raised his eyebrows. 'If he is, he'll only be in his mid sixties. Still young enough to kill. But like I said, he's dead.'

Sunny had always had an optimistic streak.

When Karl Dremmer returned to Boothgate House he pressed Beverley Newson's buzzer. After a few minutes, he saw her through the glass door, tiptoeing towards him like an overweight ballerina in her wide floral skirt, a smirk of suppressed excitement on her face. When she opened the door, she looked round as if they were fellow conspirators on a dangerous assignment. This was probably the most exciting thing that had happened to her in ages, he thought. That and the burglary in Lydia Brookes's flat.

'Well?' she said. 'Did you see anything on the tape?'

'It was inconclusive.' He knew he had to keep up his scientific detachment. 'But I'd like another look down there while it's still light. There might be something I've missed.

'Shall I come with you?' Her eager smile made his heart sink.

'That won't be necessary. I know how busy you are with your mother. How is she, by the way?' He asked more out of politeness than interest.

She sighed. 'As well as can be expected at her age.'

She stood there with him at the cellar entrance for a while, shifting from foot to foot as though she was reluctant to leave. But when he made no move to open the door she turned and retraced her steps, tripping delicately down the passage towards her flat. When she was out of sight he drew back the two strong bolts on the cellar door and pulled until it creaked open. He wondered why the bolts had been placed there. To keep something in, perhaps. He took his torch from his pocket and picked his way down the stone steps. He'd brought a stronger torch this time and, as he shone it round, he could see the grubby painted walls and the flagstone floor. And something else. Something he'd noticed last night.

As he began to cross the floor he heard a voice at the top of the stairs. Not Beverley's girlish, high pitched tones, but a deep male voice with a faint local accent. He spun round and saw Patrick Creeny standing there, blocking out the light from the hall.

'What the hell are you up to?' he asked.

And Karl couldn't really think up a convincing answer.

There was an atmosphere of shock at the offices of Cuthbert, Prideaux and Parkland, Solicitors. When Joe and Emily had visited the converted Georgian house on Sheepgate to break the news of Melanie Hawkes' death, the universal reaction of her colleagues was disbelief followed by puzzlement. Who on earth would have wanted to kill Melanie who was a nice person, a good solicitor and a valued member of the team? The idea of her killer being anybody but a random madman was unthinkable. And the madman option meant that everyone, especially any woman out on her own, was at risk.

They had been shown into Andrew Parkland's comfortable office and given a cup of tea. Parkland, the senior partner – Cuthbert and Prideaux having retired and died respectively – was a big man in his fifties, well built rather than fat with a physique that suggested a youth spent on the rugby field. His thick hair was peppered with grey and he had a tan redolent of sunnier climes.

He was keen to be of any help, he said as he leaned forward, his hands arched as if in prayer to emphasize his sincerity.

'Melanie hasn't been in work since the day before yesterday,' he said. 'We were expecting her and I did try to ring her but there was no answer. I must say I was afraid something might have happened.'

'What made you think that?' said Emily quickly.

'Melanie was usually so conscientious and not turning up like that . . . Well, it was out of character and I was worried.'

'Did you know her daughter had been kidnapped?' Joe watched the solicitor's face for any tell tale signs that he was lying.

'No. Goodness me, if I'd known . . . I thought you said Melanie had died. Are the two things connected?'

'That's what we're trying to find out, sir,' said Emily.

'The child . . .?'

'Hasn't turned up yet.'

Parkland shook his head. 'What a mess. It's unbelievable. Poor Melanie. How did she . . .?'

'We're treating her death as suspicious.'

'You mean she was murdered?'

'We won't know the details until after the post-mortem but it does look like murder, yes. That's why we need to know everything we can about her. And that includes her work here. Did she deal with any criminal cases?'

'No. She specialized in wills and inheritance matters.'

'Are there any disputes that you know of? Could anybody bear a grudge against her?'

'Not that I'm aware of. She was a very well-liked and respected member of staff and there have never been any complaints about her work.'

'We'll need to see her files.'

The man looked as if he was about to argue but he thought better of it. 'Very well. I can arrange that.'

'What do you know about her private life?'

'Her husband is an architect and she had a daughter from a previous marriage . . . not that she allowed domestic matters to interfere with her work here.' He suddenly frowned. 'One of the secretaries did mention that one of her clients had been making a bit of a nuisance of himself. A man who was trying to trace what happened to a relative of his . . . an aunt, I think. He kept calling Melanie, wouldn't leave her alone.'

Emily caught Joe's eye. 'When did he call last?'

The solicitor caught on fast. 'I'm not sure but I don't think he's been in touch for a couple of days.'

'We'll need this man's name and address,' said Joe.

An hour later, after they'd spoken to all Melanie's colleagues and learned very little, they set off for the home of Christopher Arnold Torridge.

Lydia had to face spending the night at her flat sooner or later. Amy had offered to put her up for as long as she wanted but, sensing Steve's horror at the suggestion, she'd declined.

Coming home that evening, she half expected to find the furniture piled up in the hallway again. But she told herself not to be so ridiculous. And she couldn't help smiling to herself when she remembered how DI Plantagenet had moved it for her once the Forensic people had done their bit.

In view of the note the burglar had left, he'd promised to make sure that more security measures were put in place. Somehow she hadn't expected such kindness from a policeman and she hoped she'd get the chance to thank him. She wondered whether he was married. Men like that were usually married . . . or maybe gay.

On returning to the flat she found she'd run out of bread and milk so she headed for the convenience store on Boothgate, hoping she wouldn't bump into Alan Proud. The thought of him living next door made her uncomfortable, like knowing there is only a thin membrane of material between you and a poisonous snake.

As she left the building she noticed that the door beneath the stairs was standing slightly ajar and she heard a faint scraping sound; maybe the builders had started work again and they were getting in a bit of overtime. She walked down the drive and out on to Boothgate.

'Hello. Lydia isn't it?'

She'd been so engrossed in her own thoughts that the male voice made her jump.

'Did you have any luck with the woman who sold the clock?'

When she'd seen Seb Bentham before in his uncle's shop, she'd had a vague impression that there was something a little dangerous about him. But here on Boothgate in the watery sunshine he looked harmless, an ordinary, rather attractive man, walking towards the city, minding his own business.

'Yes, I did call on Mrs Dodds and I think the mystery's been solved.'

'Really?' He paused as if he was waiting to hear the explanation.

'Her father was a doctor and so was my grandfather so he probably visited him and took me along. If it had scared me when I was tiny it might have stayed there in my subconscious. I take it you haven't sold it yet?'

Seb shook his head. 'I wouldn't give the thing house room.' There was a short silence before Seb spoke again. 'I saw you come out of the gate to Havenby Hall.'

'Boothgate House,' she corrected. 'I've got a flat there.'

He fished in the pocket on his shorts and pulled out a sheet of brightly coloured paper. Lydia recognized it at once as a flyer for the new production at the Playhouse. *Mary*. He handed it to her. 'Sorry, but I'm obliged to publicize it.'

'Why?'

He gave a modest smile. 'I wrote the thing, that's why?'

She wondered why his name had seemed vaguely familiar and now she knew why. She took the flyer and studied it. She must have seen it written in small letters underneath the title of the play. *Mary* by Sebastian Bentham.'

She looked up at him accusingly. 'You never said you were a writer.'

He shrugged. 'It's not something I tell everyone on first acquaintance. It's my first play, or rather the first I've had produced. It's set in the 1950s but I got the idea because my aunt was admitted to Havenby Hall in the late 1970s. I started reading up on what happened in institutions like that in the earlier part of the century.' He gave a coy smile. 'I had to exaggerate a little but that's art for you.' He tilted his head to one side. 'I'm sure the place is quite unrecognizable now it's been gutted and done up. I've heard the apartments are very . . .' He searched for a suitable word. 'Nice.'

'Yes, they are.' She looked down at the flyer. 'I might go and see your play. A friend of mine works at the theatre box office and she keeps offering to get me free tickets.'

'Story of my life. I've been wondering how many tickets they've actually sold rather than given away.'

She gave him a nervous smile, feeling a little guilty. 'I'd better go.'

She began to walk away, hardly daring to turn to see if he was still watching her. She continued on towards the convenience store on the corner. The encounter with Seb Bentham had lifted her spirits unexpectedly and almost made her forget about Alan Proud. And maybe, having met the author, she fancied seeing the play after all.

But when she returned to the flat, the plastic bag containing her milk hooked over her arm, she glanced at Proud's door warily as she passed, realizing that she was walking on tip toe. The last thing she wanted was another encounter.

Whenever she entered her flat now she experienced a stab of apprehension. The words of that note haunted her. *I'll see you next time I call. Be ready.*

And when she heard a knock on the door, she almost jumped out of her skin.

Christopher Torridge lived in the Pickby district, not far from Jack Hawkes but in a street of much smaller semi-detached houses. As Emily rang the doorbell she breathed in the strong aroma drifting across the city from the chocolate factory and the very smell made her feel hungry.

As soon as the doorbell sounded they could hear a dog barking. Emily liked dogs in general but this one sounded a brute. When Torridge opened the door he was holding the collar of a fat boxer dog, pulling it back. However Emily's instincts told her that they were more likely to be licked to death than savaged. She put her hand out to pat the dog's head and it began to jump up, grateful for the attention. Torridge dragged it away and locked it in a back room before inviting them in.

'Nice dog,' said Emily. 'They run some good obedience classes these days, you know.'

Torridge looked sheepish. 'She's only a puppy. Maybe I'll get round to it.'

But they weren't there to discuss animal training. Emily saw Joe take his notebook from the inside pocket of his linen jacket, his eyes fixed on Torridge.

'Do you know why we're here, Mr Torridge?' he asked.

Torridge shook his head.

'You're acquainted with a solicitor called Melanie Hawkes?'

'She's been doing some work for me.'

'When did you last see her?'

'A couple of days ago.'

'Where exactly?'

Emily saw his face redden. 'Pickby. I was walking Jezebel in the park and I met her.'

'Was that a coincidence?' said Joe. 'Or did you follow her?'

For a few moments the man didn't answer. Then he bowed his head. 'OK. I admit I saw her going into the park with her kid and I followed her. I hadn't been able to get an appointment that day and I wanted to know if she found anything out.'

'Couldn't it have waited?'

Torridge shrugged his muscular shoulders. 'I didn't think she was taking me seriously.'

'You mean you'd had a disagreement?' Emily glanced at Joe.

'I wouldn't describe it as a disagreement. I just thought she should be doing more, that's all.'

'What did she say when you spoke to her in the park?'

'She said she made some progress and she told me to come to the office to see her. I called the next day but she wasn't at work so I rang her house. She shouted at me down the phone.' He sounded quite indignant, hurt almost. 'After that I kept trying the office but they told me she wasn't there.'

'She's dead, Mr Torridge,' said Joe bluntly. 'We believe she was murdered.'

Torridge raised his hands in a defensive gesture. 'Now don't look at me. I never hurt her. Why should I? She was going to find out what I needed to know. She said she'd made a breakthrough.'

ELEVEN

Lydia looked through the peephole in the door but whoever was there had stepped to one side so they couldn't be seen. She stood there in the hallway, frozen to the spot, uncertain what to do.

Then she made a decision that she knew was probably foolish. She opened the door a crack, just to make sure that Beverley hadn't knocked for some reason then been summoned back by her mother. Poor Beverley was forever at the old woman's beck and call.

But her initial reservations were justified when the door swung open a little wider and suddenly a looming figure stepped forward. Alan Proud was smiling. A leering, triumphant smile.

'Glad I've found you in.'

He was moving towards her now, stepping into her personal space. She backed away.

'I thought we could go for a drink in town,' he said.

'I can't tonight.' She felt curiously detached from the situation, wondering how long it would be before good manners gave way to a scream and a forceful push.

He edged towards her. 'I never take no for an answer once I've made up my mind. You must be nervous . . . girl on her own after what's happened. He won't come back while I'm here, will he? If he thinks you've got a boyfriend around the place . . .'

'No.' All manners were forgotten now and she was surprised that the word came out so forcefully when she was shaking with fear.

He raised his hands in a gesture of appeasement. 'Very well. But you'll regret it.'

There was a hint of a threat in his voice but he turned and left. When she heard his front door open and close, she closed her eyes and uttered a silent prayer of thanks. It could have turned nasty. Maybe next time it would.

She stood there in the open doorway wondering whether to call at Beverley's to tell her what had happened. But she decided against it. Beverley had her own problems.

She retraced her steps and found her handbag in the living room. She still had Inspector Plantagenet's card. He'd told her to call him any time she was worried.

And she was worried now.

Once Torridge decided to talk it was difficult to stop him. And they now understood why Melanie Hawkes had given the man the brush off until she was ready to deal with him in her own time.

Torridge's desire to discover what had happened to his maternal aunt had certainly come to dominate his life. When Joe asked him what he did for a living he learned that he was self-employed, although what that employment involved remained a little vague. Perhaps deliberately so.

Torridge had been much keener to tell them why he'd engaged Melanie Hawkes' services and he'd told them the whole story in graphic detail. His mother's sister, Dorothy Watts, had had some sort of mental breakdown back in the late 1970s and had been admitted to Havenby Hall. She had remained there for about a year, rarely visited by her relatives who hadn't known how to deal with the situation, and she had died unexpectedly of a stroke. She had been forty-two years of age and, as far as everyone knew, in good physical health.

According to Torridge's elderly mother, his Aunty Dot, as he called her, had always been a nervy woman and her marriage hadn't helped the situation. Her husband had been a cold, uncaring man and the couple had been childless. Because of her bleak existence, Dot hadn't been a happy woman and her eventual fate had preyed on the mind of her surviving sister, Torridge's mother. Something had happened in Havenby Hall to cause Dorothy's premature death, Torridge said and, as his mother had become increasingly desperate to know the truth, his sister had suggested that he look into the matter. Since their mother was in her eighties, the matter was rather urgent. That was why he'd been putting pressure on Melanie Hawkes.

'Did anybody benefit from your aunt's death?' Joe asked.

Torridge hadn't mentioned money directly but the hints were there in the background.

'Only her husband . . . my uncle Frank,' he said. 'My mum never liked him. All charm when he wanted something but . . . My mum and Aunty Dot were left some money by their dad and Dot was left a considerable sum by her godfather too. I presume Uncle Frank got it all when she died. He'd been in financial difficulties so . . .'

'Her death came at the right time.' Emily finished his sentence for him. 'Where's your Uncle Frank now?'

Joe looked at her. It seemed that she was developing a fresh interest in the fate of Dorothy Watts. There was something about Torridge's story that had drawn them both in.

'Robins Cemetery. He died five years back. Mrs Hawkes said she'd found Dot's will and all the related probate documents and she left over a hundred grand. It all went to Frank but what happened to it? That's what I want to know, 'cause when he died his estate was only ten grand and, as far as I can see, he didn't have anything to show for it.'

Joe sighed. 'He could have blown it on travelling . . . or gambled it away. Money just slips through some people's fingers.' He spoke as though he knew what he was talking about. He had never been particularly good with money himself.

'He never went on holiday and he never gambled. He were a miserable old bugger.'

'Maybe he gave it away to charity.'

Emily's suggestion was met by a sceptical snort. 'No way.'

'People change, Mr Torridge.' Emily stood up. 'You're sure you've no idea what Mrs Hawkes' important breakthrough might have been?'

'Sorry. No idea.' He looked from Joe to Emily. 'Look, I'm sorry she's dead but you've got to believe me, I had nothing to do with it.'

'Why did you go to a solicitor in the first place? Wouldn't a private detective have been more useful?'

'I knew she specialized in wills and inheritance. I thought she'd know if there was something dodgy about Aunty Dot's will and all that.'

As Torridge showed them out Joe felt inclined to believe his story. However, he had harassed the murdered woman, phoned her home and followed her to the park on the day her daughter disappeared so he couldn't be eliminated just yet.

They hardly exchanged a word as they drove back to the police station. When they were nearing their destination Joe's phone rang and after a brief conversation he turned to Emily who was concentrating on negotiating her way past a bright red tour bus.

'The ransom money's been found,' he said. 'Ten grand in a holdall stuffed through a gap in the wall of the Roman tower in the Museum Gardens. A council cleaner found it and handed it in. Refreshingly honest.'

'Any CCTV in the area?'

'Afraid not. The holdall's gone to the lab. Let's hope for some nice fingerprints,' said Joe.

But when they got back to the CID office the news wasn't good. The bag had been wiped of prints. And there was still no sign of Daisy Hawkes.

When Joe's phone rang again he answered it, hoping it was good news. And when he heard Lydia Brookes's voice he wasn't disappointed.

The post-mortem on Melanie Hawkes' body had been arranged for five o'clock, the earliest time Sally Sharpe could fit it in. Joe and Emily stood watching behind the glass screen in the sparkling new mortuary. Joe felt oddly detached from the proceedings. Perhaps it was the new arrangement, the screen and the microphones. In the old mortuary they'd had to stand at the side of the table close to the sounds and the smells. As far as he was concerned the new development was an improvement.

He'd watched while Sally conducted her detailed examination and he'd seen her open the dead woman's mouth and extract the mush of sodden flower heads carefully with tweezers and deposit them in a stainless steel dish.

'So what's the verdict, Sally?' Emily asked as Sally's assistant was sewing up the Y-shaped incision on the dead woman's torso.

Sally looked across at them, her heart-shaped face solemn. 'The PM's confirmed my initial findings. There's a head injury so I think she was rendered unconscious and strangled some time later. We'll be lucky to get her killer's DNA off her body because she was immersed in water but I'll send the flowers in her mouth off for analysis, just in case.'

'Is there any indication that she put up a fight?' Joe asked.

'There's no sign of her attacker's skin under her finger nails, if that's what you're thinking. I think she was taken by surprise. I don't suppose her clothes have turned up?'

Joe saw Emily shake her head.

'Are you sure she hasn't been sexually assaulted?' he asked.

'As sure as I can be,' said Sally, staring at the body. 'But the bruising on her wrists and ankles does indicate that she was restrained.'

'Just like Peter Brockmeister's victims,' Joe said softly. 'He always said that he liked to exercise a different kind of power over his victims. That's what turned him on. Watching them tied up and helpless.'

'And there's something else,' Sally said. 'There are a number of small marks on her torso which look like cigarette burns. And there are cuts to her thighs and genital area. I think she was tortured.'

Emily gasped. 'So you're saying she was knocked out, restrained and when she came round she was tortured before being strangled?'

'That's the likely scenario,' said Sally. She wrinkled her nose. 'Nasty.'

Joe looked at his watch. Sally's words had disturbed him but there was something he had to do. Besides, he was anxious to get away from that place of death. 'Sorry, Emily, I've got to see someone.'

'Who?' He knew Emily found it hard to suppress her inquisitive nature.

'Lydia Brookes. She's . . .'

'The Builder's latest victim. Is there something new?'

'That neighbour of hers, Alan Proud – the one with the collection of Brockmeister letters – he's been round to her flat. And she's scared.'

'Why?'

'He said some things that made her suspicious and after that note The Builder left . . . Anyway, I said I'd pay her a visit.'

'Just to make sure she's all right?' There was a wide grin on Emily's face. 'The trouble with you, Joe Plantagenet, is that you're so predictable.'

Joe looked away. Perhaps Emily was right. He'd been without female company since Maddy left . . . and that was too long. Years ago he'd discovered that he wasn't cut out for the single, celibate life. Lydia Brookes was attractive. And she was single . . . and vulnerable. There was something about playing knight in shining armour to a frightened woman that appealed to him just at that moment.

'How long will you be?' Emily asked.

'An hour, maybe two.'

'Make it one. And if Proud looks a likely candidate, bring him in.' She stared at the body on the table. 'Melanie here . . . was it a random attack? Was the torture sheer sadism or was there a reason behind it? Was the killer trying to obtain information? And why the hell wasn't the money taken? You kill someone then you pass up the added bonus of ten grand in used notes. Weird.'

'Perhaps the money was irrelevant to him,' said Joe. 'He was only interested in the killing.'

'Which makes him all the more dangerous.'

'We need to know whether it's possible that Brockmeister survived,' said Joe. 'I've requested the files on his death from Scarborough and I've asked our computer people to age his photograph so that we have an idea of what he might look like now.'

'You think he's managed to fool everyone and started killing again after all these years?'

'We've got to consider every possibility, haven't we?'

'And we've also got to find that kid.' She paused. 'Oh God, Joe, you don't think he's killed Daisy as well?'

Joe didn't answer. It wasn't something he wanted to think about.

After saying goodbye to Sally and Emily he left the mortuary and drove through the rush hour traffic to Boothgate House. There were parking spaces in front of the building and he swung the car between the wrought-iron gates that had replaced the massive ones that used to keep the former residents in. But now the new gates stood open and welcoming.

Lydia answered her buzzer almost immediately, as though she'd been standing in her hallway waiting, and the few words of greeting she spoke sounded rushed and anxious. The voice of a frightened woman.

She buzzed him in and as he crossed the hall he saw a man in a suit talking to another man dressed entirely in black who he recognized as Karl Dremmer, the man who'd been with Lydia when she'd discovered the burglary. They were having a heated discussion but Joe failed to catch the drift of the conversation. Joe could make out the odd phrase about access and damage to the fabric of the building. But he had more important things on his mind.

When he reached Lydia's door she stepped out on to the corridor and took a furtive look around before opening the door wide to let him in.

'I believe you've been having trouble with your neighbour,' he said. She was dressed in a thin summer dress, low cut, and she smelled of some half-familiar perfume.

'He came round. Asked me out and implied I needed his protection. I felt he was threatening me but he'll deny it, of course . . . say it was my imagination . . . but I'm scared, Inspector.'

'Joe, please. I take it the Crime Prevention Officer's been round?'

She gave him a weak smile. 'I can't complain about the service. I've had new locks fitted. But he's only next door . . .' She hesitated. 'I think it might have been him who broke in.'

'I'll have a word.'

'Would you?'

Joe turned and made straight for the flat next door. He knocked and when the door opened Alan Proud stared at him blankly before standing aside meekly. Joe followed him into the lounge where they'd spoken before and this time he paid more attention to the framed letters on the wall, pausing to read them while Proud stood behind him. Joe could hear him breathing; a slightly asthmatic wheeze which Joe hoped had been brought on by nerves. He wanted the man afraid and cooperative.

He spun round, taking Proud by surprise. 'I've come to give you a bit of advice.' Proud stared at him, his eyes wide and unblinking. 'Ms Brookes next door said you'd been round.'

'Just being a concerned neighbour.' The words came out in a self-righteous whine.

Joe fought a strong urge to punch the man. But instead he clenched his fists and inhaled deeply. 'You frightened her.'

Proud looked genuinely surprised. Whatever he'd been expecting it clearly wasn't this.

'You told us where you were when her flat was broken into but your alibi told us you only stayed half an hour. Hardly the whole afternoon, like you said. I believe you already have a conviction for stalking a woman.'

'That was a misunderstanding.'

Joe ignored his words and pointed at the framed letters. 'If you're such an expert on Peter Brockmeister you'll know about the way he trapped his victims in their homes.'

'Not at first. He always chose empty houses at first.'

'Until he discovered that it was more exciting to have a terrified victim at his mercy.'

A faraway look came into Proud's eyes. 'He was a forceful personality, Inspector.'

'And he was here . . . in this building. Is that why you chose this flat? Because of the Brockmeister connection?'

Proud's lips twitched upwards into a secretive smirk. 'I admit it was an added attraction.'

The urge to wipe the smirk off his face came again but Joe summoned all his self-control. 'I'd like you to come to the police station to answer some questions regarding the death of a woman called Melanie Hawkes.' He recited the familiar words of the caution. It was official now. They had a suspect and he needed to be interviewed properly with the tape running and everything done by the book.

He phoned Emily to tell her but she didn't sound as delighted as he'd expected. She'd probably been hoping to get home at a reasonable time to see her kids – but in the job, things didn't always work like that.

As he led Proud out on to the corridor, he saw Lydia's other neighbour, Beverley, peeping out of her front door but when she saw him glance in her direction, the door closed quickly. He was glad someone was keeping a lookout for Lydia's sake. Nosy neighbours are sometimes worth their weight in gold.

Two hours later, when he took a break from questioning Proud, Joe grabbed the opportunity to call Lydia to tell her what was happening. And at the same time he asked if she fancied going out the following night.

Karl Dremmer's heart was pounding after his meeting with Patrick Creeny. In his world of academic research any confrontations were subtle and superficially civilized so the argument with Creeny left him feeling shaken. And he hadn't told Creeny about his suspicions. If he had, he knew the man would probably have banned him from the premises altogether.

However, even if that happened, he knew he could always rely on Beverley Newson to let him into the building. He recognized the light of fervour in her eyes and he knew she was hooked as he had been once. He understood her motivation, especially as the poor woman led such an isolated life. Being involved, albeit at a distance, in something with a whiff of exoticism was light in her darkness – and she didn't even have to abandon her elderly mother to access the vicarious excitement.

Creeny had said that he didn't want any adverse publicity, anything that would put the punters off – the flats were hard enough to shift as it was – but Karl had been straight with him: the instruments had definitely picked up something unusual in that basement, something that needed further investigation. Perhaps he should just have lied to Creeny. Kept him sweet. But lying wasn't in his nature.

He hadn't eaten since he'd grabbed a quick sandwich at lunchtime and now his stomach was rumbling. But curiosity gnawed at him more than his hunger as he took the screwdriver and began to scrape away at the mortar between the painted bricks. If he could remove a couple to see what was behind . . .

'Cooee.'

Recognizing the voice, he lowered the screwdriver. Beverley might be useful to him but he didn't particularly want her to know what he planned to do so he stepped away from the wall.

Beverley's bulky outline blocked out the light from the hall as she appeared at the top of the stairs.

'I just wondered how you were getting on.' Her voice was breathless with anticipation.

'I'm fine, thanks, Beverley.'

'You haven't told me what happened last night. Did you see anything? Any ghosts or presences?'

Karl smiled indulgently. He couldn't see her face in the shadows but he could sense her excitement. 'I haven't reached any firm conclusions.'

'Do you need anything? Anything to eat or . . .?'

Karl thanked her profusely and said he was going home to eat before returning later.

'I'll bring some hot chocolate down tonight then. Got to keep your strength up.' She giggled like a schoolgirl. 'What time will you be back so I can be ready to let you in?'

'Around ten. Is that OK?'

'I'll look forward to it.'

As soon as she'd gone he began to tidy up. And when he left he shut the cellar door firmly behind him and shot the bolts across before driving back to his flat near the university, just outside the city in the Hasledon district.

Once back home he ate a microwave meal and watched his favourite soap opera – an indulgence he kept secret, even from his closest friends. When he emerged again into the fading light he heard footsteps crunching on the gravel behind him as he walked towards his car.

It happened so quickly. The violent shove and the kick in his ribs as he landed heavily on the ground.

He was aware of a dark figure leaning over him and he curled his body into a foetal position, bracing himself for a further assault. Then the figure bent slowly towards him and he felt its warm, slightly putrid breath as it hissed in his ear.

'Don't poke your nose into things that don't concern you.'

Karl stayed quite still until he was sure his assailant had gone. Then he struggled to his feet and brushed his clothes down with his grazed hands.

He wasn't used to being on the receiving end of violence. But he wasn't going to let it deter him.

The Builder didn't know why he hadn't thought of the notes before. They certainly added an extra frisson of excitement and he could imagine the women's terror when they read those nine words on the sheet of white paper. *I'll see you next time I call. Be ready.*

He pictured them in bed, tossing and turning in their thin nightclothes, unable to sleep because they were listening for his return. Those few words endowed him with so much power that he was starting to feel invincible.

It was an older woman this time but she was still quite attractive. He'd seen her go out half an hour ago and she'd left the house in darkness so he knew it was empty. He was in the back garden now and he was delighted to see that she'd left a window open for him. Some people would never learn.

He reached in and fumbled with the latch of the large lower window. Then, once he'd climbed in, proud of his own agility, he began to carry some of the lighter pieces of furniture through to build his barrier behind the front door. When he'd finished, he made his way upstairs. He could tell which of the two bedrooms was hers so he went in and sat on the bed. He took her nightdress from under the pillow and put it to his face, breathing in the smell of her, imagining her there with him. At his mercy.

Eventually he stood up, walked over to the dressing table and opened the top drawer. The stupid bitch had made it so easy for him.

TWELVE

Beverley looked into Mother's room at nine o'clock to make sure all was well and she'd found the old lady snoring gently, lost in the deep and peaceful sleep brought about by her medication. When Beverley returned to the lounge, she'd poured herself a glass of white wine – a rare treat – and waited for the buzzer. She had everything ready in the kitchen – the saucepan filled with milk and the chocolate powder in the new mug she'd reserved specially for Dr Dremmer.

When ten o'clock passed and he hadn't arrived she felt disappointed that he'd let her down. His secretive visit was to have been the highlight of her day.

At ten forty-five she heated the milk in the saucepan, poured it into the waiting mug and took it into her bedroom. After reading for a while she put the light out and lay down, pulling the duvet up to her throat even though the night was warm.

She was in that no-man's land between sleeping and waking when something woke her with a jolt. It was the doorbell. The glowing red numbers on her alarm clock told her it was eleven thirty.

He was late but he'd probably still want his hot chocolate. She struggled out of bed and shuffled out into the hallway in her fluffy slippers. When she picked up the receiver of the entry phone she heard his abject apologies. Something had come up – an unavoidable problem.

So she buzzed him in. It would do no harm.

On Saturday morning Joe arrived in the CID office at seven thirty. He hadn't slept well and he felt tired. But he felt hopeful . . . about the Builder investigation at least. As for Melanie Hawkes' murder and her daughter's disappearance, they hadn't made much progress. The sodden flowers found stuffed in

Melanie's mouth were all too common and could have come from many places round and about Eborby and its surrounding countryside. There had been no word of Daisy and Jack Hawkes hadn't received any further calls or instructions. Perhaps the kidnapper had heard about Melanie's death and panicked. There could be another, more sinister possibility of course, but he didn't want to think about that until he had to.

Emily had wanted an early start, especially as Alan Proud had spent the night in the cells and would be nicely softened up for further questioning, but her office was empty so he sat down at his desk, intending to go through the files he'd taken from Melanie Hawkes' office. As soon as he'd taken off his jacket, Sunny hurried up and placed a report in front of him, an 'I told you so' look on his face.

'There was another burglary last night. Same pattern. And he left a note and all.'

Joe picked up the sheet of paper and read it. The Builder had broken into another house. And he'd left his calling card – a note printed in neat capital letters, identical to the one left at Lydia Brookes' flat.

I'LL SEE YOU NEXT TIME I CALL. BE READY.

'Do you think he means it or do you think he does it just to scare the pants off 'em?'

Joe hoped it was the second alternative, but he was keeping an open mind. 'No idea, Sunny. What do you think?'

'He's copying Brockmeister's MO, and the flowers in Melanie Hawkes' mouth were his MO too. But where's the kiddie, that's what I want to know.'

Joe considered the question for a while. 'Daisy's abduction might have nothing to do with her mother's murder. But I could be wrong.'

'It's funny that her killer didn't take the ransom. Why chuck away the chance of ten grand?'

Before Joe could answer, Emily marched in like a ship in full sail. Young detective constables who'd been chatting round the coffee machine scattered and made for their desks and computers, trying to look busy. Joe sometimes wished that he had that effect on his underlings. Maybe that's why he'd so far been passed over for promotion.

'Right.' Emily brought the room to order like a teacher preparing to take the register. 'Anything new come in?'

Joe handed her the report Sunny had given him. 'The Builder's struck again in Bacombe. Same pattern. Single woman. Furniture piled behind the front door. Only underwear and cash taken. And he left another note. Identical to the one he left for Lydia Brookes. Standard A4 sheet of paper and printed on a laser printer.

Emily rolled her eyes. 'Why can't they use their own handwriting or a good old fashioned traceable typewriter? Alan Proud was in custody so he's out of the frame. I was so sure . . .'

'So was I.' He looked round and saw that several of the team were watching them, listening in to their conversation. 'I presume the crime scene people have done their bit.' he said to nobody in particular. 'Any prints?'

'Nothing yet, sir,' said DC Jamilla Dal. 'I'll get on to them.'

Joe thanked her and Emily pulled up a chair and sat down beside his desk. It was time they made some progress.

'I'll send Jamilla round to have a word with the latest victim.' He'd have liked to go himself but with Melanie Hawkes' murder, he hadn't time. 'And I'll get tests run on the note,' said Joe.

'All bases covered then. Unless he decides to carry out his threat, in which case Lydia Brookes will be first on his list.'

Joe looked her in the eye. 'I suppose we'll have to let Proud go.'

'You're right. He might have the best alibi of the lot – for the burglary at least – but I still think he's up to something. I think his interest in Peter Brockmeister is . . .' She searched for an appropriate word.

'Unhealthy?' Joe suggested.

'That's the word. And he hasn't got a convincing alibi for the time Melanie Hawkes was abducted and murdered.' Her eyes focused on the large white board that covered one wall of the CID room. 'So I'm not taking his picture down off that board just yet.'

Joe knew Emily was right. Alan Proud was hiding something. And the thought of him living next to Lydia made him uncomfortable. He remembered his date with her that evening – if he could call it a date. She'd obtained free tickets for the Playhouse from a friend and he could hardly think of a visit to the theatre as a romantic tryst. But he felt an unexpected frisson of anticipation whenever he thought about it.

'Are you going to tell him he can go or shall I?' said Emily.

'I think it would be better coming from you,' he said quickly. He didn't feel up to facing Proud so early in the morning. The man made his flesh crawl.

Jack Hawkes had told Janet Craig, the motherly, well-meaning family liaison officer with a permanently sympathetic expression, to go. He didn't need her. He wanted to get his life back to some semblance of normality and get back to work.

But now he realized that this had been a mistake and the police could well interpret it as indifference to his wife's fate. As for Daisy, the kidnapper hadn't been in touch since Melanie's death so they'd probably seen it on the news and were planning their next move. He imagined they wouldn't want the police to think they were involved in the murder so they'd release Daisy unharmed. It was best not to think of the alternative.

Patrick Creeny had called in first thing that morning but Jack hadn't been in the mood to deal with his anger. A man claiming to be a researcher in paranormal phenomena had been down in the basement of Boothgate House; aided and abetted by one of the more gullible residents, he'd even installed monitoring equipment and spent the night down there.

Creeny had reckoned that if there was something malevolent lurking in the building, it would be nigh on impossible to shift the remainder of the flats. It was bad enough that a few of the workmen claimed to have had strange experiences. One had mentioned going to an exorcist and it had taken a great deal of persuasion on Creeny's part to stop him going to the press. Several men had left without explanation too. And with half the population of Eborby knowing the history of the place, any extra adverse publicity would probably doom the entire project. Punters were squeamish and prone to all kinds of weird superstitious misgivings when it came to investing in bricks and mortar. Patrick Creeny had already taken steps to get rid of Dr Karl Dremmer. If that didn't work, he said he'd have to take things further.

Jack let him rabbit on. He'd sunk most of his money into the Boothgate House development but he'd realized long ago that the whole thing was cursed, most likely due to the prevailing economic conditions rather than some supernatural agency.

He sat in the large kitchen, staring at the dirty dishes he'd been intending to stack away in the dishwasher. His wife had met her death in a terrible way. He had no idea what had become of his step-daughter and he wasn't sure how he'd cope if she came back. Perhaps he'd be able to palm her off on her real dad. After all, he already had a family and he'd only accepted Daisy for Melanie's sake. The whole thing was a mess.

His thoughts were interrupted by the sound of the telephone ringing. He picked it up, thinking it was Patrick calling to report some new disaster, then he suddenly remembered that his calls were still being monitored by the police so he pressed the button which alerted them and started the recording machine. Just in case.

When he heard the voice on the other end of the line he knew he'd done the right thing. He hadn't heard from Daisy's kidnappers since Melanie's death but now they were back. Making demands he couldn't fulfil.

'We still want the money. Ten grand as arranged.' It was an electronic voice just as before.

'Is Daisy all right?'

'She's fine. But she won't be if you don't pay up.'

'Does she know about her mother?'

There was silence on the other end of the line.'

'I want to speak to Daisy. How do I know she's OK if I can't speak to her?'

The silence continued. Then Jack heard a small voice. Daisy's voice. She said hello but nothing more because the phone was taken off her. It was hard to judge from that single word whether she was frightened or happy.

The police had told him to keep the kidnapper talking so

that the call could be traced. But whoever was on the other end was obviously wise to this because they said they'd be in touch and ended the call abruptly.

Jack sat there for a while listening to the dialling tone. Even though the money had been found, the police were keeping it as evidence. He pressed the button to make another call. DCI Thwaite would know what to do. She might even give him his money back.

It was Lydia's turn to do the Saturday shift at the Tourist Information Office and she was late for work. Even though she knew Alan Proud was safely in the cells at Eborby police station she'd had a restless night. The dream had returned and she'd woken with a start at four in the morning. Then she'd drifted back to sleep and overslept by half an hour. As soon as she got out of bed she'd put the radio on and heard about the burglary in Bacombe. Then she'd switched the TV on, hoping to find out more from the local news bulletin and by the time she'd looked at the clock, she'd been running behind.

The phone rang and she answered it, hoping it wouldn't delay her any further.

'Am I speaking to Lydia Brookes? It's Judith Dodds. Oriel House.'

In her tired state it took Lydia a few seconds to place the name. 'Hello, Mrs Dodds. How are you?'

She didn't answer the question. 'I've found something that might interest you. I didn't realize it was there until your visit made me curious and I decided to go up in the attic and look through my late father's things. Can we meet?'

Lydia did a rapid calculation and remembered that she had to work through her lunch hour that day because she needed to get away early for her visit to the theatre with Joe Plantagenet. 'I'm busy today but can we meet tomorrow lunch-time? Is that OK? I know it's Sunday but . . .'

'That suits me quite well,' said Mrs Dodds. 'The cathedral café should be open. I'll meet you there at twelve o'clock?'

'That's fine,' she said. 'See you then.'

Lydia put the phone down, wondering what Mrs Dodds had

found that was so important. And whether it had anything to do with the clock she saw in her nightmares.

Joe hurried into Emily's office. She'd just returned from a meeting with the Superintendent and as he walked in he saw that she looked harassed.

'What is it, Joe? Tell me there's been a breakthrough.'

'Jack Hawkes has had another call from the kidnappers. They put Daisy on the phone this time but not for long.'

Emily sighed. 'Well, at least we know she's still alive.'

'I've sent the family liaison officer back there. I don't care what he says, I think someone should be on the premises. They're going to call him back. And he'll need the money.'

'I'll square it with the Super. I reckon dangling the bait of ten grand in front of the perpetrators is the only way we're going to make an arrest.'

Joe sat down, stretching out his legs, making himself comfortable. 'I couldn't agree more.' He hesitated. 'I've had someone checking out Jack Hawkes' background.'

'That's been done already.'

'I know he hasn't any convictions or even come to our attention, but I wanted to find out more about him.'

Emily sat forward, interested now.

'I've found out that his father, Edward Hawkes, was a detective sergeant. And he was stationed here at the time of the Peter Brockmeister murders. He was on the investigation team.'

'In that case we need to talk to our Mr Hawkes,' she said, folding her arms. 'Let's pay him a visit.'

Jack Hawkes sat with his head in his hands, the picture of despair.

Emily had made them a cup of tea, playing the homely mother card. It was a performance that had lulled a lot of suspects into a false sense of security. She set the mugs of tea down in front of them and smiled.

'You must be worried sick, Mr Hawkes,' she said. 'But don't worry. Someone will be here with you day and night until we get Daisy back safely. The call you received earlier was made from a call box in a village three miles south-east of the city. No CCTV I'm afraid. But the abductor's bound to slip up soon.'

Joe took his first sip of tea. It was too hot and he put it down on the worktop again. 'At least we know Daisy's alive. As soon as they give you instructions we'll get the money to you and you can deliver it as arranged. Then, fingers crossed, they'll let Daisy go and we can make an arrest. You must miss her.'

Joe watched Hawkes as he nodded and swallowed as if he was trying to choke back a sob. He could tell it was an act. And the man wasn't a particularly good actor. Now that Melanie had gone, it might be that he didn't want to have to bring up another man's child. He already had three children of his own from his first marriage so perhaps he'd never bonded with Daisy. There was no predicting these things.

Emily caught his eye. It was time to change the subject. 'You never mentioned your father was a policeman, Mr Hawkes,' Joe said casually, as though he was making conversation.

'I didn't think it was relevant.'

'It probably isn't. But you are aware that there are certain similarities between your wife's death and the murders committed by a man called Peter Brockmeister – he killed four women back in the late 1960s?'

Hawkes opened his mouth to speak but no sound emerged.

'Your father worked on the Brockmeister case.'

A flicker of panic appeared in Hawkes' eyes, there for a second then gone as he composed himself. 'He never talked much about his work.' He looked straight at Emily. 'Surely you understand that. You don't want to bring all that nasty shit home with you.'

'Is your father still alive?' Emily asked.

'He died two years ago.'

'And he never talked about Brockmeister?'

Hawkes shook his head.

But Joe was sure he was lying.

THIRTEEN

Joe managed to slip away from work at six, feeling a little guilty about abandoning his post. He'd left Emily sifting through paperwork but she'd told him to go and enjoy himself . . . and find out anything he could about Alan Proud and the set up at Boothgate House. She'd expect him in early in the morning, she said with a knowing wink.

He walked back to his flat in the small, stone-built block in the shadow of the city walls. It was a warm evening with just a hint of light rain in the air and as he passed beneath Canons Bar, one of the city's great medieval city gates, the smell of garlic wafted from a nearby Italian restaurant, making him hungry.

He didn't know why he felt a little nervous about the evening. Maybe it was the fact that Emily regarded it as work. Was he just using Lydia? And if he was, would she realize? He didn't know the answer. But sometimes you just have to see what happens.

When he reached his flat he closed the door behind him and stood for a few moments in the silence. The light on the answering machine was flashing so he pressed the key. There were two messages: the first from his sister saying that his mother was worried that she hadn't heard from him for a while, the second from an old university friend who was coming up to Eborby in a couple of weeks' time for a stag weekend. He wondered if Joe would like to join him, but, with murder and an abducted child on his mind, enforced enjoyment was the last thing he could face. He'd call the friend back and say it depended on his work commitments. Work always provided a good get out if one was needed.

He looked at his watch. If he was going to make the theatre by seven, he'd have to get a move on. He didn't know much about the play as he'd been too preoccupied with work to pay much heed to Eborby's artistic life, but as Lydia had obtained free tickets from a friend, at least they'd have no worries about sneaking out if it was bad. He made himself something to eat and flicked through the evening newspaper that had been lying on his doormat. Melanie Hawkes' murder had made the headlines again but the news blackout meant that there was no mention of Daisy's abduction. And half way down the page he saw the words 'The Builder: serial burglar strikes again. Could this be a copycat?' It seemed some observant journalist had picked up on the similarity between the recent burglaries and Peter Brockmeister's MO. But there was no mention of Brockmeister in the reports of Melanie's death – the detail of the flowers was something the police had been careful to keep to themselves.

He put on a fresh shirt and jeans and looked at himself in the mirror. He had thick, black hair that badly needed a trim and there were shadows beneath his blue eyes. His face looked pale, which was hardly surprising, given that he'd spent most of the recent good weather stuck in the police station, his desk piled with work.

He walked because it wasn't far to the theatre and, besides, parking was difficult in the centre of Eborby – a city designed centuries before the internal combustion engine was a spark in its creator's eye. When he arrived he saw Lydia standing in the corner of the foyer, studying a display of blood-coloured posters arranged around a set of black-and-white cast photographs. Joe watched her for a few moments. She looked good and she'd obviously taken more trouble with her appearance than he had. She was engrossed so he walked up to her and tapped her on the shoulder, which was a mistake because she jumped at his touch. He really should have realized that her nerves wouldn't be good after what she'd been through.

'I'm sorry,' he said.

'That's OK.' She gave him a nervous smile. 'You've released Alan Proud. I saw him as I was leaving my flat. Got a bit of a shock.'

'We had to let him go. There was an identical burglary last night so we know it wasn't him.'

'As long as he keeps away from me,' she said.

'If he gives you any trouble, just let me know.'

She took a deep breath. 'The play's had good reviews.'

'I believe so,' he said, trying to sound knowledgeable.

The bell sounded, telling them to take their seats for the first act. Joe bought a programme and gave it to Lydia as they made their way into the auditorium. They chatted a little until the house lights went down.

And when they went up again they both sat for a while in stunned silence.

'I hadn't expected that,' Lydia said as they made their way to the bar. Joe was in need of a drink after the catalogue of misery they'd just witnessed being acted out on the stage. The eponymous heroine, Mary Downes, was a young woman in the 1950s who had become pregnant by an itinerant fairground worker so her family had had her committed to Havenby Hall, saying she was 'morally degenerate'. The girl's journey of suffering had been hard to watch.

He told himself that the play had sprung from the author's imagination rather than any real life events. There had been a harrowing scene when a woman had been tormented by a sadistic member of staff who used subtle and imaginative ways of inflicting degradation. He could still hear the actor's sobs echoing in his ears.

'I expect most of it's made up,' he said as he handed Lydia a glass of white wine, trying to sound cheerful.

'There's the writer so why don't we ask him?'

She was pointing to a young man in a black T-shirt who was talking earnestly to a group of young people dressed in similarly funereal clothes.

'You know him?'

'His name's Sebastian Bentham.' She didn't make any effort to explain further. She just set off in his direction, pushing her way through the crowd of interval drinkers with mumbled 'excuse me's' and Joe felt obliged to follow.

When the man spotted Lydia he muttered something to his companions and moved forward to meet her, a slightly nervous look on his face. 'You made it then?' he said. He looked at Joe. 'Aren't you going to introduce us?'

Joe held out his hand. 'Joe Plantagenet. Friend of Lydia's. Did you do much research?'

Sebastian began to look more relaxed. 'I did. As a matter

of fact I interviewed a number of people who were at Havenby Hall when it was a hospital.'

Joe suddenly made the connection. 'Ever heard of Peter Brockmeister?' said Joe

He frowned. 'His name came up while I was doing my research. I haven't named him in the play, of course but . . . let's say he influenced events.'

'In what way?'

'Well, I learned that he was highly intelligent and very charismatic and some of the staff – how shall I put it? – fell under his influence. My play's set twenty years earlier, of course, but I've used him as a shadowy presence.'

'The madman? The one who frightens the main character?'

'That's right. But from what I've heard Brockmeister was more evil than mad. If you believe in that sort of thing.'

Joe nodded. He did believe in that sort of thing. Throughout his life he'd seen too much evidence of evil to be a doubter.

Joe handed Sebastian his card. 'I'm interested in talking to anybody who knew Brockmeister.'

Sebastian studied the card and his eyebrows shot up. 'Is it about those burglaries? I read about them and . . .'

'Did you speak to anyone who was at Havenby Hall at the same time as Brockmeister?'

'Yes.'

'If you could let me have their names and addresses . . .'

'No problem. I spoke to a former nurse, the chaplain and a former patient.' He took his mobile phone from his pocket, studied it then scribbled the names and phone numbers on the back of Joe's card. 'They were all very helpful,' he said as he handed it back. 'None of them wanted to see the play but I don't suppose that's surprising.'

Joe said nothing. When Sebastian returned to his friends and his playwright's role, Joe whispered in Lydia's ear. 'Do you want to stay for the second half or shall we go for a drink?' He prayed that she'd choose the second option.

'Let's have the drink afterwards,' she said.

His heart sank. But he'd just have to brace himself for putting duty before pleasure.

* * *

The clock was watching Lydia again with its hard, painted eyes. Her heart was pounding and she was trapped, unable to move. It was looming nearer and she knew it would consume her, crush her body.

She jerked awake and found she was covered in perspiration. It took her a few seconds to realize that she was in her own room and she could make out the familiar shapes of her furniture in the moonlight streaming through her thin cotton blinds.

Since she'd actually set eyes on the clock in that shop she'd been free of the nightmare. Perhaps it was seeing Sebastian and his awful play. According to Judith Dodds, the thing had come from Havenby Hall so the associations had most likely mingled in her head and brought it all back.

She turned over and stretched her arm across the pillow beside her own on the double bed. She'd asked Joe Plantagenet back for coffee but he'd seemed reluctant. He'd said he had to be at work early in the morning. Working on a Sunday morning may have been an excuse, but, as there had been a murder as well as another burglary, she supposed it could well be the truth.

When they'd escaped the theatre they'd hurried through the narrow streets to the Star where she'd drank more wine than was advisable while Joe downed several pints of best bitter like a man who was trying to forget the trials of the day. There had been something about him that invited confidences and she found herself telling him her life story. How she'd married young. How she'd given birth to a beautiful baby girl who'd died after only two hours in this world. How her marriage hadn't survived the tragedy of loss. How she'd come to Eborby and had been establishing her life again until The Builder came and dented her new-found confidence.

He had reciprocated and told her of his days in a seminary training to be a priest, of his meeting with Kaitlin who was to become his wife and of her tragic death in an accident six months after their wedding. Then there was the shooting while he'd been working in Liverpool when his colleague had died and he'd been seriously injured. He still had the scar where the bullet had entered his body, he said. Emboldened by white wine, she'd replied that she'd like to see it. He'd given her a distant smile and said perhaps one day. But she was sure she'd messed up.

She looked at the red glowing numbers of her alarm clock and discovered that it was two fifteen.

She closed her eyes. She had to be in work in the morning so she needed some sleep. But a distant sound made her haul herself upright and listen.

It was there again. A faint scraping, a distant door closing. Then silence.

FOURTEEN

Beverley had let Dremmer in when he'd arrived at eleven thirty the previous night and given him a mug of hot chocolate but he'd made it clear that he wanted to be alone, and she'd managed to hide her disappointment.

That morning she'd risen early and dressed in her new beige trousers and a red T-shirt. She'd even applied some make up to her blotchy skin, but one glance in the mirror was enough to tell her the effect wasn't the one she'd wished for. She'd put on three stone since she'd left work to look after Mother and, as food had become her greatest comfort and pleasure, that particular situation was unlikely to change in the foreseeable future.

After she'd given her mother breakfast, she poured an extra cup of tea. Dr Dremmer was bound to need it after spending the night down there. And she liked to be useful.

She put the door of the flat on the latch and carried the mug of hot tea carefully down the corridor. When she reached the entrance hall she saw that the door to the basement stood half open. Dr Dremmer had told her that he wasn't to be disturbed. But she was sure that didn't apply to the morning.

She pushed the door open and began to make her way down the stairs, calling Dremmer's name softly. There was no answer and it too dark down there to see much but she could make out the outline of his recording equipment, the night vision camera on the tripod. Strange that he should leave it there unattended.

She turned and as she reached the hall she noticed that the front door was ajar, which was odd because most of the residents were careful about shutting it properly, especially since the burglary. She crossed the hall and stepped outside into the watery morning sun. It was Sunday morning and everything was quiet; no sound apart from birdsong and the occasional car passing along Boothgate.

She looked round and her eyes were drawn towards the

graveyard to her right. Something was lying half hidden amongst the blackened headstones so she clutched her cardigan around her and walked towards it, her feet crunching on the new gravel path.

As she drew closer she could see it was a human body laying face down, flattening the overgrown grass, its arms raised as if in surrender.

She'd found Karl Dremmer at last.

Joe almost wished he hadn't told Emily about his night out with Lydia. She was taking too much of an interest in his private life for comfort. She meant well, of course, but he'd know better for next time.

As soon as he'd set foot in the office she greeted him with a quizzical 'Well, how did it go?' The question was packed with innuendo.

He'd given her an enigmatic smile in return. It appealed to some innate sense of mischief that he'd thought had left him long ago to keep her guessing.

There was something on his 'to do' list, something he'd been putting off that needed to be checked out in connection with Melanie Hawkes' murder. He needed to contact the people she'd interviewed in relation to the Torridge case, three of whom had also helped Sebastian Bentham with his research. But first he had to have a word with Chris Torridge's mother to see if she backed up his story about her sister being committed to Havenby Hall and the ensuing mystery about what had become of her money. He could have given the job to one of the junior officers but he felt he wanted to check it out himself.

He had obtained her address during his interview with her son. She lived in a nursing home in Hilton so he bagged himself a pool car and drove out there, passing Boothgate House on the way. He noticed that an ambulance was parked outside and he experienced a sudden feeling of dread that something awful had befallen Lydia. He wondered whether to stop but he told himself not to be so imaginative; there were ten occupied flats in the building so the odds were that it was nothing for him to worry about.

The Yelland Grange Nursing Home, once the home of a nineteenth-century Eborby worthy who'd chosen to live out of town away from the smoke and dirt of the city's ancient crowded streets, stood in well-kept gardens at the far end of Hilton, not too far from the ring road and the park and ride. Joe parked the car on the driveway, glad that he'd called ahead to warn of his arrival.

He was met at the door by an overweight middle-aged woman in a blue overall. She wore her hair in a severe pony tail and there was a wary look on her round, pale face.

Once he'd showed his warrant card she led the way through a maze of carpeted corridors, eventually stopping at a door with a small card bearing Edna Torridge's name attached to it with a drawing pin, as though to emphasize the temporary nature of her stay.

The young woman suddenly fixed a determined smile to her face and pushed the door open. 'Visitor for you, Edna. It's a nice policeman.'

Joe smiled too, trying to live up to his billing, and stepped into the room.

Mrs Torridge was sitting in an armchair, her knees covered with a blanket in spite of the oppressive heat in the room. She was a small woman with thin grey curls. She reminded Joe of a small, delicate bird. But when she looked up at him he could see a strength of spirit in her watery blue eyes.

'Sit down then,' she said. She looked at the woman who had brought him there. 'And you can go and all. I don't need a nursemaid.'

Joe had expected her voice to be weak and quavering but it was as strong and determined as Emily's. The woman in the blue overall hesitated for a second before leaving the room, and once she had gone Joe made himself comfortable on a chair which he suspected doubled as a commode.

'I expect you've come about my sister. It's about time we got to the bottom of what happened to her. That son of mine's been faffing about with solicitors and all that but I told him to tell the police. I want to get to the truth before I go and meet my Maker. Our Dot was a silly woman, always suffering with her nerves, but she never deserved what happened to her in there.'

'What did happen?'

'I think she was murdered.'

'Her family were told she'd had a stroke.'

'That's rubbish. Apart from her nerves she was as fit as a flea until they took her into that place. I fought it, you know, but that husband of hers . . .'

'Your son said you didn't visit her when she was in Havenby Hall.'

She shook her head in exasperation. 'I didn't visit her because *he* told me not to. I wish now that I'd taken no notice and gone anyway. Forty-two she was. No age at all.'

'How do you think she was murdered?'

'I don't know how they did it. I just know that her death wasn't natural. And I want to get justice for her before I go. Sixty grand she had left her by her godfather and there was half our dad's money she hadn't touched. And when *he* died his estate was only worth ten grand so what became of all that money, that's what I'd like to know. Trouble is, I've no proof – just a feeling. That's why my Christopher wouldn't tell the police. Him and my daughter said they'd just laugh at me if we didn't have more evidence.'

'I'm not laughing, Mrs Torridge,' said Joe. 'The solicitor who was enquiring into your sister's death was murdered. That's why I'm here.'

Edna Torridge's eyes shone. 'You think it was because of something she found out about Dot?'

'That's only one possibility among many. We've got to check everything out and this is the only case she was dealing with that seemed to be . . .' He searched for the right words. 'Out of the ordinary.'

'Well there was something going on in that Havenby Hall place. Other people died unexpectedly and all.'

'How do you know?'

'There was a nurse there called Betty.'

Joe nodded. Betty Morcroft was one of the names Sebastian Bentham had given him. One of the people he'd spoken to when he'd researched his play. And Melanie Hawkes had spoken to her too.

Edna continued. 'Betty was there at Dot's funeral – horrible little hole-in-the-corner affair it was because *he* didn't want a fuss. Crematorium and no hymns, I ask you. Betty was the only one from that place who turned up and bloody worried she looked and all. I spoke to her afterwards and I could tell she was scared. She didn't say much but she did admit there'd been a few unexpected deaths. Then she clammed up as if she realized she shouldn't have said it. Like I said, she was frightened of something . . . or someone.'

'Did you meet anyone else from Havenby Hall?'

'*He* made sure I was kept well away. But Betty mentioned a couple of names. The matron was a Mrs Chambers . . . and there was a doctor called Pennell. I'd hoped Christopher would be able to find out more but . . . He's always been a lazy lad so I'm not surprised he left it to some stranger to do the work for him.'

'That stranger was murdered, Mrs Torridge.'

Edna leaned forward. 'Maybe she found something out after all,' she said in a loud whisper.

But before Joe could reply his mobile phone began to ring. And when he answered it he discovered there'd been a death at Boothgate House. And this one was definitely suspicious.

Patrick Creeny's face was so red that Emily feared for his health.

As soon as he'd heard about the death on the radio news he'd driven to Boothgate House and found half the grounds sealed off with police tape and the whole panoply of a murder investigation in progress. And, when Joe arrived, Emily was about to interview the man to find out what he knew.

A woman in one of the flats had raised the alarm. The victim, she said, worked at the university and he'd been spending the night down in the basement. Her account of his work had been a little vague but, as Emily understood it, he'd been carrying out research down there with an array of scientific equipment. She'd already been down to the basement and seen the cameras and meters so she knew the story was true.

The university had already confirmed that the dead man, Dr Karl Dremmer, was a well-respected researcher in paranormal phenomena who specialized in debunking Eborby's many ghostly sightings, which meant he probably wasn't a popular man with the tourist board. Patrick Creeny had already admitted that he'd opposed Dremmer's presence, saying that the remaining flats were hard enough to sell as it was without the place getting a reputation for being haunted. Dremmer hadn't had his permission to be there last night and it seemed that one of the residents had let him in – foolishly, in his opinion.

Creeny had an alibi for the previous night. Not only was his wife able to vouch for him, but his in-laws were staying and, according to him they were the most reliable of witnesses because there was no love lost between them and their son-in-law. Someone had already checked and it seemed he was telling the truth. At no point during the night did Patrick Creeny leave his luxury five-bedroom house in Abbotsthorpe. Besides, Dremmer might have been a nuisance but that was hardly worth committing murder for. Somehow he didn't sound very convincing.

When the interview was over Emily told Creeny he could go. They'd be in touch. But Joe had a couple more questions for him.

'Do you know why Dr Dremmer chose to conduct his research here?' he asked.

Creeny looked round as though he was afraid of being overheard. 'Presumably because he reckoned the place was haunted. All nonsense, of course.'

'It's not in any of the usual books on Eborby hauntings. And the ghost tour doesn't come here.'

'That's what I told him. But he'd heard stories from one of my workmen. If I found out who it was, they wouldn't have a job for long, I can tell you.'

'Some people think a good ghost story adds a bit of interest to a house,' said Emily.

'This wasn't a ghostly monk or a grey lady – Dremmer said the workmen had sensed something evil. I've had a few workers leave, saying the place gave them the creeps. If that got out it would drive the punters away. And I can't afford that in the current economic climate.'

They let Creeny go because they had no reason to keep him there. And when Joe asked if Lydia had been interviewed,

Emily told him that Sunny had had a word with her but she hadn't been able to tell him anything useful. She'd heard what she thought might have been voices at around two fifteen but that was all she knew.

The woman who'd found the body was being looked after by Jamilla who was doing the tea and sympathy bit. Emily had left Alan Proud till last because she wanted to see his reaction for herself. Joe said he'd help her conduct the interview but there was something he wanted to do first.

Emily had already seen the body but Joe felt he needed to see for himself exactly what they were dealing with. He left her and made for the graveyard. It was close to the building and he could see iron scaffolding bars, pallets and dusty floorboards piled up near the walls. The whole area had been sealed off with police tape and Sally was packing up her crime scene bag so he guessed she had finished her preliminary examination and pronounced life extinct. She looked round when he said hello and smiled.

'You're keeping me busy,' she said. 'At least this one hasn't got flowers stuffed in his mouth. He was killed with a good old-fashioned blunt instrument.'

She stared down at the body. Joe had only met Karl Dremmer briefly; he'd been with Lydia when she'd discovered that her flat had been violated. Now he looked at the shell that had once been a man. He was lying face down and the back of his head had been hit with some force, cracking the skull like a boiled egg so that in places the grey matter of the brain was visible.

'Think he died here?' he asked Sally.

'I think so.'

'Any sign of the weapon?'

Sally shook her head. 'Not so far.'

'He was supposed to be down in the basement. Wonder what he was doing here.'

Sally thought for a moment. 'Could someone have lured him out here somehow? Someone who knew he'd be down there . . . or found him down there.' She gave him a wide smile. 'But I'm glad to say that's your problem. I'm only the pathologist.'

There had been a time when Sally had made it plain that she wanted him to be more than a colleague. But he had missed his opportunity and now she was engaged, to another doctor, so he'd heard. Life was full of missed chances. He wondered whether to see how Lydia was. But he didn't really have time.

He returned to Emily and told her about his meeting with Edna Torridge.

'Think it's relevant?' she asked.

He considered her question for a while, ideas and theories flitting through his head, refusing to settle. 'If our two deaths are linked, this place could be the common denominator.'

'I'm not sure they are linked,' Emily said. 'Different MO for a start. And Brockmeister only killed women.'

Joe remained silent as they entered the building and made their way to Alan Proud's flat. He was bracing himself for another encounter with the man and the thought of him living in such close proximity to Lydia made him uncomfortable.

Proud swore that he hadn't known Dremmer was down there and that he hadn't heard a thing. He'd never met the man and he certainly didn't believe in ghosts. All that was a load of rubbish to fleece the tourists. And why were the police harassing him? Just because he was interested in true crime and the stupid bitch next door had misinterpreted his actions, it didn't make him a murderer.

Joe didn't feel inclined to argue. He was just glad to get away from the man. But Emily said they should keep a careful eye on him. If Proud so much as dropped a piece of litter in the street, she wanted to know about it.

It was almost midday when they finally left Boothgate House. Emily looked strained, as though this new development was too much for her. Joe knew how she felt. Not only would they be delving into Melanie Hawkes' life and work but now they'd have to find out everything they could about Karl Dremmer. Someone had already talked to some of his colleagues at the university and discovered that he lived alone. A wife hadn't been mentioned. But that, Emily said, didn't mean there wasn't an ex-Mrs Dremmer lurking somewhere in the background – a woman who'd tired of her husband spending his nights hunting ghosts.

They were driving back to the police station when Joe's phone rang. He answered it and heard a familiar voice.

'Hello, George. How are things?'

But the Rev George Merryweather clearly hadn't rung for a social chat. 'I've just come out of morning service and I've been trying to ring a man called Karl Dremmer. His phone was answered by a policeman who said there'd been an incident. He took my name and told me someone would be in touch. Can you tell me anything? Has something happened to him?'

'Are you free for lunch?'

'The cathedral café in an hour? I've a lot to tell you.'

Joe glanced at Emily who was trying to keep her eyes on the road. 'Sounds interesting. See you later.'

Lydia had met Karl Dremmer. He'd been the one who helped her when she'd found the furniture barricaded against her front door. Perhaps he'd been a little strange, a little intense, but he'd been gentle and sympathetic. She'd hardly known the man but she'd liked him.

Although it was Sunday the tourist office was still open and she was down to do a shift. She'd been about to set out for work when she'd heard someone knocking on her door. Fearing it was Alan Proud, she'd opened it cautiously, glad that she still wasn't in her night things, and found a short, middle-aged detective with nicotine-stained fingers standing there. DS Sunny Porter had broken the news and she'd felt stunned. Then she'd recalled how she'd been woken by a sound in the night. Voices, perhaps, or a distant door opening. She knew the time – two fifteen – because she'd looked at the alarm clock. But that was all she knew. She hadn't even realized that Dr Dremmer was in the building.

The morning passed quickly and after she'd finished helping out some American visitors who were trying to find out the times of the river trip, she looked at her watch and realized it was almost time for her lunch break. Her appointment with Judith Dodds had been on her mind all morning. She wondered what the woman had to tell her.

As soon as the Americans left the office a Canadian couple

came in enquiring about theatre productions. Lydia took a deep breath and told them she'd seen the new production at the Playhouse, *Mary*, and she couldn't really recommend it as an enjoyable night out. She put it tactfully, of course, but she thought they'd got the message. She felt no qualms of guilt about her negativity; she hardly knew Sebastian Bentham and she didn't owe him anything. She would have felt more guilty about condemning a pair of innocent visitors to an evening of unadorned misery. Besides, there was an Alan Ayckbourn play on at the Opera House so she had no problem suggesting a more digestible alternative.

Once the couple had gone away happy, her colleague tapped her on the shoulder. 'Didn't you say you wanted to take an early lunch?'

It was time to go and suddenly she felt afraid, although she didn't know why. Surely anything Mrs Dodds had discovered wouldn't make things worse.

It was a beautiful day and the only clouds in the sky were small, fluffy and white so she didn't bother taking a jacket as she hurried through the streets to the cathedral, weaving her way through crowds of strolling tourists. The cathedral bells began to ring as she crossed the road, narrowly avoiding being mown down by a cyclist. She could see a line of horse-drawn carriages lined up on the street, and she watched as one set off carrying a pair of middle-aged tourists, trotting at a leisurely pace and holding up the traffic. On a pleasant Sunday like this it would be easy to forget the darker side of Eborby life. But she felt the darkness would always be with her while she lived at Boothgate House. She had made an impulsive decision and it had been wrong.

She passed beneath Boothgate Bar and found herself on a narrow street where small shops with jutting upper storeys jostled with cosy pubs and busy restaurants, eventually arriving at the great paved square in front of the cathedral. The bells were louder here, drowning out all other noise. She stopped for a few seconds, drawing comfort from the sound before skirting the great church and arriving at Vicars Green.

The cathedral café was housed in an ancient stone building

once used by the clergy. She made her way past the glass cabinet full of fattening cakes and scanned the room for a familiar face. Sure enough Mrs Dodds was there waiting for her, sipping a coffee.

She looked up as Lydia approached. 'I haven't eaten yet. Do you want . . .?'

They served Sunday lunch there but recent events had robbed her of her appetite. 'Just a sandwich,' she said. Mrs Dodds said she'd have the same and Lydia queued up at the counter.

She ate quickly, sensing Mrs Dodds wouldn't reveal the purpose of the meeting until they'd finished. Once the plates were empty Mrs Dodds delved in her floral shopping bag, took out what looked like a ledger and passed it to Lydia.

'After you'd left I went up in the attic and had a root through my father's things. My father went into hospital for an operation in early 1980 and it looks as if your grandfather acted as locum at Havenby Hall for a couple of weeks.'

A yellow Post-it note marked the appropriate page and Lydia opened it. There was her grandfather's signature against the notes. Dr Reginald Speed. The page was filled with his sloping handwriting: when she'd helped to clear her grandmother's house out after her death she'd found many examples, kept as treasured mementos by his widow.

As she began to read she realized that it was an account of the various treatments he'd given to patients, mainly antibiotics and painkillers. However, as she continued to read, things became more interesting. After the first few days at Havenby Hall her grandfather had no longer confined himself to matter-of-fact notes of medications he'd administered. He had begun to record his observations of various patients, even though he was supposed to adhere strictly to dealing with physical ailments. And there were observations about the staff too and comments on the way they treated the patients. Then a name caught her eye. Brockmeister. After the first three pages he featured a lot and it seemed that her grandfather had made a special point of observing his behaviour. When she turned the page she saw that several sheets of paper had been torn out. Whatever her grandfather had written there had been removed.

The rest of the ledger was filled with another handwriting, presumably that of Mrs Dodds' father, Dr Pennell. And he had confined himself to routine medical matters.

She looked up and saw that Mrs Dodds was watching her closely. 'Why are you showing me this?'

'Because I thought there was something unusual about the way your grandfather wrote about Havenby Hall. And those pages were torn out. I wondered if my father did that when he took over again.'

Lydia stared at the ledger. 'You're right. I think my grandfather was worried about something. Something to do with this Brockmeister.' She hesitated. 'I know who he was.'

'So do I,' Mrs Dodds said almost in a whisper.

Lydia delved into her purse and pushed her share of the lunch money across the table. 'I'm sorry, I've got to get back to work. Thanks for . . .'

'You can keep the ledger if you like. It's no use to me.'

Lydia picked it up and slipped it into her large handbag. But as she walked out of the place she regretted her action at once. She didn't want to be reminded of Brockmeister or that clock. On the other hand, she was curious.

As she hurried out of the café, suddenly anxious to be out of there, she was startled to see Joe Plantagenet standing in the doorway. He wore what she presumed were his working clothes which reminded her that he was bound to be on duty after what had happened to Karl Dremmer. When he spotted her he smiled. He had a nice smile, slightly crooked, and all the darkness she'd sensed in him last night seemed to have vanished.

'On your lunch hour?' he asked. But she sensed his mind wasn't on her as his eyes began to search the room as though he was looking for someone.

'Yes, I . . . I've just found out something about my grandfather. He . . .'

'Joe. Good to see you. How are you?'

She turned her head and saw a small bald clergyman bearing down on Joe. From his wide smile of greeting she could tell the two men knew each other well and she had the feeling she'd be in the way.

'Look, I'll have to go,' she said.

'I'll call you,' he said, touching her arm gently. 'Take care.'

Joe watched Lydia as she walked away. Perhaps he should have made more effort to find out what she had to say about her grandfather. But time was tight. He grabbed a sandwich from the display, ordered a coffee and sat down opposite George who was about to tuck into a plate of roast beef and Yorkshire pudding – his weekly treat after Matins.

'So what happened to Dr Dremmer?' George sounded concerned but worry didn't seem to have dampened his appetite, judging by the speed with which the roast beef and Yorkshire pudding was vanishing from his plate.

'How do you know him?'

'He contacted me. He was conducting paranormal research in Havenby Hall on Boothgate – it's been converted into apartments and renamed Boothgate House.'

'I know. Dr Dremmer was found dead there first thing this morning. We think he was murdered.'

George put down his knife and fork. 'He seemed a quiet sort of chap . . . an academic. Although I believe academics can make a lot of bitter enemies amongst their colleagues . . . professional rivalries and all that.'

'We think his death might be connected with the building. You've heard of the other recent murder – Melanie Hawkes?'

'Yes. That was terrible.'

'Her husband was the architect who's been working on the Havenby Hall conversion. And the woman I spoke to earlier lives there. Her flat was broken into by this serial burglar.'

'The Builder?'

'That's right.'

George gave him a mischievous grin. 'And there was me thinking you might have found yourself a woman.'

Joe decided to say nothing. If anything came of the relationship he'd tell George in his own good time. 'I'm sure there's some connection to that place but I don't know what it is yet.'

George continued to eat and Joe waited until he'd finished before he asked his next question. 'In view of what happened I need to know what Dremmer said to you.'

George took a sip of his tea. 'He was a sceptic, a serious researcher. I try to take that attitude myself, of course. Most allegedly paranormal phenomena can either be explained away or they're the result of someone's overactive imagination. But now and again you come across the genuine article: something inexplicable or just plain evil.' He put his cup down and looked Joe in the eye. 'That's what Dremmer thought he'd found in the basement of Boothgate House. He called me because he wanted a second opinion. He said his equipment had picked something up. And he said he'd found something down there, something he intended to investigate.'

'Did he say what it was?'

'I'm afraid not.'

'You haven't been down there yourself?'

'He was going to spend another night there and he said that if he hadn't come up with a feasible explanation, he was going to ask me to go down with him. Dremmer's not the first person to sense something amiss in that building; a few workmen have reported disturbing experiences. He said he'd encountered opposition from the developer but one of the residents was happy to admit him to the building.'

'We've met her. She's a retired spinster with a sick mother and I think Dremmer's arrival was the most exciting thing that had happened to her for years. Everyone loves a good ghost hunt.'

'True. But I didn't get the impression there was anything entertaining about this one. I think Dremmer was genuinely disturbed by what he experienced down there.'

'I'm going back there now so I'll have a look for myself. And I'm sure we'll find someone to have a look at his equipment and interpret the findings.' He drained his coffee cup. 'I'd better go, George. I'll be in touch.'

'Have you given any thought to my suggestion . . . that work with the homeless shelter?'

Joe turned. 'Sorry, George. Things have been a bit hectic. Maybe when things ease up a bit.'

He left reluctantly. He'd have liked to spend more time with George, who'd helped him through the worst time in his life: the time when he'd moved to Eborby after Kaitlin's death and his own injury in the course of duty. George had saved his faith and his sanity. He owed the man. Maybe when the case was resolved, he told himself. Maybe then he'd give George the attention he deserved.

As he walked back to Boothgate House he couldn't help wondering about Daisy Hawkes. There was something odd about the kidnapping. But that was only one of the things he had to worry about.

Janet Craig was bored. Being a family liaison officer was a difficult job, requiring a great deal of sensitivity, but she had never come across anybody like Jack Hawkes before. Even though his wife had been murdered and his stepdaughter kidnapped, he seemed determined to carry on as normal, spending much of his time in the large office at the other end of the house, conducting phone conversations and disappearing off to meetings. She'd even heard him laughing. She knew people dealt with grief in different ways but this was a first.

One of her duties was to monitor the phone in case Daisy's kidnappers called with more demands. She'd never dealt with a kidnapping case before but, again, she sensed this one was unusual. Something about Hawkes didn't add up. And she'd said as much to DCI Thwaite.

Hawkes was in his office, a spacious room with the model of Boothgate House, once known as Havenby Hall, at its centre, recently returned there after a spell in the drawing room. In his absence she stood up and wandered around the room, wishing something would happen; that Daisy's abductor would make contact or that there'd be some breakthrough in the murder enquiry that she could convey to the not-so-grieving widower. After staring out of the window at the quiet street outside for a while, her natural curiosity got the better of her and she opened the glazed doors of the large mahogany bookcase that stood against one wall. When she pulled out a couple of books and examined them, hoping to find something interesting to read to pass the time, she was surprised to see another row of books behind the first. And these looked far more interesting with their garish covers.

She removed some of the books in the front row carefully

– she didn't want Hawkes to know she'd been prying – and found that the second, hidden row was made up of true crime books, all about one particular subject. There were a couple of box files too, tucked away in the corner. With one eye on the door, alert for Hawkes' return, she took them out and when she opened them she saw that they were full of notes.

And they, like the books, were all about Peter Brockmeister and his crimes.

FIFTEEN

Joe knew that Emily was expecting him back at the police station but he called her to say there was something he had to do. She told him not to be long.

When he arrived at Boothgate House, the place was still buzzing with police officers. He knew that Alan Proud had already been interviewed and had sworn that he knew nothing and that he hadn't been aware of anything out of the ordinary the previous night. Proud had already complained of police harassment so Joe's instincts told him it would probably be best to take it easy until they had some reason – however slight – to put the pressure on.

There was no sign of Beverley Newson. According to one of the constables guarding the scene, she was in her flat with her mother, recovering from her ordeal. Of all the residents, Beverley had had the closest dealings with Dremmer so Joe thought it might be worth having another word. But there was something he wanted to do first.

The heavy wooden door beneath the staircase which led down to the basement had been dusted for fingerprints and, when Joe had opened it, he brushed the fine grey powder off his hands. He took his torch from his pocket, wondering why no electric light had been installed down there, and retraced his steps, calling to a uniformed constable who was stationed at the front door.

'Any chance of getting some proper lighting down here?'

The gangly young constable, who looked as if he should still be in the classroom, gave him a blank stare for a few moments then said he'd ask someone. Passing the buck, Joe thought. But fifteen minutes later a pair of arc lights were carried down to the basement and Joe felt a little guilty about misjudging the lad.

Joe walked down the cold stone steps into the brightly lit cellar and took in the scene. A pair of cameras had been set up on tripods, presumably night vision models as the darkness in this place would have been impenetrable at night despite the tiny barred window at the top of one wall which now let in a trickle of watery light.

A sleeping bag lay against one wall, with only a thin foam mat to protect its user from the cold stone flags. Joe marvelled at Karl Dremmer's dedication. Or perhaps he'd become so obsessed with his research that such hardship had become irrelevant. Obsession, in Joe's experience, could lead to danger – and in Dremmer's case it had probably led to his death.

He noticed a plain white mug containing the muddy dregs of what was probably hot chocolate standing beside the sleeping bag. A battery powered lantern stood next to the mug and the sleeping bag looked as if its occupant had climbed out of it in a hurry. He put on a pair of plastic gloves and tested the lantern but nothing happened. It had probably been left switched on since Dremmer had abandoned his post for whatever reason and the batteries had run down. A rucksack lay near the makeshift bed and Joe began to examine its contents. Two sets of spare batteries, a chocolate bar, a banana, a towel, a spare pair of socks, a notepad and a pen. Dremmer had scribbled a few words on the pad: 12.32 orb; 1247 voice; 1.23 temperature drop; sobbing. Then a single word in large scrawled capitals – WALL.

Dremmer had placed his sound recording equipment at the back of the chamber and, as Joe drew closer, he realized that it was recording. He suddenly felt a new bout of optimism – if it was triggered by sound, then it might have recorded the murderer's voice. He switched it off. The scientific support people could examine it, sooner rather than later.

Looking round the room he spotted a screwdriver lying on the floor by the brick wall at the far end of the basement. His heart beat faster as he began to examine the area. There was a small pile of grey mortar dust on the dark stone flags and he could see the patch in the centre of the wall where someone had tried to scrape the mortar away from between the bricks. However, there had been builders crawling all over the building for months so it might have been them who'd been working on the wall rather than Dremmer.

As he stared at the wall he suddenly experienced a feeling of cold dread. According to George, Dremmer had talked about something evil being down there and, as he looked down at his hand he realized it was shaking.

Alan Proud knew that it was best to keep out of the way because the police and the CSIs were downstairs and out in the grounds with their crime-scene tape and their white overalls that made them look like giant maggots crawling over the dead. They'd been knocking on all the flat doors and they'd already interviewed him – just routine, they said. But he hadn't told them anything.

He pulled back the rug. He'd created the hiding place for his really precious things – the loose floorboard he'd prised up, a result of shoddy workmanship he imagined, had given access to a perfect hidey-hole. He knelt on the floor and lifted the section of board, peering down into the hole at the wooden box which had once contained expensive cigars.

He lifted the box out and opened it, breathing in the faint whiff of tobacco that still clung to the wood. Inside were the letters from Peter Brockmeister that he couldn't display on his wall; the ones that could cause a lot of damage. These were the ones that would turn Eborby's smug, cosy world upside down.

SIXTEEN

'Why did he leave the basement, Joe?' Emily asked quietly.

'I don't know. But Lydia told me she'd heard something that sounded like scraping and some of that mortar on the far wall's been scraped away. Dremmer might have done it for some reason.'

Emily smiled. 'Lydia, eh.'

Joe ignored the suggestion in her voice. 'We need to find out what he was up to. Could the cellar extend beyond that wall?'

'If it did it would be on the plans and the builders would have used it to gain access to services and all that. Jack Hawkes is the architect so he should be able to tell us for sure. Anyway, my gut feeling tells me that if the basement was any bigger than this, Creeny would have used it to incorporate some basement flats and squeeze a bit more money out of the place.'

Joe knew she had a point. 'We should have a word with Hawkes and Creeny anyway.'

'Talking of Hawkes, I've just had a call from Janet, the family liaison officer. She'd found some material about Peter Brockmeister in his house.

Joe gave a low whistle. This was something he hadn't expected.

'Jack Hawkes is the one who would have drawn up all the plans for this place,' said Emily. 'And he's the one with the dead wife.'

What would the police do without vigilant neighbours? That's the question DC Jamilla Dal asked herself as she recited the familiar words of the caution at ten thirty on a cloudy Monday morning.

The burglary had taken place at a new block of flats in Bacombe and the burglar had selected the flat of a single woman on the ground floor, gaining access through the French windows leading to the communal gardens which had been one of the flat's major selling points. He had broken in at nine thirty but he'd been heard by the next door neighbour who happened to be taking a day off sick and knew the flat's owner had already left for work.

The neighbour had heard crashing and dragging sounds, as if furniture was being moved around, and by the time the patrol car arrived, his attack of man-flu had diminished in the excitement. The two constables picked up the intruder as he left the premises the same way as he went in, and all the neighbour saw was a middle-aged man being led away, still carrying a handful of what looked like ladies' underwear.

It seemed that The Builder had been caught at last and, in view of the major investigation at Boothgate House, Jamilla had been called upon to conduct the initial interview.

The man sitting opposite her in the interview room could only be described as ordinary, the type she wouldn't have glanced at twice in the street. He was average height with receding hair and the face of a rather dim weasel. But, thanks to the Police National Computer, she knew who he was and she knew what he'd done in the past. He was a small-time career criminal of the sort she'd met so often before; the sort who considered themselves a cut above the riff-raff because they never used violence.

'So if you never use violence how do you explain the notes you left?' Jamilla asked, pushing the plastic exhibit bag containing the note he'd left his last victim across the table.

I'LL SEE YOU NEXT TIME I CALL. BE READY.

The burglar, whose name was John Jones – alias Arthur Smith, alias Michael Grogan, also known as David Beech – gave the duty solicitor a sheepish look. 'I didn't mean it. I just did it for a laugh.'

'Your victims weren't laughing. And why did you pile the furniture up by their front doors?'

'If they came back unexpectedly it'd give me time to get away, wouldn't it,' he said as though Jamilla should have realized this.

'And you took their underwear.'

'Yeah . . . well, I've always had this thing about . . . I was after cash and jewellery but the knickers were a bonus.' He looked Jamilla up and down and she squirmed in her seat. 'What colour are you wearing today, love?'

Jamilla felt like landing a punch on his smirking face but instead she assumed her sternest expression and didn't grace the question with a reply.

'Where did you get the idea of piling the furniture up?' She studied the print out of his criminal past that lay on the table in front of her. 'It isn't your usual MO.'

'A lad I was inside with knew someone who used to do it and I thought I'd give it a go. Trouble is . . .' He tilted his head to one side, as though considering the matter. 'Trouble is it takes a while to move the stuff so you're in there longer and there's more chance of some nosy neighbour hearing what's going on.' He rubbed his back. 'Besides, I'm not as young as I was so all that shifting . . .'

Jamilla watched the man's face. 'Who gave you the idea?'

He thought for a moment. 'I once shared a cell with a lad called Darren Carter. He was done for murder – I don't usually share with murderers but with space being short and all that . . . Anyway, he said he was innocent and I believed him. He was inside for killing his girlfriend but he swore it wasn't him. He reckoned it was this bloke called Peter Brockmeister and he tried to get him to admit it, not that he had much luck in that direction. Now, Brockmeister was a man to avoid. He got put away in some hospital in the end . . . cushy number. Don't know how he wangled it but . . .'

Jamilla sat upright. 'You knew Peter Brockmeister?' In view of DCI Thwaite's interest in the Brockmeister case, this could be something that could earn her a few brownie points.

'I didn't actually know him but, like I said, I knew Darren who'd shared a cell with him at one time. Brockmeister had a reputation for being a scary man but Darren had been determined to get friendly with him 'cause he thought he could get him to confess to his girlfriend's murder so he could appeal his conviction. But Brockmeister ran rings around him – kept him dangling by hinting that he was going to confess, but of course he never did. He was just playing with the lad.'

'And you knew Brockmeister used to pile furniture up at his victims' front doors in the same way as you did?'

'I told you, that's where I got the idea from. Darren wouldn't stop going on about Brockmeister and what he'd done. Obsessed with him he was.'

'Do you know where Darren is now?'

'In the cemetery, poor lad.' Jones bowed his head as if in respect. 'He got killed inside. I sometimes wondered . . .'

'What?'

Jones hesitated. 'Whether Brockmeister gave the order. Darren kept writing to him, you see – pushed things too far. Brockmeister might have got sick of it.'

Jamilla suddenly remembered what DCI Thwaite had said about Alan Proud's collection of letters written by the killer. 'Brockmeister wrote back to him so he couldn't have minded that much.'

He raised his eyebrows as though he was surprised at how much Jamilla already knew. 'Until Darren got too close. There were people inside ready and willing to do whatever Peter told them, believe me. He had charisma, that man. There were some who thought he had powers, if you see what I mean.'

The words sent a chill through Jamilla's body. But she was determined not to show it.

'But he's dead,' she said. 'His body was found shortly after he was released from hospital.'

Jones leaned forward, a knowing leer on his face. 'I heard on the grapevine that he was still alive. They found that solicitor woman in the river, didn't they? I reckon he's at it again.'

'Jones has made a full statement,' said Emily as she ended the call. 'At least we've got the burglaries cleared up.'

Joe watched her, sensing there was something else, something she hadn't told him yet. 'You don't look happy.'

She sighed. 'One string of burglaries down, two murders and a kidnapping to go. Jack Hawkes was out last night – he told Janet he was going to see his ex-wife and his kids but he didn't get back till the early hours. She was woken up by the sound of his car returning at three in the morning. Which means his kids must have late bedtimes if he was telling the truth.'

'He could have been seeking solace from his ex,' Joe suggested. He knew some relationships were never cut and dried.

'We've asked her and she says he left at nine. I don't think there's any love lost there. Anyway, I've sent a patrol car to pick him up. I've got a feeling he's in this up to his neck. And we can ask him about the plans of Boothgate House while he's here.'

Joe knew Emily could be right. The husband is usually the first suspect when it comes to a murdered wife and Karl Dremmer's interference could have deterred prospective buyers of the Boothgate House flats, adversely affecting Hawkes' bank account. And they couldn't forget that Hawkes was in possession of material relating to Peter Brockmeister's crimes. Which meant that not bringing him in would be tantamount to a neglect of duty.

They stood in the entrance hall at Boothgate House, directly beneath the elaborate chandelier put up by Creeny to introduce a touch of luxury to the building.

'There's someone else I need to see,' said Joe.

'If you're thinking of Alan Proud, he's been interviewed. Swears he was fast asleep all night and didn't leave his flat. Not sure if I believe him but . . .'

'I didn't mean Proud. I've asked George Merryweather to come over and have a look at that basement.'

Emily stared at him with a mixture of puzzlement and disbelief. 'Isn't that your exorcist mate? What do you want to bring him in for?'

'Because Karl Dremmer was a paranormal researcher. I want to find out more about that particular angle.'

Emily emitted a sceptical snort. 'Well, whoever killed Dremmer, it wasn't a bloody ghost.'

Joe felt the blood rising to his face. 'The lab's going through Dremmer's recording equipment but I've read through his notes and I think there might be something unusual there. I also want to trace some of the people who worked here when the place was a hospital. I can't help feeling this whole thing's connected with Peter Brockmeister. And he was here. He lived in this building.'

Emily paused for a few moments, deep in thought. 'You're right, Joe. Someone certainly copied his MO for Melanie Hawkes' murder. And we've got two people round here with detailed knowledge of his crimes: Jack Hawkes and Alan Proud.'

'Our burglar, John Jones, was in prison with Brockmeister's old cell mate, Darren Carter, who was the recipient of the letters in Proud's collection. It seems Darren gave Jones chapter and verse on Brockmeister's crimes. According to Jones, Darren became obsessed with him and ended up dead. I'd like another look at those letters.'

'From what Janet's said about the material in Hawkes' house, it looks as if his father became fixated with the case. Brockmeister seemed to be the kind of criminal who affected people like that. Word has it that he was so charismatic that he even had experienced officers eating out of his hand. And a charismatic killer is a dangerous beast. Good job he's dead and he can't do any more damage.'

Joe knew the truth of Emily's words. It seemed that Brockmeister's evil spell had endured even after he was gone. 'What if he's not dead?' he said softly, almost reluctant to utter the words.

Emily shook her head. 'According to the files he was identified. There was no mistake.'

'Identifications can be wrong. Everyone says he was charismatic – what if he charmed the landlady into identifying the body as his? There was no DNA in those days and there's no mention of dental records in the file.'

Emily suddenly looked worried. 'No, Joe, I'm as sure as I can be that Melanie Hawkes was just a copycat killing. Someone's keeping Brockmeister's flame alive. And, according to Sally, she was tortured. There's no record of Brockmeister ever doing that.' She looked at her watch. 'I've sent a patrol car to pick Hawkes up. He should be at the station by now.'

'I'm meeting George here, he's due any moment. I'll join you later.'

She gave him a sideways look. 'Make sure you don't get sidetracked. I want your input on this one.'

'Don't worry. I also want to ask Creeny if he knows any

reason why Dremmer should have taken a screwdriver to that basement wall. But, in view of his attitude, I'm not getting my hopes up.'

'I don't see how it's relevant to our murders, Joe. I wouldn't waste time on it.'

'It's niggling at me, that's all.'

She rolled her eyes before sweeping out through the front door. As he watched her disappearing back, Joe's phone chimed to tell him he had a text message. He read it and discovered that Lydia wanted to see him that evening. From where he stood he could almost see her flat door but he knew she was at work. After a few moments of hesitation, he texted back. I'll pick you up at eight. He hoped he was doing the right thing and that the investigation wouldn't get in the way.

George arrived on the dot, looking round nervously as he walked in as though he feared he was intruding. Joe saw him start to make a shy approach to one of the uniformed officers who were hurrying in and out of the building and he walked forward to the entrance to greet him.

'George. Good of you to come.'

George looked relieved, as though he'd been rescued from an awkward social situation. 'No problem, Joe. Glad to help.' He pointed to the graveyard which was cordoned off with tape, suddenly solemn. 'Is that where . . .?'

'Yes.' Joe saw George bow his head in a moment of silent prayer. 'Dremmer had his equipment set up in the basement so I don't know what he was doing outside. We think he was killed where he was found.' He took the clergyman by the elbow and guided him to the basement door. 'I'll show you where he was working.'

George halted at the top of the basement steps, looking down at the bright scene below, lit like a stage set.

'You OK, George?'

George nodded. Joe noticed that he had been fingering the wooden cross around his neck and he knew that he wasn't the only one who sensed something evil in that place.

'This was where he spent the night.' He saw George staring down at the sleeping bag and the empty mug with the dried brown crust of chocolate in the base that still stood on the cold stone flags. 'A lady from one of the flats took pity on him and brought him a hot chocolate down. He'd set up his recording equipment here but that's been taken to our lab for analysis. I've seen some of the notes he made – just rough jottings with times and observations. He mentions orbs and noises . . . and a temperature change.'

'Pretty standard stuff. I'd like to know what's on the recordings.'

'We're hoping the killer's voice might have been recorded.'

George smiled. 'That would be useful.' He paused, standing absolutely still and staring at the far wall. 'I definitely feel something hostile in here, Joe. I know you'll think it fanciful but I've been to a lot of reputedly haunted sites and this . . .'

'How do you mean exactly?'

'You know as well as I do that it's not an exact science . . . however much Karl Dremmer was trying to make it one. It's just a strong feeling that something doesn't want us here. But it could be my mind playing tricks. I always like to eliminate the earthly explanations first – that's why I'd like to know what's on Karl's recordings.'

'I'm sure that can be arranged.'

George approached the wall and turned to face Joe. 'I make no claims to be a psychic, you know that, but even I can sense that dreadful things have happened here.'

Joe would have been lying if he said he hadn't felt an atmosphere of terror and deep sadness down there. He had tried to convince himself that it was his imagination, something conjured from his knowledge of the building's past. But if George felt it too . . . 'I think Dremmer was trying to scrape the mortar away from the bricks in that far wall. I think he might have been trying to see what was beyond it.'

'Is there anything?'

'We're going to speak to the architect and find out.'

'Let's get out of here,' George said.

Joe didn't need asking twice.

On his way to the police station Joe dropped George back at the cathedral. Both of them would rather have walked but time was tight. George had been uncharacteristically quiet during the short journey. The basement had disturbed him and George wasn't an impressionable man. In all the time he'd known him, Joe had found him to be remarkably down to earth – he had to be if his role in the church wasn't to become a laughing stock. A diocesan exorcist – or rather a deliverance minister – dealt with unquiet souls and Joe trusted him to recognize true evil when he came across it.

Melanie Hawkes had been given the task of finding out what had happened to one of Havenby Hall's residents who had met an unexpected end. And Karl Dremmer had been investigating the place. Maybe there was something there somebody hadn't wanted them to find. And Peter Brockmeister's name kept coming up again and again. Peter Brockmeister, the killer who had been transferred from prison to Havenby Hall and had met his death soon after the place had been closed down.

He knew Sebastian Bentham had interviewed several people with connections to Havenby Hall when he'd been researching his play and speaking to those individuals was at the top of Joe's list of things to do. But Emily had told him to join her down in the interview room to speak to Jack Hawkes as soon as he returned so it would have to wait. In view of Janet Craig's report that Hawkes hadn't returned home till three in the morning they knew he'd been out and about around the estimated time of Dremmer's death.

Joe parked the car and he was making for the police station's front entrance when his mobile rang. It was Janet Craig and she sounded anxious.

'There's been a call from the kidnapper,' she said breathlessly. 'Jack wasn't here so I had to let it go on to the answering machine and he left a message. Is Jack being held?'

'For now. The DCI wants to question him. What did the message say?'

'The kidnapper was annoyed that Hawkes didn't answer and he said he'd call back in two hours with instructions. The call's been traced to a phone box in another village. No CCTV coverage again.'

For someone whose attempts at obtaining money had so far failed, the kidnapper was showing remarkable presence of mind. Joe said he'd pass on the information and hurried straight to the interview room where he summoned Emily out into the corridor to relay Janet's news. He looked at his watch. They'd have to be quick. Hawkes had to be back at his house when that call came through. Getting the child back unharmed was their top priority.

They had ninety minutes before the call. Ninety minutes to discover whether Hawkes had murdered his wife. And perhaps Karl Dremmer too. He followed Emily back into the interview room and they sat down side by side opposite Hawkes and his solicitor.

He left it up to Emily to break the news of the phone call from the kidnapper and Hawkes' only comment was that he'd better be back at the house when the call came through. If he didn't make it he'd hold the police responsible for anything that happened to Daisy. Joe sat in silence, watching him carefully. He could detect no warmth or worry when he spoke Daisy's name and he had a strong feeling there was something artificial about his show of concern. Perhaps he'd only accepted Daisy because Melanie had insisted she was a non-negotiable part of the package and, already having three children of his own, he resented her presence in his new marriage. Or perhaps he already knew she was safe. Perhaps he'd arranged her abduction, maybe to get at Melanie, and now he was forced to keep up the charade to avoid detection.

'Where did you go last night?'

'I told you. I went to see my ex then I went for a drive. I knew I wouldn't be able to sleep so . . .'

'Where did you drive to?'

'I visited a friend.'

'What's this friend's name?'

He hesitated, weighing up his options. 'Yolanda,' he replied after a long period of silence. 'She'll vouch for me. I just needed some company.'

Emily pushed a notebook towards him and told him to write down the address. After passing it on to the constable by the door with orders to get it checked out, she leaned towards Hawkes.

'We'd like to talk to you about Peter Brockmeister,' she said, sweetly threatening.

Hawkes' surprise wasn't faked. This was something he hadn't expected. 'What about him?'

'Your father worked on the case.'

'Yes.'

'And you have a collection of books on the subject. And some case notes, presumably belonging to your late father.'

Hawkes half rose from his seat, his hands clenched. His solicitor touched his arm and he sank back but there was no mistaking the fury in his eyes. 'How the hell do you know that?'

Joe saw Emily glance at him. 'Never mind how we know. Is it true?'

'Has that Janet been snooping? Because if she has . . .'

He looked pleadingly at his solicitor who cleared his throat. 'If my client's house has been searched without his permission or a warrant . . .'

'We can easily get a warrant,' said Emily sweetly. 'But if your client has nothing to hide it shouldn't be necessary.'

The man's bluster subsided, as though he sensed it might be unwise to make waves.

'It's just that you seem to be taking a great deal of interest in Peter Brockmeister's crimes, Mr Hawkes,' said Joe. 'And as there are strong similarities between those crimes and the death of your wife, surely you can understand why we have to ask you a few more questions.' He made the statement sound so reasonable that it would have seemed churlish for the solicitor to challenge it.

'OK, I admit I've got some stuff about Brockmeister. It all belonged to my dad. I think he was planning to write his memoirs only he never lived long enough. I found them when I was clearing out his house after he died.'

'And you kept them.' Emily's words were a simple statement of fact.

'I knew Brockmeister had spent time in Havenby Hall so when I started working on the plans for the place I read up on its history, that's all. Look, I had nothing to do with Melanie's death and I can't believe why you aren't out trying to catch the bastard who killed her,' he added self-righteously.

'The bastard who killed her copied Peter Brockmeister's modus operandi, Mr Hawkes,' said Joe. 'I wonder why that is.'

Hawkes squirmed in his seat. 'Because he's famous around here. Everybody knows what he did to his victims. It's all in the public domain.'

'He didn't torture his victims though. He didn't burn them with cigarettes and cut their flesh.'

Hawkes' eyes widened, horrified, and Joe thought that either this was news to him or that he was a very practised deceiver.

'That's what happened to Melanie,' he continued. 'Why would anyone want to do that, do you think?'

'I don't know. But doesn't it mean it might not be connected with Brockmeister after all?'

Joe caught Emily's eye. The man could be right. This was a deviation from Brockmeister's MO. This was the work of an even more savage mind.

'Let's talk about Havenby Hall . . . sorry, Boothgate House. I noticed that the basement doesn't extend underneath the whole building.'

'That's not uncommon.'

'Can I see the plans?'

'Be my guest. Now unless you're going to charge me, let me go and see if I can at least get Daisy back and salvage something from this bloody disaster.'

Emily stood up. 'Very well, Mr Hawkes."

'And I've got a funeral to arrange. When are you going to release Melanie's body?'

'We'll keep you informed,' said Joe, suddenly feeling sorry for the man.

'I'll tell you something for nothing,' said Hawkes, leaning forward, prodding a finger in Joe's direction. 'My dad always believed that Brockmeister was still alive. He reckoned he was living under another identity. In fact he said he saw him once.'

Emily leaned forward. 'When was this?'

'It was just before he died two years ago. He said he saw him in Eborby by the castle. Said he looked quite different but he knew it was him. My dad was sharp as a knife till the end. And he never forgot a face.'

SEVENTEEN

Emily provided a patrol car to take Hawkes home. His solicitor had been right when he'd said they had no reason to hold his client . . . certainly not on the strength of a few true crime books and his late father's notes. And his alibi had checked out. He was with Yolanda from nine thirty until around three in the morning when he'd returned home in the hope his absence wouldn't be noticed. But with Janet Craig wise to his nocturnal wanderings, he was unlikely to abscond again without them knowing.

There was only half an hour to go before the kidnapper made contact and Janet had instructions to let them know as soon as it happened. The holdall containing the cash had been returned to Hawkes as Emily didn't want to take any risks with the child's safety. But a tracking device had been concealed in the fabric of the bag and technical support was on hand to put a trace on the phone call.

She had called Daisy's biological father, Paul Scorer, to keep him up to date with developments. He'd sounded more worried than Hawkes and frustrated because he didn't have the wherewithal to do anything about it. It was Hawkes who could lay his hands on ransom money. Scorer, she observed to Joe, didn't have two halfpennies to rub together.

Emily said she'd covered all bases and Joe hoped she wasn't being over-optimistic.

As soon as Joe returned to the CID office, he found the card with the numbers of the individuals who'd helped Seb Bentham with his research scrawled on the back: the chaplain, the nurse and the former patient. Melanie Hawkes had the first two names in her file, along with another name, a Cecil Bentham.

Joe wondered which one to call first but, as there was no reply from the nurse, Betty Morcroft's number, the decision was made for him.

The Reverend Kenneth Rattenbury lived in a small terraced house in Hilton, a couple of miles down the road from Boothgate House. Rattenbury answered the door as soon as Joe had rung the bell, as though he'd been hovering in the hall waiting for him.

The former chaplain of Havenby Hall was a tall man in his mid to late sixties with thick white hair and clothes that hung loosely off his large frame as though he'd recently lost weight. He wore an open-necked checked shirt but no dog collar.

Once inside the house Joe was shown into a small lounge dominated by a pair of tall bookshelves either side of a pretty cast-iron fireplace and a large TV in the corner of the room. The former chaplain invited Joe to sit and made himself comfortable in the armchair opposite.

'I must say I was intrigued by your call, Inspector.'

'Sebastian Bentham, the playwright, said you'd helped him with his research.'

Rattenbury looked down modestly. 'I think he's overestimating my contribution. I don't remember telling him anything much apart from my impressions. I had a parish back then you see, and I only visited Havenby Hall a couple of times a week . . . and I gave communion on Sundays of course.'

'Do you know Cannon George Merryweather by any chance?'

Rattenbury's rheumy eyes lit up. 'Yes, I believe I've met him.'

'So you know all about his current role . . . the Deliverance Ministry?'

'I had heard about it, yes.'

'George and I are old friends. There was a time when I was considering joining the priesthood . . . Catholic that is.'

'Lost your faith?'

Joe smiled. 'Found a wife.'

Rattenbury's face clouded. 'I lost mine five years ago.'

Joe hesitated. 'Kaitlin died six months after our wedding. I know what it's like.'

'I'm sorry to hear that,' the retired clergyman said softly. 'Now what is it you want to know?'

'Peter Brockmeister was a patient at Havenby Hall while you were working there.'

'Yes, he was.' The answer was guarded and Joe suspected the mention of Brockmeister's name had disturbed him.

'What can you tell me about him?'

Rattenbury considered the question for a few moments. 'What do you want to know?'

'Did he ever talk to you about his crimes?'

'I never had much to do with him. I don't think he liked clergymen. The one time I had a conversation with him he ranted on about Satan being more powerful than my God. Satan was his master, he said. As you can imagine, I found the encounter . . . rather disturbing.'

'He was insane?'

'Some people – some experts – thought so but I think he knew exactly what he was doing and saying. I think he derived pleasure from evil. Mercifully people like that are rare but I'm sorry to say they exist.'

'Do you know anything about a woman called Dorothy Watts?'

Rattenbury frowned, trying to recall the past. 'Yes, I remember Mrs Watts. She used to come to communion every week. I seem to remember that she died rather unexpectedly.'

'Did she confide in you?'

'At times. She was an unhappy, unstable woman who was convinced her husband wanted her dead. A lot of people in that place had paranoid tendencies so I didn't set too much store by what she said.'

'Did you ever meet her husband?'

'No, I didn't.'

'Dorothy Watts' sister asked a solicitor to investigate her will. She wanted to find out what had become of her money. She was quite a wealthy woman.'

'I didn't know that.'

'Your name was in the solicitor's file. Her name was Melanie Hawkes. Did she visit you?'

'No . . . although I did receive a phone call from her. She asked me if I remembered Dorothy Watts and I told her exactly what I've just told you. I was sorry I couldn't be more help.'

'Did anybody else die unexpectedly at Havenby Hall?'

'As I said, I only visited the place a few times a week. You'd be far better asking any of the nursing staff. Or Dr Pennell – he was the Medical Superintendent. And of course there was Mrs Chambers.'

'Who's she?'

'She was the matron. If she's still alive you should ask her. I'm sure she'll tell you everything you'll need to know.' He looked Joe in the eye. 'Nothing happened in that place without Mrs Chambers knowing about it.'

The call came as arranged. On the dot. Emily had decided to be there with Janet Craig, watching and listening to everything that was said.

The instructions were terse and the call only lasted a few seconds. The kidnapper was clearly wise to the fact the police might be listening in and he wasn't taking any chances, although they already knew the call had come from an unregistered mobile situated somewhere in Eborby city centre . . . which really wasn't much help.

Daisy was well, the electronic voice said, and Hawkes would receive more instructions in the morning. Emily knew the kidnapper was stalling and, in her opinion, this wasn't a good sign. There must be some reason why they were playing for time and the only one she could think of was that the kid was dead. The very thought made her feel sick.

But she wasn't going to give up hope. And tomorrow – as they said in Emily's favourite film of all time, the one she always watched on her birthday with a box of chocolates and a bottle of wine – was another day.

EIGHTEEN

As soon as Joe left Rattenbury's house, he tried Betty Morcroft's number again. This time she answered her phone and explained that she'd been at an afternoon social in the communal lounge of her retirement flats, adding that she'd won a bottle of vodka in the raffle. Even over the phone Joe detected a twinkle of mischief in her querulous voice and he was rather looking forward to meeting her.

Betty lived in sheltered housing in Hasledon, half a mile down the road from the university campus and well away from Boothgate House. It was a new complex set in well-tended gardens. When Joe opened the double doors he could see into a thickly carpeted communal lounge where four elderly women with identical grey perms sat at a baize-covered table playing cards with the intense concentration of seasoned gamblers. The glazed inner door was locked so he looked for Betty Morcroft's name on the entry phone panel to his left. The voice that answered sounded excited, like a little girl anticipating a treat.

As he pushed the inner door open the card players didn't look up and he turned left down a corridor, following the signs for Flat Twelve. When he arrived at his destination, he found the flat door standing wide open and his eyes travelled downwards to focus on the woman in the doorway. She was small with fluffy grey hair and a large nose and she reminded Joe of a bird perched on a state of the art electric wheelchair that engulfed her thin body. But her blue eyes were bright and inquisitive and his instincts told him that this visit wouldn't be a waste of time.

She invited him in and fussed about, making tea. When it was ready he helped her by carrying the tray over to the tiled coffee table and sat down on a sofa so soft that he feared getting out of it might prove difficult.

'Have you seen Sebastian Bentham's play?' he asked as she poured the tea.

She shook her head vigorously. 'He offered me free tickets but I didn't fancy it. I didn't want to spend an evening thinking about that place.' She looked directly at him. 'Besides, it sounded a miserable sort of play and at my age you want something a bit more cheerful, if you know what I mean.'

Joe nodded. He knew what she meant all right. When you'd been surrounded by death and suffering all your life you hardly want to be reminded of it in your leisure hours. 'I went to see it but I found it a bit heavy going.' He gave her a conspiratorial grin. 'In fact I needed a stiff drink afterwards.'

She chuckled sympathetically. 'Now what did you want to talk to me about?'

'Havenby Hall.'

'Why is everyone so interested in that dreadful place all of a sudden?'

'You worked there?'

'Two years. And that was two years too long. But jobs were short and my late husband couldn't work 'cause he'd had an accident so I had to take what I could get.'

'You must have worked as a psychiatric nurse before. You knew what to expect.'

The old woman bit her lip, as if something was bothering her. It was a few moments before she spoke. 'Oh yes, I'd worked in various hospitals and I'd always enjoyed the work but . . . Havenby Hall was different. It wasn't a nice place, Inspector.'

Joe had a feeling that he was about to discover something important. He asked her what she meant and she drained her tea cup before she spoke, as though she needed time to consider her words.

'Odd things happened. Patients died unexpectedly. As far as I knew there were never any post-mortems but the doctor – Pennell his name was – always signed the death certificates.'

'What about the relatives? Didn't they kick up a fuss?'

'They just seemed to accept it. I think Dr Pennell and the Matron, Mrs Chambers must have . . .'

'Must have what?'

She shook her head, a little unsure of herself. 'I don't know.

Sweet talked them into not asking any awkward questions? I'd seen those patients and there'd been nothing wrong with them. I asked Dr Pennell, of course, but he just came up with some story about them dying of heart attacks or strokes. Another odd thing is that I was never allowed to see the bodies. Whisked away they were. Now I'm not saying there was anything untoward . . . nothing I could prove anyway. But I felt something wasn't right.'

'Were the dead patients buried in the graveyard at the side of the building?'

She shook her head. 'Oh no. That hadn't been used for years. They were all cremated as far as I know.'

'How many died like that while you were working there?'

She frowned. 'I'm not sure . . . six or seven perhaps.'

'You never reported this to anyone?'

'Havenby Hall was a private concern, not part of the NHS. And besides, I had absolutely no evidence, did I? And I didn't live in. I only worked days because of my husband not being well so I didn't know what went on the rest of the time.'

'What about the rest of the staff?'

'There were some odd people working there, I can tell you. Worse than the so-called patients, some of them.' She hesitated. 'And a few of them seemed very close to Mrs Chambers – like her chosen circle. They never had much to do with the rest of the staff.'

'What happened to them after the place closed?'

'I've no idea. I never kept in touch.'

'And Mrs Chambers, where did she go?'

Betty shrugged her thin shoulders. 'Who knows? I never heard of her again. But I do know that Dr Pennell retired. He died about eighteen months ago. I read his obituary in the local paper.' She shuddered. 'I didn't like that man.'

'Did Mrs Chambers have a family?'

'Not that I know of.'

'Do you remember a patient called Dorothy Watts? She died unexpectedly.'

Betty's expression changed, as if a cloud had passed over the sun. 'Oh yes,' she said softly. 'I remember Dorothy. Dot she liked to be called. Poor woman. I told Dr Pennell she was on the wrong medication but he gave me an earful for my trouble. Threatened to get me sacked for questioning his medical judgement. I needed the job so I kept quiet but I feel bad about it now. I always believed as a nurse that my first duty was to my patients and I fear I let Dot down badly.'

Joe leaned forward and touched her bony, liver-spotted hand. 'There was nothing you could have done.' He could see tears were starting to form in her eyes and he felt an overwhelming desire to reassure her. 'Pennell called the shots in that place so don't blame yourself. Dot's sister has been trying to find out what happened to her. Her son hired a solicitor called Melanie Hawkes to make enquiries.'

'I know. She came to see me. Very nice she was.'

'I've got some bad news, I'm afraid,' he said gently. 'She's dead. She was murdered.'

Betty's hand fluttered up to her mouth. 'Oh dear God,' she muttered.

'Do you remember a patient called Peter Brockmeister?'

Betty sat there, her mouth agape. From her reaction Joe knew that she remembered Brockmeister all right. And that memory disturbed her.

'I hardly had anything to do with him and I didn't want to, thank you very much. He gave me the creeps, the way he looked at you. But of course I knew what he'd done. Maybe if I hadn't known . . . He was very charming, you see. Very plausible. He charmed some of them, I can tell you.'

'Who?'

'The staff. After he'd been there a while he really got his feet under the table, had the run of the place and spent a lot of time with Dr Pennell and Matron. I reckon it suited him to be there. He'd been transferred from prison because they said he was insane. But the insane can be cured and the theory went that once he'd had treatment and taken the right medication he wouldn't be a danger any more. Only I'm sure the whole insanity thing was all a ruse to get out of prison. I don't think he ever took any medication.'

'Surely he was supervised.'

'By Dr Pennell. And I reckon Brockmeister had him in his pocket.'

'How?'

'Who knows? And Pennell's dead so we can't ask him, can we? But I do know one thing: when one of the night staff started asking questions she disappeared.'

Joe held his breath and waited for her to continue.

'Jean Smith her name was. I met her in town one day and she looked worried sick. Anyway, she asked if she could speak to me and we went into a café. She said she'd found some tablets hidden in Brockmeister's room – the patients all had private rooms, you see. She was certain he hadn't been taking his medication and she wondered whether she should tell someone but she didn't trust Dr Pennell or Matron. I said she should report it, that's when she told me she was really scared. She'd heard things, she said. Screams. And patients had died unexpectedly. She said something about the basement then she seemed to lose her nerve. I said we should meet again and talk about it away from work and she said maybe. Then . . .'

'Then what?'

'I never saw her again. And when I asked, Mrs Chambers said she'd left. She said she'd been stealing from the tea money. I never believed it but I couldn't prove anything, could I?'

'Did you ever try and investigate the basement?'

Betty shook her head. 'I worked during the day and there were always people around so I never got the chance. Pity.'

Joe felt glad that Betty hadn't decided to risk going down there. If she had, she might have met the same fate as Jean . . . whatever that was.

'Do you think Dr Pennell and Mrs Chambers could have been under Brockmeister's influence?' he asked.

Betty nodded slowly, as if he had just voiced something she'd already known but barely dared to acknowledge. 'You don't think Mrs Hawkes' murder had anything to do with all this?'

'We're considering all possibilities at the moment,' said Joe. Although his words were non-committal, his instincts told him that Melanie's death was no coincidence. Now he'd spoken to Betty he was more convinced than ever that there was a connection with whatever had gone on at Havenby Hall. But now he had to prove it.

NINETEEN

The flat door was half open and Beverley peeped out. The police were still there and she wondered what they were doing that took so long. Some of them wore white suits and swarmed purposefully in and out of the door under the stairs which stood propped open. She could see that the basement was brightly lit now and she almost wished she could venture down there. But she made no move. She didn't dare.

She could see Lydia had just come through the front door, back from work early. She was standing in the hall now chatting to one of the constables, looking relaxed. Sometimes Beverley envied her that easy way she had with people. Beverley would have liked to be like that, to have a job interacting with people. Beverley would have liked to be popular. She had seen Lydia with that good-looking detective and she knew by the way they behaved together that there was an attraction. Beverley had never had a boyfriend. Mother had never encouraged that sort of thing.

Lydia was walking towards her flat now and when Beverley opened her own door a little wider Lydia spotted her and smiled as she came closer. Beverley edged past her mother's wheelchair which had been left neatly folded against the wall, and stepped out on to the corridor, preparing to begin a conversation. It was something that didn't come easily to her, but then she hadn't had much practice since she left work.

'You're home early,' she said, fixing a smile to her face.

'I only work till three on a Monday,' Lydia replied. 'How's your mum?'

Beverley suspected she only asked this because she couldn't think of anything else to say. 'Not too bad.'

'I haven't seen her for a while.'

'She's been spending most of her time in bed. Old age, eh.' She saw Lydia nod sympathetically. 'I took her out for a walk this morning . . . put the wheelchair in the car and drove down to the river. She likes to watch the boats and the swans. But I think it wore her out because she's asleep again. Dead to the world.'

Lydia fumbled in her bag for her key. 'If you don't mind leaving her for half an hour why don't you come in for a cup of tea?'

Beverley glanced back at her mother's bedroom door. 'OK. But I can't be long and I'd better leave the door on the latch.' She closed the door over and crept across the landing on tip toe as though she was frightened of waking the old lady up.

'Have you seen anything of . . .?' Lydia nodded towards Alan Proud's door.

'No. But I'm sure I heard him go out earlier.' Beverley looked around as if she feared someone might be listening. 'He doesn't seem very nice. And the way he tried to get into your flat . . .'

'But the police have caught my burglar so we know it wasn't him. For a while I thought . . .'

'Yes. I know,' said Beverley with a shudder that set her chin wobbling.

Lydia unlocked her door and Beverley followed her in. 'It's rather reassuring having all those policemen downstairs, isn't it.'

'In a way. Poor Dr Dremmer seemed a nice man.'

Beverley bowed her head. 'In a way I blame myself for what happened. If I hadn't let him down there . . .'

Lydia touched her arm, a gesture of reassurance and Beverley could feel the warmth of her hand on her bare flesh. 'It's not your fault. The police think he opened the front door to his killer and followed him outside for some reason.'

'Did your detective friend tell you that?'

She saw Lydia blush. 'That's right.'

Lydia hurried to the kitchen. Beverley followed and stood in the doorway watching as she put the kettle on and dropped two tea bags in a brown china pot.

'Did your detective say anything else interesting?'

'He doesn't talk much about his work. I suppose it's confidential.'

'Yes, of course.' She fell silent for a moment and watched

Lydia take two mugs from her cupboard. 'Dr Dremmer – Karl – was in touch with a clergyman from the cathedral.'

Lydia looked round. 'Why's that?'

'The clergyman is an exorcist and Karl was worried there was something here he couldn't explain. Since we moved here, Mother's been much worse. And she's been having dreams – nightmares.'

Beverley saw Lydia's eyes widen in alarm, as she leaned towards her, speaking in a whisper. 'Don't you feel there's something about this building that's not quite right?' She saw Lydia shudder.

'I think the tea's brewed,' Lydia said, turning away.

And from the look on her face, Beverley knew that she had felt the evil too.

Joe had called Lydia at the tourist information office to say he'd be working late but he'd suggested they meet for a drink at nine thirty.

It might have been his imagination but he thought she sounded quite excited at the prospect of seeing him again and he wasn't sure how he felt about this. When he was with her he enjoyed her company. But since Kaitlin's death he'd found it hard to make close relationships – maybe that's why he'd let Maddy go so easily without a fight. He'd felt sorry for himself at the time but now he realized it had probably been his own fault. No other woman could match up to his late wife, still perfect in his memory after their all-too-short time together. But one day he knew that things had to change if he wasn't to be condemned to a life of bitter solitude.

He tried to feel positive about that evening's meeting, even though he kept telling himself that Lydia had probably picked up from every cop show she'd ever watched that policemen hardly make the best partners in life.

It was a fine night so they walked into Eborby, stopping for a drink in the Star. Joe had been a little late but he'd apologized profusely. During a murder enquiry there was a lot to do. But he didn't mention that they were still waiting for Daisy's kidnappers to name the time and place of the drop. The less that was said about that, the more chance they had of getting the kid back safe and sound. Not that he didn't trust Lydia. It was just that he didn't know her that well . . . yet.

They sat in a dimly lit corner of the bar, a room of dark oak panels and well-worn red upholstery. On one wall was a framed account of the pub's history and Lydia made a point of reading it carefully before she settled in her seat. The place was haunted, she told Joe, by Civil War troops – Royalists who'd been injured during the siege of Eborby in 1644. The dying men had been brought to the inn and, according to legend, their ghosts still lingered in the place. Joe said he couldn't blame them – if he had to haunt anywhere a pleasant pub was as good a place as any.

He made a feeble joke about serving spirits and he was glad when it made Lydia smile. In her unguarded moments there was an air of sadness about her. She did her best to conceal it but he knew it was there; he'd known tragedy himself so he could recognize the effects in others.

When they left the pub they linked arms and strolled slowly down to the bottom of Boargate, keeping close to each other as though for protection.

'There's something I want to show you,' she said after a period of amicable silence.

Joe allowed himself to be led down a snickleway that ran between two medieval buildings. It was barely wide enough to walk two abreast but they soon emerged on to a wider street of small shops and cafés, now mostly closed. She turned right and Joe realized they were in the street that housed many of Eborby's antique shops. Intrigued, he followed her as she marched purposefully towards one of the smaller shops. Compared to some of the others it looked rather run down and the interior was lit by a single overhead bulb, no doubt left on for security.

She took his arm and steered him towards the window where they had a clear view of the dusty furniture piled up inside. 'You know I told you about that nightmare I keep having. Well, that's the clock. There at the back. The one with the face painted like the moon.'

Joe could see it. Even if Lydia hadn't told him about her nightmare, he would still have thought the clock's face had a sinister, leering look. The sunken painted eyes were still now but he imagined that if it was working they would move from side to side, looking this way and that. Watching.

'It used to be in Boothgate House when it was known as Havenby Hall. It belonged to the Medical Superintendent.'

'Dr Pennell?'

'That's right. He was the father of that Judith Dodds I told you about.'

Joe wished Lydia had mentioned this before. But they'd been too engrossed in their own concerns to give much thought to the recent horrific events that had occupied Joe's long working day.

'I'd like to speak to Mrs Dodds. I've already talked to a couple of people who worked at Havenby Hall and Dr Pennell's name has come up quite a bit.' He looked at his watch. 'I suppose it's too late to go round there tonight.'

He was half hoping the answer would be no, it wasn't too late. However Lydia said she thought it was. 'But I'm free first thing tomorrow,' she said. 'She knows me so if you want me to come with you . . . if it's just for a chat . . .'

Joe considered her offer. Lydia was right; it was just an unofficial chat and Lydia's presence might help Mrs Dodds relax and speak more freely.

'Want to come back for a coffee?' she said as they began to walk back.

Joe felt as though he'd been plunged into an abyss of indecision and for a few moments he didn't answer. From the look in her eyes he knew her meaning. Coffee would be more than a caffeine-packed hot beverage. Then he felt her fingers touching his and he suddenly knew what his decision would be. They'd almost reached the shadows of Boothgate Bar before he gave his answer. Yes. He'd come back for coffee.

Alan Proud switched on his computer – a new laptop he'd bought from a man in a pub. It was a fairly recent model so he hadn't asked too many questions.

He checked his emails and saw that a new one had come in – an answer to the plea he'd sent out into cyberspace. When he saw the name of the sender his heart began to beat faster and he prayed to a god he didn't believe in that it was genuine and not some sick hoax. His hand travelled to his wrist and he took his own pulse. He'd experienced a few chest pains recently and his father had died of a heart attack at quite a young age so he knew he'd have to take care. But this was something he'd craved for ages and he didn't want to back out just in case the excitement was bad for his health; according to the TV news, most pleasurable things are bad for your health these days so why should this be an exception?

He began to type. 'I've got the letters you sent to Darren Carter. And other letters you wrote of a more delicate nature. I'd like to ask you some questions so can we meet?' Did this seem too impertinent, he wondered? The last thing he wanted was to scare him off.

He sent the message and waited for the reply. If the thing was real, he thought, it was great that a man of that age was so au fait with technology.

He heard a distant door closing. He knew from the sound it was Lydia's and he felt the blood rise to his cheeks when he thought of the stuck-up bitch. She needed teaching a lesson. Perhaps the man who'd just contacted him would have some ideas. The thought made him smile and he felt a familiar tingling in his loins.

He heard voices through the party wall – a man and a woman – but he couldn't hear what they were saying. She had a man in there. Perhaps if he listened with a glass to the wall he'd be able to hear them. It was an old trick his mother used to use to spy on the neighbours. She'd never felt guilty about it and neither would he. Perhaps it would provide some entertainment while he awaited the reply.

But when he checked he saw that the email had already come in. He had replied. Peter Brockmeister had deigned to get back to him.

Judith Dodds decided to have an early night so she locked up the house as she did every night, checking the doors and windows and setting the alarm.

Since the break up of her marriage she hadn't slept well but she felt she should make the effort to get some rest so, after a lavender-scented bath, she put on a clean nightdress and climbed into bed, picking up her book off the bedside table.

She read for ten minutes, her eyelids heavy with sleep. But she knew that even if she dropped off straight away, she'd wake up in the early hours, her mind filled with images of the past. Her father standing in the doorway, staring at her with cold eyes as though she was some unpleasant laboratory specimen; her mother crying hysterically as she pleaded with him to stay. Her mother had had no pride but she hadn't repeated that mistake in her own marriage. As soon as things weren't to her liking she'd sent her ex-husband on his way, ensuring that she kept everything that was hers and most of what was his, including Oriel House.

She put the book down, switched off the light and pulled the duvet around her shoulders, making herself a cosy nest. Sleep had almost come when a sound jolted her back to wakefulness.

It came from downstairs. A tinkling sound of breaking glass. She hugged her duvet around her for protection and sat up, listening. She heard the distant shriek of an ambulance siren heading for the bypass. And the wind rustling the trees at the foot of her garden.

Then the soft, muffled tread of footsteps on the carpeted stairs. She switched on the light and swung her legs to the floor, feeling around for her slippers. She picked up the phone extension by her bed but there was no dialling tone. The line was dead. She had a mobile phone which she rarely used but that was on the hall table downstairs.

The intruder was on the landing now. She could hear him.

She switched off the light and slid down to the floor. As she squeezed underneath the bed, the rough woollen carpet dug into the bare flesh of her arms and cheek but she hoped that if she lay still, he might not come for her.

TWENTY

That night, after they'd made love, Joe had fallen into a deep sleep, only to wake again in the early hours. As he looked at Lydia sleeping peacefully like a child free of cares, he experienced a hollow feeling of unease. Maybe he'd been too impetuous; maybe he shouldn't have let his urgent desire for communion with another human body override his misgivings. In those dark, silent hours he lay awake, trying to get things straight in his head, before succumbing once more to a fitful sleep.

He woke at seven the next morning and opened his eyes to see Lydia, propped up on one arm watching him as a mother watches a sleeping child. She smiled, kissed him gently and rested her head on his chest. She'd slept well for the first time in ages, she said. And she hadn't dreamed that the clock with eyes was pursuing her into some terrible abyss.

He lay quietly for a while, absent-mindedly stroking her hair, until a glance at the alarm clock told him it was time to move. With an apology to Lydia, he sat naked on the edge of the bed and picked up his mobile phone to call Emily to check whether there'd been any developments in the Daisy Hawkes kidnapping case and to tell her about his intended visit to Mrs Dodds. It was time they had a breakthrough in the case which was becoming more complex and elusive by the minute.

Emily sounded alert as usual. Sometimes Joe didn't know how she coped with her family and working all hours on two murder cases, not to mention the kidnapping. But some people were just born that way. On occasions he'd heard Sunny calling her Wonder Woman – he sometimes wondered whether Sunny had a nickname for him, too.

He learned that they were still waiting for Daisy's kidnapper to get in touch again. His gut feeling told him that something about it didn't quite ring true. Perhaps the lack of viciousness in the half-hearted threats, as though the kidnapper couldn't quite bring himself or herself to utter the appropriately heartless words. He mentioned this to Emily but she said nothing, which meant she probably disagreed with him. She told him to find out what he could from Mrs Dodds and ended the call.

Lydia had lain back on her pillow and she was staring upwards with a slight smile on her lips.

'We'd better go and see Mrs Dodds,' he said.

She rolled over to kiss his back. But when he turned round the smile had vanished.

'Do you think she's in any danger?' she said.

Joe didn't know the answer so he said nothing and began to get dressed.

'Do you think I'm in danger?'

Joe froze. It was something that had been at the back of his mind, something he had barely liked to acknowledge.

'I wouldn't worry about it,' he said, forcing out a comforting smile.

She climbed out of bed and tiptoed to the bathroom as Joe finished dressing. As he looked at himself in the mirror he suddenly realized that there'd still be a police presence downstairs dealing with the scene of Karl Dremmer's murder, still sealed off with blue-and-white tape. He'd have to exercise all the discretion he could muster if he wasn't going to be the talk of the police station.

But his plans went awry when they bumped into Sunny Porter as they were leaving the building together. Sunny gave him a knowing smirk and said good morning, the words loaded with innuendo.

Joe felt eyes watching him as they walked to the car and he experienced another wave of uncertainty, so sharp it almost hurt. Perhaps the speed of his relationship with Lydia had been a mistake. They had been two lonely people seeking comfort and now he feared the situation might raise more problems than it had solved. But he tried to put it out of his mind as he drove down the road to Hilton.

He parked outside Judith Dodds' house and he walked to the front door with Lydia by his side, feeling a tingle of anticipation that he might be about to learn something about what went on in Havenby Hall all those years ago. He'd heard talk and rumour about Dr Pennell – none of it good – but now he needed to get at the truth.

He left it up to Lydia to ring the doorbell but there was no answer. She tried again. And again.

'Her car's there.' Lydia sounded slightly worried.

Sure enough, a small blue Peugeot was parked in front of the detached garage which stood to the left of the house.

'She might have walked to the local shops or gone to see a neighbour.' Joe tried to sound positive. However, looking up at the house with its closed curtains, he sensed that something was wrong. 'I'll have a look round the back. Stay there in case she comes back.'

He walked slowly around the side of the house until he reached the back. Here a large kitchen extension jutted out from the main building. He could hear the sound of running water from a stream that flowed past the bottom of the well-kept garden, shaded by mature trees.

He returned his attention to the house and noticed that one of the glass panes in the back door was broken. He walked over and looked inside. Glittering splinters were spread out on the kitchen floor and he waited there for a few seconds, his heart beating fast, wondering whether to call for back up.

Suddenly remembering that Lydia was waiting round the front, he hurried back to her and told her to get back in his car and stay there. The tone of his voice meant that she didn't question the instruction. But she looked frightened and he felt a new tenderness for her.

'I think there's been a break in. I'm just going to have a look.'

'Be careful.'

He didn't reply.

Once he'd returned to the back door he put on the plastic gloves he'd taken from his pocket and tried the handle. The door was unlocked so he pushed it open, avoiding the glass as best he could, and crept on tiptoe through the kitchen and morning room. When he reached the hall he peeped into each of the downstairs rooms but nothing seemed to be out of place. If the glass had been broken by a burglar, he'd left many items of value that could have been disposed of easily in any number of shady pubs.

He stood in the hallway, listening to the silence and staring at the thickly carpeted staircase. If there was anything to find, it would be up there.

He climbed the stairs slowly, pausing every so often to listen, and, once on the landing, he went from room to room but found nothing amiss. He'd left the room at the back of the house till last. The door stood ajar and when he pushed it with his gloved hands it creaked open to reveal a large, tastefully decorated master bedroom, dimly lit by sunlight seeping in through the closed floral blinds. The double bed was unmade as though somebody had just got out of it a few seconds earlier. There was a telephone extension on one of the matching pair of bedside tables and Joe picked it up, only to discover that the line was dead.

A feeling of dread snatched at his heart as he stood and observed the room as he'd been trained to do. The stool by the dressing table had been knocked over and a book and a pair of reading glasses lay on the floor by the bed as though they had been dislodged in a struggle. Something had happened here but it wasn't until he noticed the smear of blood, drying russet on the pink carpet that he knew for sure that the room had been touched by violence.

Stepping out on to the landing he noticed two parallel lines in the pile of the carpet as if a body had been held beneath the arms and dragged from the master bedroom, across the landing and down the stairs. There were a couple of faint smears of blood on the parquet hall floor and when Joe retraced his steps into the kitchen he saw that the parallel tracks continued through the broken glass.

Avoiding the glass again, he stepped outside and started to look round the garden. It was a pleasant day, warm and dry but with clouds that occasionally scudded across the sun. The garden was in full bloom with its well-established bushy shrubs, any of which might conceal the dead.

He searched systematically, finally reaching the foot of the garden where a row of trees shielded the lawn from the stream. To his right a willow dipped its delicate branches into the stream. And, caught in the fronds, he saw a naked human body.

Words he had learned by rote at school popped unbidden into his mind – 'There is a willow grows aslant a brook.' Then there was something about 'fantastic garlands'. It was almost as if the woman's killer was familiar with Shakespeare's words because the corpse was indeed lying beneath the willow, but rather than being garlanded with flowers, the blooms had been stuffed into her mouth, a white rose protruding from the side like a cigarette.

Just like Peter Brockmeister's victims.

The undercroft of the abbey. Two o'clock. It was an appointment etched on Alan Proud's brain. He was about to come face to face with Peter Brockmeister. His hero.

His excuse was that he needed the letters authenticating. But the truth was that he longed to meet the man. He already felt he knew him so well. It was just the physical meeting that would give Alan the thrill he craved.

I met Peter Brockmeister. I shook the hand of a famous killer. It was something to boast about . . . if there was anybody willing to listen.

TWENTY-ONE

Joe had been reluctant to ask Lydia to confirm that the body was that of Judith Dodds, but she had insisted. She wasn't afraid, she'd said, although he'd seen the colour drain from her face when she'd gazed down at the dead woman. He suspected that she was being brave to impress him – but he couldn't help admiring her a little for it.

He had taken her home straight afterwards. A crime scene was no place for her. Besides, she had to be at work, although he wasn't convinced she was in any fit state to face the public after what she'd just witnessed.

He was standing in the front drive, waiting for Sally Sharpe to arrive and examine the body which had been photographed and videoed in situ before being pulled out of the stream to lie on a plastic sheet in the garden. The CSIs were in the house and garden and now he was alone. As he stared at the front gate, now covered in fingerprint powder, he imagined the killer opening it and holding it carefully so the sound of it clattering shut wouldn't wake Judith Dodds or her neighbours who, frustratingly, hadn't seen or heard anything suspicious.

A car rounded the corner and parked down the road at the end of a line of police cars and CSI vans. When the driver emerged, he saw that it was Emily and, for some reason he couldn't quite fathom, he felt relieved.

As soon as she spotted him she waved and he raised his hand in a tentative greeting. She looked determined. He knew the signs: the pursed lips; the swift walk; the focused eyes.

'Any word from the kidnapper?' he asked, fearing bad news.

'We're still waiting for him to get in touch again. Paul Scorer's been calling us to ask if there's any news. He seems more worried than Hawkes does. And so he might. It's been so long now, Joe. I can't help thinking the worst. What happened here?'

Joe brought her up to date.

'So you were here with Lydia when you found the body? Anything I should know?'

Joe felt the blood rise to his cheeks. 'How do you mean?' Emily seemed in a better mood now, especially with the spice of gossip on offer.

'You and Lydia.' She gave him a look of mock disapproval. 'Sleeping with witnesses . . . tut, tut. What would the Chief Constable say?'

Joe felt awkward enough without the whole station knowing, so he ignored her words and stuck to work matters. 'Judith Dodds gave Lydia an old record book from Havenby Hall that her father had kept. Lydia's grandfather got a mention in it. I think these murders are linked to that place. Melanie's, Karl Dremmer's and now Judith Dodds'.'

'A Peter Brockmeister connection?'

'Dremmer wasn't killed using Brockmeister's MO. I take it there have been no developments on that front?'

Emily shook her head. 'There was nothing useful on those tapes he made down there, only the odd bang and crash, a lot of scraping noises and the door opening. No voices. Creeny was supposed to have installed CCTV and a decent security system in the building but it's not up and running yet. Place is only half finished. Our bloody luck.'

Joe led the way round to the back of the house. Emily needed to see the body and Joe wanted to take another look inside the house. If Judith Dodds had been killed because of something she'd found, the killer had probably taken it. But there was always a chance.

He left Emily deep in conversation with Sally Sharpe. He had no wish to hang around Judith Dodds' pale, naked body for longer than was necessary and, besides, there was something he wanted to check back at the house.

Joe had helped in the search of Oriel House. But there was no sign of anything that would throw any light on why Judith Dodds was killed so, after telling the search team that he was to be informed immediately if anything mentioning Dr Pennell or Havenby Hall turned up, he returned to the garden to see if Sally had come up with any new conclusions.

As usual Sally was hedging her bets until the post-mortem, although she did remark on the cuts and cigarette burns; signs of torture identical to those of Melanie Hawkes' body. Joe tried hard not to imagine the woman's last hours and he noticed that Sally was looking uncharacteristically concerned, as though she shared his thoughts. Some things even got to the professionals.

He made for his car and drove back towards the city, passing Boothgate House before turning right by Boothgate Bar. The Tourist Information Office was on his left and he thought of Lydia working in there. His initial, niggling feeling that last night had been a mistake, something to repent in his leisure hours, was growing by the minute. But they'd both been yearning for something; love, perhaps, or just the reassurance of human contact. So why did he feel as though there had been a betrayal? Of Kaitlin's memory, perhaps, or just his old-held – and some would say outdated – principles. But he knew he hadn't time to think about that now.

He parked in the police station car park but, instead of entering the building, he walked on to the street and crossed over Wendover Bridge, heading again for the centre of the city, obeying a sudden instinctive impulse to check out something that was bothering him. It would probably come to nothing but he told himself it would do no harm.

He walked quickly – he always did – and he soon reached the antique shop belonging to Sebastian Bentham's uncle. Melanie Hawkes' file had contained the name of a Cecil Bentham but no address. Perhaps he was a relative of Sebastian's. It would certainly do no harm to ask. He looked into the window and saw the clock with the moon face standing at the rear of the shop. Sebastian was there too, sitting at a roll-topped desk, a broadsheet newspaper open in front of him. When Joe entered the shop he looked up expectantly and folded the paper.

'DI Plantagenet. What can I do for you?' He sounded slightly worried.

'I'd like to take a look at that clock if that's OK with you. Does it work by the way?'

'No idea. I don't think my uncle ever tried to get it going.

Why? Not thinking of buying it are you?' he added hopefully, as though he'd be glad to get the thing off his hands. Or perhaps he just needed to make a sale, any sale.

Joe shook his head. 'How's the play going?'

Sebastian's face lit up. This was a subject more to his liking. 'It's had some good reviews. The Yorkshire Evening Post described it as 'powerful and thought provoking'.

'That's good. I've spoken to the Reverend Rattenbury and Betty Morcroft by the way. Is there anyone else you can think of who might be able to tell me more about Havenby Hall?'

Sebastian shook his head. 'I tried to trace the matron, Mrs Chambers but I had no luck.'

Joe nodded. His own team had tried to track down Mrs Chambers too but she seemed to have vanished without trace. There was no record of her death so presumably she was still out there somewhere. Perhaps he would get them to try harder.

'Do you mind if I look inside the clock?' he asked.

'Help yourself.' His lips formed into a sad half grin. 'If you manage to get it going we can put the price up.' He opened the desk drawer and, after fumbling around for a while, produced a key which he handed to Joe.

Joe walked over to the clock and used the key to unlock the door in the tall base. But all he saw was a dusty pendulum drooping sadly in the dark, cobwebbed space.

'Are you looking for anything in particular?' Sebastian asked. Joe could tell he was doing his best to hide his burning curiosity.

Joe turned to him. 'The woman who sold your uncle this clock was murdered last night.'

Sebastian stared at him in disbelief for a few moments. 'Fuck. I mean . . . oh God.'

'Did you know that she was the daughter of Dr Pennell, the doctor who worked at Havenby Hall?'

Sebastian's eyes widened in surprise. 'No.'

'You didn't contact her when you were carrying out the research for your play?'

'Dr Pennell's name came up a lot and I soon learned that he'd died. I tried to find his relatives but . . .'

'Mrs Dodds had been estranged from her father since she

was very young. But it's odd that the doctor's clock ended up with you, isn't it? You'd really no idea it came from Havenby Hall?'

Sebastian stared at the clock and shook his head.

'Havenby Hall was the inspiration for your play and the clock just happened to end up here. As a policeman, I don't tend to believe in coincidences like that.'

Sebastian scratched his head, as though he was trying very hard to think up a convincing answer. 'My uncle deals with lots of house clearances. As far as I know this was just another one . . . routine.'

'Is Cecil Bentham a relative of yours?'

'Yes. He's my uncle.'

Joe felt a thrill of triumph.

'Then I'd like a word with him.'

Sebastian looked uncertain for a moment. 'I'll give him a call.'

Joe watched as Sebastian picked up the old Bakelite receiver and dialled. It was a long time since he'd seen a telephone like that but anything more up to date would have looked out of place in this emporium of old and shabby things.

After a short conversation Sebastian replaced the receiver and turned to Joe. 'He says he's not feeling too good today.' He frowned, puzzled. 'He seemed quite lively when I saw him last night.'

The last thing Joe wanted was to be accused of bullying a sick old man but he needed to speak to him. 'What's wrong with him?' he asked.

Sebastian shrugged. 'He's had a virus. He was on the mend but . . .'

Joe turned his attention to the clock again. There was somewhere he hadn't looked but it was a long shot. 'Mind if I have a look behind the face?'

He pointed to the clock and Sebastian folded his tattooed arms as though he was weary of the whole subject. 'Help yourself.'

'Will you give me a hand to turn it round?'

Sebastian left his desk and walked over the bare floorboards to where the clock stood, pushed against the shop wall. They both manoeuvred it round until the back was visible, covered in dust and cobwebs. A large spider scuttled in panic down the case and out of sight and Joe saw what he was looking for. There was another door behind the clock face and when he used the key he'd used for the lower case, he found that it fitted perfectly.

The door opened with a stiff creak revealing the inner workings of the clock. And something else. A small black notebook, dusty and battered, had been stuffed into the gap between the workings and the clock case. Joe took a plastic evidence bag from his pocket and scooped the thing into it.

'What is it?' asked Sebastian, craning his head for a better view.

'I don't know yet. I'll give you a receipt for it and . . .'

'Don't worry. It's nothing to do with me,' he said as if he was anxious to dissociate himself from the whole thing.

'I'll need your uncle's address,' said Joe as he slipped the notebook into his pocket.

Maybe it was time for visiting the sick.

Beverley had seen Lydia go out that morning with a man in tow. And she'd recognized the man at once as the police inspector. Plantagenet, he was called – not a name that's easy to forget. She found herself wondering whether some distant ancestor of his had had royal blood. Not that he looked anything special or particularly regal. Perhaps when she saw Lydia again, she'd ask her. It would be something to talk about. An excuse to open a conversation.

Mother was still in bed. Since her last bout of illness her health had deteriorated and she needed the wheelchair all the time now. It was a good job, Beverley thought, that her hatchback car could accommodate it; at least it meant she could get out of the flat on a regular basis. In the hospital they'd talked about physiotherapy and rehabilitation, but Mother had showed little interest in that sort of thing. The only thing that preoccupied her these days was the past.

She put the door on the latch, walked out into the corridor. The police presence had dwindled to a single uniformed constable sitting on a plastic chair next to the basement door, separated from the rest of the world by a barrier of blue-and-white crime-scene tape festooned around the hallway like bunting at a fête. She toyed with the idea of taking the young man a cup of tea. But as she watched he answered his radio and began a conversation. She'd missed the moment.

Besides, she had something else to do. She returned to her flat and picked up a scrap of paper bearing a neatly written number. It was time she made the call.

'Is that Canon Merryweather? The Deliverance Minister?' she asked when the call was answered. 'It's Beverley Newson here, from Boothgate House. I knew Karl Dremmer. Look, I think I need your help.'

She listened carefully to George's reply.

The undercroft was the only part of the abbey near the city centre that had been left intact after Henry VIII's commissioners had done their worst. Standing near the entrance to the Museum Gardens, it served as a gloomy covered passageway with its elaborately vaulted ceiling and its huge Roman sarcophagi, placed there in the shelter to protect their ancient carved stonework.

Alan Proud leaned against one of the sarcophagi, watching the passers-by; the mothers with pushchairs, the teenagers on bicycles and the couples holding hands. A few of them gave him a wary glance. Some people considered that a man waiting in the shadows must be up to no good. Little did they know his real interest – if they did, they would have fled screaming.

The time of his appointment had passed long ago but he still waited. He'd give him another fifteen minutes before he abandoned hope.

He fixed his gaze on the entrance to the gardens, a pair of huge wrought-iron gates erected at a time of Victorian civic pride, and watched as tourists, young families, pensioners and workers on their lunch break streamed through. He felt a stab of disappointment. He'd been anticipating this moment for so long and now he'd let him down.

With a sigh, he turned to leave his post. Perhaps there'd be a message on his computer when he got back to the flat. Perhaps he'd get a second chance.

'Alan?'

The voice, soft as a whisper, made him swing round.

'You've changed,' was the only thing he could think of to say to the man who'd killed so many people.

TWENTY-TWO

Karl Dremmer's post-mortem was already booked for that afternoon and Emily reckoned they were lucky that Sally had agreed to fit Judith Dodds' in as well. But he supposed it depended on your definition of luck. To him there was nothing lucky about watching a corpse being taken apart.

There were few surprises about Dremmer's cause of death. A blunt instrument, probably the hefty chunk of wood left over from the renovations that had been found discarded, bloodstained and wiped clean of fingerprints, in the overgrown grass of the graveyard during the routine search. The blow had caused massive head injuries that had resulted in death and Dremmer had been attacked from behind so he probably hadn't known a thing about it. There were signs that he'd been the victim of some violence before death. There was some bruising to his torso, as though he'd been punched or kicked in the ribs, and a cut on his cheek. But whether this was linked to his murder, Sally couldn't say.

Once she'd finished with Dremmer, Sally turned her attention to Judith Dodds.

'She died in exactly the same way as Melanie Hawkes,' Sally said once she'd completed her gruesome business. 'She was rendered unconscious by a blow to the head and then strangled with a ligature – a scarf perhaps or a pair of tights – and then there are the cuts and burns. The bruising on her wrists and ankles is identical to that on Melanie Hawkes which suggests that she'd been restrained at some point. I think the flowers were stuffed into her mouth once she was dead but I can't be absolutely sure.'

'Fresh flowers?' Emily asked.

'Well, they weren't fresh when we found them but I think they must have come from her garden.'

'So he probably used anything that was handy?'

'Looks like it. The ones in Melanie Hawkes' mouth were wild flowers mostly, found in any piece of wasteland or hedgerow.'

'A bloke picking flowers would stand out like a tart at a convent,' said Emily.

Sally considered the question for a moment. 'Didn't Peter Brockmeister sometimes gather them and keep them in a vase till he was ready to use them?'

'That's right,' said Joe. 'It was part of his ritual.'

'So this killer's trying to copy him,' said Emily. 'But the cigarette burns and the cuts make it different. Brockmeister never tortured his victims; he just knocked them out, tied them up and strangled them . . . slowly. If he was alive, I'd say he could be branching out, trying something new.'

'But he's dead,' said Emily.

Before Joe could reply Emily's phone rang. When she answered it he could tell from her expression that the news was to her liking.

'That was Janet,' she said, returning the phone to her pocket. 'The kidnappers have been in touch again. They wanted to check whether Hawkes still had the money. They even put Daisy on the line for a second to prove she was still alive. Janet said she just said hello and she didn't sound frightened.'

'Could have been a recording.'

Emily suddenly looked solemn. 'Could be. They cut her off before Hawkes could start a conversation with her. Oh God, Joe, I hope you're wrong.'

'So do I. When's the drop?'

'Tonight. They're going to call with further instructions. 'We could have a chance to get the kid back,' she said. 'So let's not blow it.'

As Joe followed her out of the mortuary, he felt in his pocket and his hand touched the plastic bag containing the book he'd found hidden in the clock. But examining it would have to wait. There were things he had to do.

Seeing Judith Dodds' body like that had shaken Lydia but she tried not to show it at work. And when her boss had told her to take her lunch break while they were quiet, she'd decided to buy a sandwich and eat it in the Museum Gardens. It was a fine day and the place was always lively.

She strolled in through the gates, lunch in hand, wondering what Joe was doing at that moment. She hoped he'd be free that evening, partly because Judith Dodds' murder had made her nervous about being alone in Boothgate House and partly because she needed reassurance that last night hadn't been a mistake. He'd seemed a little distant that morning, but then he'd had a lot on his mind. She told herself that if Joe wasn't free she should visit one of her friends, Amy perhaps . . . but that would mean coming home in the darkness to that empty place and somehow that prospect seemed even worse.

Something, a movement caught out of the corner of her eye, made her glance to her right at the medieval undercroft. Alan Proud was standing there, watching her with a self-satisfied smirk on his face and her heart began to race as she began to half walk, half run towards the abbey ruins. He looked as though he was waiting for somebody but the way he'd stared at her so intently made her uneasy. She walked on quickly, relieved when she reached the tourist-filled shelter of the abbey walls.

Sanctuary.

When Joe had taken a quick look inside the notebook he'd found in the clock he'd discovered that half the words were abbreviated and the handwriting was appalling, little more than a scrawl. Deciphering it would need considerable thought and effort so it would have to wait till later.

He looked at his watch. He needed to speak to Cecil Bentham and although his nephew had implied that he wasn't up to visitors, he was sure that a casual word would do no harm. He had the old man's address, Flower Street, just outside the city walls. He knew it would take less time to get there on foot than it would take to struggle through the traffic in a car so, after telling Emily where he was headed, he left the police station and crossed the road. He took his jacket off. It was a warm day even though a shroud of cloud hid the sun from view.

Cecil Bentham lived in a small Georgian cottage, plain and sober unlike the pub next door which was festooned with baskets containing cascades of colourful flowers. When Joe raised the black lion head knocker he heard a shuffling behind the door which opened to reveal a tall, elderly man with thinning grey hair, combed across to hide his bare, shiny scalp. Joe introduced himself and Bentham made a careful examination of his ID, as though he suspected him of being an impostor, but eventually he stood aside to let him in. There was no sign of ill health. In fact Joe thought he looked pretty sprightly for his age.

'How are you, Mr Bentham?' he asked, following the old man as he made his slow progress down the narrow hall and into a claustrophobic drawing room crammed with antique furniture and ornaments. The fruits of his labours over the years, the reward of being in the know.

'I'm feeling much better, thank you.' His thin, pale lips, still bearing faint traces of toothpaste, twitched upwards in a half-hearted smile. 'My nephew will be relieved when I finally get back to work so he can get on with his writing.' He said the last word with a faint touch of irony, as though he didn't quite approve.

'I need to ask you about the long-cased clock you purchased from a Mrs Dodds. She lived at Oriel House in Hilton.'

Bentham nodded with polite interest, giving no hint that he'd noticed Joe's use of the past tense.

'You knew her father, I believe . . . Dr Pennell?'

It was a long shot but when the old man gave a cautious nod it seemed that Joe had struck lucky and he suddenly felt hopeful that his visit wouldn't be a waste of time.

'How well did you know him?'

There was a long silence before he answered. 'I don't know how much my nephew's told you.'

'Only that Pennell was the Medical Superintendent at Havenby Hall. Did you know him socially . . . or maybe you were a patient of his at one time?' Joe hoped that if he kept on digging, he'd eventually strike gold. But when Bentham stood up and asked him to leave, he was surprised. And curious.

'What is it you don't want to tell me, Mr Bentham?' he

asked. 'Is it something about Havenby Hall . . . something that happened to one of your family?' This was pure guesswork but it seemed to get results. Bentham looked angry.

'Whatever you've heard, it's all lies.'

'Then why don't you give me your version of events?' Joe leaned forward and waited expectantly. More often than not the tactic worked with criminals. The urge to fill a vacuum of silence is sometimes irresistible.

'My wife was ill . . . very ill. She was admitted to Havenby Hall but she suffered a stroke and died three weeks later. That's all.'

Joe said nothing but his brain was working fast. Dorothy Watts had supposedly died of an unexpected stroke. Perhaps a pattern was emerging.

'My wife died of natural causes and nothing could be done.'

'Is that what Dr Pennell told you?'

'I'm sure even a policeman can understand that it's distressing to talk about it. And as for Sebastian's play . . . he didn't know the pain he was causing when he cashed in on my grief. Because that's what he's been doing.' He turned his head away, his eyes damp with tears. 'Now I'd like you to leave.'

Joe sat there for a few moments. He'd known there was something Sebastian had been holding back and if Cecil Bentham was telling the truth, he must have been furious with his nephew for making use of such a disturbing episode in his family's past.

'I'm sorry if I've raked up painful memories but this is connected to a murder enquiry,' he said as he stood up. 'Did you speak to a woman called Melanie Hawkes? She was a solicitor and she was making enquiries into the death of a former patient at Havenby Hall.'

Bentham shook his head. 'I told her I couldn't help her and I'm telling you the same,' he said, pressing his lips together in a stubborn line.

As Joe left the house he was weighed down by an uncomfortable feeling of guilt . . . and this time it didn't concern Lydia.

* * *

When Joe returned to the police station he was glad to see that some of the old files he'd requested had finally arrived, including a report on the death of Lydia's grandfather, Dr Reginald Speed, in a road traffic accident back in 1980. He opened the file and read the typed pages inside. Dr Speed had been killed in a hit-and-run incident outside his house in Pickby. And the one woman who'd witnessed it swore to the police that the car had been driven at him deliberately. The doctor had been pronounced dead at the scene and nobody could imagine why anybody would want to kill such an inoffensive, caring man.

But Joe was sure he knew the answer. Dr Speed had acted as a locum at Havenby Hall. Somebody had torn his notes out of the Medical Superintendent's log book that Judith Dodds had passed to Lydia and then the locum had been silenced . . . permanently. Joe could only conclude that Dr Speed had discovered something going on at Havenby Hall. Something somebody wanted to keep hidden. And with the deaths of Melanie Hawkes, Judith Dodds and Karl Dremmer, he feared that anybody who might be about to stumble on that secret could still be at risk.

He wondered whether Sebastian Bentham had encountered any threats in the course of his research. He hadn't mentioned anything but perhaps he ought to have another word . . . just to be sure.

He pushed the file to one side, suddenly remembering the clock. Lydia had told him that she'd seen the thing in her nightmares and the only place she could have seen it was if she'd stayed with her grandfather at Havenby Hall. Perhaps she'd witnessed something terrible there as a small child, something that had stayed dormant in her brain until she'd returned to the building all those years later. A dozen frightening possibilities marched through his head. If the killer knew that Lydia had witnessed something . . .

'I've been checking out that Mrs Chambers, the matron you asked about.'

He looked up and saw Jamilla standing by his desk, her notebook in her hand.

'Her first name was Christabel which is fairly uncommon

so I thought finding her would be easy. I've looked through death records and the census . . . also whether she's been employed since Havenby Hall closed.' She gave an uncharacteristically dramatic shrug. 'Absolutely nothing. It's as if she just vanished off the face of the earth. Although she was never reported missing either.'

'Maybe she changed her identity.'

'It's a possibility. She was divorced from her husband back in the nineteen sixties and it doesn't look as if there were any children of the marriage. Of course she might have gone abroad. Retired to the Costa del Sol or something like that.'

Joe sighed. 'She might,' he said. 'Or perhaps she was murdered too and her body hasn't been found yet.'

Jamilla nodded. She'd considered this possibility too. 'That nurse called Jean Smith you mentioned . . . the one Betty Morcroft said had got too curious. Her full name was Jean Margaret Smith and she was reported missing by her sister in 1979. She hasn't turned up since, alive or dead.'

'Thanks for trying.' Joe gave her a grateful smile just as the phone on his desk began to ring. He picked up the receiver. It was George Merryweather. Did Joe have time for a quick word? He asked him to wait and covered the mouthpiece.

Jamilla had been about to return to her desk but Joe had a thought. 'Are you any good at deciphering bad handwriting?'

Jamilla grinned. 'I always like a challenge.'

Joe passed her the notebook he'd found in the clock. 'See what you can make of that.'

She took it and flicked through the book, raising her eyebrows as if she was wondering whether she'd been too hasty to volunteer. As soon as she'd gone Joe resumed his call.

'Sorry to keep you waiting, George. What can I do for you?'

'Beverley Newson wants me to visit the basement at Boothgate House again. She said she wants me to get rid of whatever's down there. I must admit I'm intrigued. I've talked to Karl Dremmer's colleagues at the university and they told me his instruments definitely picked up something out of the ordinary; drops in temperature and points of light that defy scientific explanation. And then there were the builders who reported strange goings on.'

'Visit the place by all means, George, but be careful. After what happened to Dremmer . . .'

'Nice of you to be so concerned, Joe.'

Joe suddenly visualized Karl Dremmer's dead body and felt a concern for his friend that verged on panic. 'Anyway, it's a crime scene so I can't let you down there unsupervised,' he said quickly. I'll come down with you if you like.'

'What about tonight?'

Joe hesitated. It was tonight that Hawkes was due to deliver the money to Daisy's kidnappers.

'I can't make it tonight. How does tomorrow suit you?'

'It's not me I'm thinking of. It's Miss Newson. She's getting very nervous, poor woman.'

'In that case go round in daylight. Tell the constable on duty you have my permission . . . and make sure he hangs around.'

He replaced the receiver hoping George wouldn't do anything risky. But he knew that if Beverley Newson was in a state of panic, George's conscience wouldn't allow him to ignore her.

He saw Emily making for his desk. She'd just been briefing the Superintendent on their progress and she looked haggard, as though he'd been giving her a bad time.

'Any luck with Cecil Bentham?' she asked wearily.

'His wife died in Havenby Hall . . . in exactly the same way as Chris Torridge's aunt, Dorothy Watts. The one Melanie Hawkes was investigating.'

'You think the deaths weren't natural?'

'I don't know. I'd like to find out why Karl Dremmer tried to chip away at that far wall. I'd like it demolished.'

Emily raised her eyebrows. 'We'd need Creeny's permission . . . and, according to the plans we've got, the basement doesn't continue under the rest of the building. I've even asked the search team to keep an eye out for another entrance but they haven't reported anything.'

'All the same, I'd like to make sure.'

Emily fell silent for a while. And when she finally spoke she sounded worried. 'If you're right and there were deaths in that place that weren't natural, this could be the biggest scandal . . .'

'Jamilla's examining a notebook that probably belonged to the Medical Superintendent. It might tell us something.'

'How did you get it?'

'Long story.' He hardly wanted to tell Emily about Lydia's nightmares. It would seem like a betrayal of trust. He looked over at Jamilla and was glad to see that the notebook was open in front of her and she was making notes, deep in concentration.

'There was somebody – a patient – who helped Sebastian Bentham with the research he carried out for his play. His name wasn't in Melanie Hawkes' file but I'd like to speak to him . . . just in case.'

'Did that play you saw contain anything about murder?'

'No. It was set twenty years earlier and it was about a girl who'd been put into an asylum by her family for getting pregnant. Nasty and disturbing but I believe that sort of thing was fairly common in days gone by. Bentham did include a shadowy character that he admitted was inspired by Peter Brockmeister but . . .' He thought for a moment. 'Could Brockmeister still be alive? Could he be killing again?'

Emily turned away. 'Oh God, I hope not.'

A worm of doubt about the authenticity of the emails meant that Alan Proud had failed to bring the letters to the first meeting. But now he knew for sure that they were genuine. He'd shaken the hand of the man who'd killed all those people. And now he was going to meet him again, he had so many questions to ask.

He sat in his flat waiting for the sound of Lydia putting her key in the lock of her front door. He listened for her every evening. He liked to think of her in there, unaware that only a thin partition wall separated them. He'd enjoyed listening to the sounds coming from her bedroom last night. Animal sounds of pleasure. Pity she'd chosen a policeman to share her passion with. Proud knew he could have given her so much more. Perhaps he still would.

There she was. He could hear her footsteps on the landing, soft and quick. Then voices. She was saying hello to that stupid, fat Beverley opposite, asking her how her mother was, making polite conversation. Then he heard the key in the lock and her door quickly opening and closing. Now she was inside the flat he was tempted to knock on the wall. How she'd panic and how he'd enjoy imagining her fear. She'd been so nervous of him since he'd made his first, ill-advised move and the thought gave him a thrill – although he realized now that he should have bided his time. He'd seen her in the Museum Gardens and he wondered how she would react if she knew his secret. What would she do if she came face to face with Peter Brockmeister?

He knew what he'd do next. He'd invite Brockmeister back to his flat and show him the rest of his collection. He was bound to be interested. And the thought that he'd entertained a killer in his humble flat would buoy up his spirits for weeks . . . even if that was only as far as it went.

Proud had never had the courage to emulate the actions of the men and women whose relics he collected and pored over so avidly. He venerated these mementos of their lives as the medieval believer venerated the relics of dead saints. But to Alan Proud, evil was so much more powerful than goodness. He packed Brockmeister's letters to Darren carefully in his briefcase and made sure everything was in place. The other letters – the more intimate and explosive ones – he'd keep for a further meeting. It would be an excuse to continue their relationship.

Only a few more hours and he would have what he wanted. This meeting was too important to mess up.

TWENTY-THREE

Joe had always known that Jamilla had a quick mind. She'd passed her sergeant's exams first time and was waiting for a suitable opening. She'd turned down a posting in Northallerton because that would have meant moving away from her close-knit Indian family and Joe, unlike some others, could sympathize. He hoped something suitable would come up for her soon. But in the meantime, he was glad she was on his team. Especially when she waved him over to her desk, a look a triumph on her face.

'I've cracked the first couple of pages. It's a list of names and dates. I've copied it out for you.' She pushed a sheet of paper towards him. Jamilla's neat, square handwriting was easy to read and a couple of names jumped out at him, making his heart beat a little faster.

The first that caught his eye was Dorothy Watts. He recognized the date beside her name as the date of her death. And then a time – four hours thirty-five minutes. Beneath Dorothy's name was another name, Frank Watts, and a sum of money: £5,000.

There were other names, amongst them that of Elsie Bentham along with her date of death. The time by her name was three hours five minutes but no actual cause of death. Her husband's name was beneath hers. Cecil Bentham: £4,000.

There were seven other names and all the entries followed the same pattern. The name of the deceased, the date of death, a time in hours and minutes, and, presumably, the name of the next of kin followed by a sum of money.

Now they had more names, they could delve further. And it struck Joe that that could be what Melanie Hawkes had been trying to do when she met her death.

He told Jamilla to keep working on the notebook and instructed one of the young detective constables to attempt to trace the relatives of the other people mentioned on the list. Presumably Dr Pennell had hidden the notebook from prying eyes and the more Joe discovered about Pennell, the more suspect his actions appeared to be. He'd heard it said that when doctors went bad, they did it very efficiently and with deadly consequences. He had a feeling that Dr Pennell had gone very bad indeed. But what he needed now was proof.

Joe was as sure as he could be that Judith Dodds had died because of something the killer thought she had or knew, possibly the notebook that was now on Jamilla's desk. But now they had it and he felt suddenly optimistic that they could be one step ahead of him at last.

The details of the former Havenby Hall patient Sebastian Bentham had interviewed were unfolded on the desk in front of him. He felt slightly apprehensive as he made the call, aware that he was probably about to resurrect unhappy memories for Dennis Younger, memories of a time of despair. But when Dennis answered the phone, to Joe's relief and surprise, he sounded quite cheerful. No, Dennis hadn't minded being interviewed by Sebastian at all, that unfortunate part of his life was over and done with long ago and he was happy to talk to Joe if it helped. No, he'd not been contacted by Melanie Hawkes – he sounded a little disappointed at this omission.

Joe looked at his watch. Six o'clock – a time when most people were arriving home from work. The delivery of Daisy's ransom was to take place later so the night would be a long one for his team. He poked his head round Emily's office door and told her where he was going, promising to be back in time for the hand over. She nodded and returned to her paperwork.

Dennis Younger lived out in the suburbs and Joe was glad the rush hour was over as he steered the car out of the city. He felt a thrill of optimism that sooner or later he'd find the piece of information that would make everything fall into place.

Mr Younger's semi-detached house was small and neat with a front garden filled with roses. It was an elderly person's house with green paintwork, snowy lace curtains and a proper garden gate while most of the neighbours had opted for double driveways.

The door was opened almost immediately by a small, round woman with grey curls. She invited Joe in and asked if he'd like a cup of tea. He said yes.

Dennis emerged from the kitchen and shook his hand before leading him into a small sitting room and inviting him to make himself at home.

'I'm sorry if all this brings back unhappy memories, Mr Younger.'

Dennis shook his head, a determined smile on his lips. 'Don't worry yourself about that.' His accent was pure Yorkshire. 'At one time the subject was off limits but at my age . . . I had what they called a breakdown caused by the stress of losing my first wife and my job at the same time.' He straightened his back. 'But I got over it and everything's been fine and dandy since. In fact I quite enjoyed helping that lad with his play. Didn't think much to the finished result though. Left at the interval.'

Joe smiled and gave him a conspiratorial nod. 'I was tempted to do the same myself. What was Havenby Hall like in those days?'

'Well it certainly wasn't as bad as it was made out to be in that play. Mind you, I was in the blue wing – that was for the cases that weren't considered so bad. I was in three weeks but I know some were there for years. The serious cases were in the red wing and we never had anything to do with them.'

'Did you come across a patient called Peter Brockmeister?'

Dennis shifted forward and looked round, as though he was afraid of being overheard. 'I knew he was there 'cause I overheard one of the nurses talking – she said he was very charming but he made her flesh crawl because she knew what he'd done. He was kept well away from us so I never actually saw him . . . well, not that I'm aware of.'

'Do you recognize the names Dorothy Watts and Elsie Bentham?'

He shook his head. 'They might have been in one of the other wings.

'Dorothy had suffered a breakdown so I would have thought she might have been treated on the same wing as you were.'

'Sorry. I don't remember the names. Of course, we might have been there at different times.'

'Do you remember the chaplain?'

'Oh yes. Nice man.'

'The Reverend Rattenbury?'

'I can't recall his name but he used to come in and chat sometimes.'

'What about Dr Pennell?' he asked.

'Now I didn't like him one little bit. Cold fish he was. The actual psychiatrists were OK but Pennell was the Medical Superintendent and he lived on the premises. Between you and me, I think he ran that place.'

'When he went into hospital for an operation he was replaced by a locum – a Dr Speed. Do you remember that?'

'Can't say I do. Maybe it was after my time.'

'You'll remember the matron, Mrs Chambers?'

'Oh aye. I heard her and Pennell were thick as thieves.' He gave Joe a theatrical wink.

'Did anything unusual happen while you were there?'

'That depends what you mean by unusual.' He hesitated. 'I don't know what's normal in a place like that. There were some sad cases in there, you know. I sometimes heard screams. Terrible screams. Like souls in torment. But like I said, there were some very sick people in there.'

'What about the basement?'

Dennis's eyes widened. 'We were told never to go near it – something to do with delicate equipment. I thought that maybe the ECT machines were down there but they weren't – they were on yellow wing. I don't know what they kept down there but . . . Well, I think that's where the screams came from. But I couldn't swear to that. When I asked one of the nurses she just said the place was haunted. I thought she was joking.'

'Probably,' said Joe.

At that moment Mrs Younger came in with two bone-china cups and saucers filled with lukewarm tea. Joe drank it gratefully.

The kidnapper had been in touch with detailed instructions and they had two and a half hours before the drop. Emily was sure she had everything covered but she felt too restless to sit there in her office pushing paper round her desk. Besides, there was somebody she wanted to visit before all hell broke loose and she just had time to fit it in.

Daisy's biological father, Paul Scorer, had been the model of patience throughout the whole thing, keeping in touch by phone but not overreacting in a way that might put the operation in jeopardy. She reckoned he deserved a quick visit, just to reassure him that they were doing everything they could.

As she drove out to his cottage, she wondered what would happen once Daisy was safely returned. She couldn't bring herself to contemplate the possibility that she wouldn't be returned. As a mother herself, there were some things she couldn't bear to think about.

The drive took twenty minutes and when she arrived at Scorer's cottage at six thirty there was no sign of life and she cursed herself for not ringing ahead. However, she had longed to get away from the office . . . and besides, some instinct had told her that it might be better to take him by surprise. According to Scorer his partner was still away in Somerset and she wondered how she had reacted to the news that Daisy had been abducted. She would have expected her to return from whatever hippy retreat she was at to provide her partner with some support. But other people – particularly those with an unconventional lifestyle – didn't always think the way she did.

She knocked at the door but there was no answer so she walked round the cottage, looking into windows.

She pressed her face up to the grimy panes and she could make out the interior of the living room; the beanbags and the old rugs and the shelves crammed with books and an eclectic assortment of objects d'art. It looked cosy and she imagined what it would be like in winter with the dusty wood-burning stove lit.

Then she saw the child lying face down on a bean bag in the corner, her arm dangling to the floor and her head bent to one side. She couldn't see the face but it had to be Daisy.

And from the position of the body she looked as if she was dead.

TWENTY-FOUR

Emily had called for back up and as soon as Joe found out he drove out of the city – too fast – to join her at Scorer's place.

When he got there he found two middle-aged constables leaning against an untidily parked patrol car as if they were waiting for something to happen.

'Where's DCI Thwaite?' he asked as he emerged from his car. 'What's going on?'

'She's round the back of the house . . . told us to send you round as soon as you arrived.' The constable, a big man with sagging jowls who looked as if he might not pass his next medical, looked solemn.

Joe didn't hesitate. He rushed round to the rear of the house, almost tripping over a discarded watering can. His heart was pounding. How could they have got this so wrong?

As he rounded the corner he found Emily standing next to the open back door with another uniformed constable. He saw that one of the French windows had been smashed.

'They said you'd found Daisy,' he said as he hurried towards her.

She gave him a bitter smile. 'As soon as I made the call I broke in. Turns out I've been a bloody idiot. Come and have a look.'

The constable stood to attention like a flunkey. 'Careful of the glass, ma'am,' he said, standing back to let Emily enter the house first.

Joe followed her in, walking on tip toe. He gasped when he saw the child lying perfectly still on the floor. Emily took a step towards her, picked her up by the hair and began to laugh.

'I only saw it in the gloom. Bloody realistic.'

Joe looked at the small figure and immediately saw what she meant.

'I should have known cause my Sarah's got one just like it.' She propped the doll upright against a chair. It was as big as a six-year-old child and startlingly lifelike from a distance with its fair hair and soft plastic face lit up by a permanent half smile, as if it was harbouring some delicious and sinister secret.

'My Sweet Friend, they're called,' said Emily, the expert. 'Horrible things in my opinion but kids seem to love them.' She pointed to a label dangling round the thing's neck like a noose. 'This is brand new and they're not cheap.' She turned to the constable. 'False alarm, I'm afraid.'

'Is it?' said Joe.

'I'll say a few prayers, if that's all right.' George Merryweather was armed with nothing more dramatic than his old Bible, a faithful friend since theological college.

'Will that be enough?' Beverley looked sceptical as she stood at the basement entrance, her hand resting on the door, ready to push it open and descend to the depths.

'It usually is,' said George. 'Deliverance ministry is about bringing peace to a place and sending any restless souls there might be to their eternal rest. It's rarely dramatic but that doesn't mean it's not effective in cases where it's appropriate.' He resisted the temptation to add that if she was expecting a scene reminiscent of *The Exorcist* she would be very disappointed.

He smiled at Beverley who looked mildly frustrated, as though she was afraid he wasn't taking this seriously enough.

'But there's definitely something here. Even in my flat I can feel it. I've heard noises.'

'Well, there has been lots of building work going on.' George always looked for the obvious first but this clearly wasn't what she wanted to hear. 'I've asked the police and they say it's OK to go down . . . if you're ready. Shall I go first?'

She nodded and George thought she looked eager rather than frightened.

George was glad that the police had left their lighting down there. He had been instructed how to switch it on from upstairs so as he descended the stairs the room below was brightly lit.

'Shouldn't the lights be out?' Beverley said.

'No. It's fine,' he replied as he reached the bottom of the steps and began to walk around the room, taking in his surroundings.

Karl Dremmer's sleeping bag was still there and George found the sight of it unnerving.

He placed the Bible lovingly on a ledge and took his prayer book from his jacket pocket. Then as he began to pray he thought he heard a faint sigh from somewhere beyond the far wall.

And Beverley screamed.

The man who had once been Peter Brockmeister walked through the streets, passing groups of tourists, out searching for a suitable restaurant. The fact that they were quite unaware of what he was about to do amused him. Poor innocent sheep, he thought. Poor potential victims.

He walked on to the meeting place, leaving the pedestrianized heart of the city, suddenly shocked when he encountered a road busy with cars and buses. He was so wrapped up in his own thoughts that he narrowly avoided being mowed down by a bus and after the encounter he stood on the kerb, heart beating fast. However, he knew he'd been saved from disaster by some unseen force – the unseen force that had ruled his life for so many years. Some called it the force of evil. But he wasn't that imaginative. He preferred to think of it as the force of pleasure and fulfilment.

The sun was just setting and when he reached Museum Gardens there were very few people about: only a few strolling couples, oblivious to anybody and anything but themselves, and some youths perched on the park benches with bottles of strong cider while others of their kind circled on bicycles like puny, sportswear-clad vultures. He avoided their gaze. Trouble was the last thing he wanted.

Ahead of him he could see the jagged ruins of the abbey in the fading light. He derived some satisfaction from the thought of all that goodness, all that worship destroyed by one man's lust and greed. He understood only too well the driving force behind that destruction.

The best-preserved section of the ruins was the abbey church and several of the great windows still stood, glassless and empty, their elaborate stone tracery like lace against the darkening sky. This was the meeting place.

He stepped into the outline of the church. He was five minutes early but surprise would give him the advantage.

He concealed himself behind a wall. From there he could see anybody approaching and another taller wall at his back gave him protection from unexpected intruders. After a couple of minutes he leaned his tired body against the stones. And exactly on time he saw Alan Proud walking towards him, his eyes fixed ahead. He watched him quicken his pace as he passed the youths but they were too occupied with their own affairs to notice.

Proud was carrying a briefcase and he looked rather self-important, like someone trying to play the role of a busy businessman. But he didn't fool the man who spied on him from the shadows of the ruined church. He knew what made Proud function. He could see into his soul.

He stepped from the shelter of the wall and when Proud spotted him he raised a hand in tentative greeting. But the watcher stood quite still and waited for Proud to come to him . . . like a supplicant.

Proud wore a conspiratorial grin on his face; the grin of a fool who imagined he was in on a secret. How wrong he was.

'I've got the letters,' he said. 'And I've printed out a certificate of authenticity so if you can sign it for me . . .' He gave a nervous little laugh. 'Well, I'd be ever so grateful. You don't know what this means to me, you really don't.'

Brockmeister put out his hand and looked on as Proud fumbled with the clasp of his briefcase. His nerves made his fingers clumsy and useless and Brockmeister was gratified to see that he could still wield that sort of power over a man. Women, of course, were a different matter. He had never met any problems with women.

It seemed like an age before the briefcase sprung open and its contents spilled on to the grass. Proud gave an irritating little laugh again and scrabbled down to retrieve them.

Proud straightened himself up, replacing the contents of his file and delving in his briefcase for something lost. Eventually he produced a sheet of paper with a triumphant flourish and handed it over.

'Here's the certificate. If you can just sign there. I've got a pen somewhere . . . hang on.' He fumbled in his briefcase again. 'Sorry about all this. I'm so grateful to you . . . I really am,' he repeated as he produced a cheap ballpoint pen and presented it with an ingratiating smile. 'I've got a few more of your letters hidden at home. They're the ones you wrote to someone called Jason. They're of a more . . . sensitive nature . . . candid, I suppose you could call them,' Proud said with a knowing wink. He began to read out loud. 'This is to certify that these letters are genuine and were written by me, Peter Brockmeister to Darren Carter between June nineteen seventy-eight and April nineteen eighty-one. Signed . . .'

Brockmeister looked Proud in the eye and saw uncertainty there. And weakness. He liked weakness. 'What makes you think I'll sign this for you? What's in it for me?'

He watched as Proud's smile vanished and was replaced by a puzzled frown.

'But I thought . . .'

'You thought wrong,' he said as he tore Proud's certificate neatly in two.

Proud stood there gaping, lost for suitable words.

'I'm surprised at you, Mr Proud. You claim to be some sort of authority on me and my kind but you really have no idea what you're dealing with, do you?'

Proud was backing away now, stuffing the file back in his briefcase.

And Brockmeister could smell his fear.

TWENTY-FIVE

All patrols were on the lookout for Paul Scorer's vehicle: a battered, blue camper van that had seen better days. Emily had gone over every reason why Scorer should have been in possession of a new My Sweet Friend doll and she could only come up with one feasible answer – it had been acquired for his daughter, Daisy, and that meant he knew she was alive.

All the worried phone calls had been a smoke screen. The most likely scenario was that he had kidnapped his own daughter in order to extract some money from an ex-partner he knew was considerably better off financially than he was. She thought of Scorer's ramshackle cottage, comparing it with the Hawkes' pristine and prosperous villa. Of course, there might have been another reason. Perhaps Scorer thought that Daisy wasn't being cared for, or perhaps he'd got wind of Jack Hawkes' indifference to the child. But, whatever his motive, he'd made a big mistake.

Emily was sitting in the car watching the arranged location of the drop, the park and ride near the bypass. She imagined the place had been chosen because it would be busy at that time with sightseers returning to their cars after a day out enjoying Eborby's medieval splendours . . . and the bypass provided an ideal getaway for a kidnapper in a hurry.

Joe had been following some leads on their murders but it didn't seem he'd made much progress. She wondered if he was right to pursue the Havenby Hall angle. Was he just pursuing some hunch about Peter Brockmeister that would ultimately lead nowhere? But if the identification of Peter Brockmeister's body all those years ago had been wrong, it changed everything.

But if Brockmeister had survived to resume his murderous activities, what had he been doing in the intervening years and where was he now? Covering every angle, she had asked one of the team to contact several police forces abroad – in places favoured by British ex-pats – just to see whether they had any similar killings on their books. There had been no response as yet . . . and at that moment Daisy's fate seemed more urgent.

She had been looking out for Joe's car and at last she saw it. He parked near the entrance and she watched as he got out and walked casually towards her. She pressed the button to unlock the passenger door and he climbed in beside her, arranging his legs, making himself comfortable.

'Anything new come in?' she asked.

'I managed to confirm that Scorer's partner, Una Waites, hasn't been in Somerset as Scorer claims. She's been using her credit card in Sainsbury's in Scarborough. Buying sweets, crisps and kiddies' yogurts amongst other things.'

Emily put her head in her hands. 'Shit. We should have checked before. I think that clinches it. Let's hope we can get this tied up tonight, eh.'

'Do you think Scorer and Waites have anything to do with Melanie Hawkes' murder?'

'Do you?'

'I'm keeping an open mind.'

'Here's Hawkes.'

They fell silent as Hawkes' huge black SUV swept by. He'd been instructed to leave the money in one of the litter bins right at the far end of the car park, a quiet spot where very few people had bothered to park because of the long walk to the park-and-ride bus.

Emily started her engine and drove slowly round the car park, stopping where she could get a better view. She saw Hawkes climb out of his car and look round before taking the holdall from the passenger seat and strolling over to the litter bin, hesitating before he dropped it inside. Then he returned to the car and waited a few moments before driving off.

The drop was done now. It was just a question of waiting.

And they didn't have to wait long before a battered white van drove towards the end of the car park at a stately pace and came to a halt near the litter bin.

Joe got on his radio right away with the registration number, only to find that it was false. This was it.

The van moved along a bit, parking right in front of the bin, blocking their view. Emily swore under her breath, took out her radio and gave the order.

'Target in place. Move in now. Repeat, move in now.'

Suddenly all hell broke lose as officers emerged from cars dotted around the car park. Emily burst from the car and ran towards the van, Joe following in her wake. She dodged round the back while Joe circled the front and soon she saw a dark, hooded figure bending over the bin, struggling to pull the holdall out.

'Hello, Paul,' she said.

But when the man swung round, she found she'd made a mistake. It wasn't Paul Scorer who stood there.

Then she heard Joe's voice. 'What the hell are you doing here?'

And Christopher Torridge dropped the bag.

Lydia had stayed at work till six thirty. Even when the Tourist Information Office closed there had been things to sort out, new leaflets to be placed in the racks and new information filed. Her boss had left early because her son was coming home from university and she wanted to cook him a meal after a term's diet of junk food. Her words had caused Lydia a stab of pain. Her own child was lying in a tiny grave. She would never come home from university and she would never cook for her . . . not in this life. As she'd placed some new river cruise leaflets in the rack she'd felt a tear run hot down her cheek. Then she'd wiped it away with the back of her hand. She had to get on with life. And Joe Plantagenet had given her a glimmer of new hope.

Joe had called earlier to say he was working that evening. She'd wondered whether his work would bring him to Boothgate House but she wasn't getting her hopes up. If she wanted their relationship to develop she told herself she'd have to accept that his job meant unpredictable hours and broken dates.

After work she met Amy for a drink at the Dean's Arms by the cathedral. She had a couple of glasses of white wine and listened to Amy moaning about her boss's attitude and

Steve's thoughtlessness and lack of domestic acumen. She nodded sympathetically and gave non-committal replies to her friend's direct questions about Joe. Their relationship seemed too new and fragile to analyse; it would seem like tearing apart a cobweb to examine its construction.

At nine thirty she walked home and when Boothgate House came into sight she experienced a feeling of cold apprehension. She'd never felt comfortable there and perhaps she should try to sell the flat on . . . if she could find a buyer who hadn't heard of the place's murderous connections.

As she reached the entrance to the building in the fading light she glanced to her left, towards the little graveyard where Karl Dremmer's body had been found. In the gloom she could see the headstones, blackened with years of grime. The promised removal of the graves had never happened and her initial enthusiasm for her spacious new flat had vanished over the months, only to be replaced by unease and nightmares. She could see the tattered remnants of the crime-scene tape shifting in the breeze above the resting place of those sad souls who had existed, suffered and died inside the glowering building.

There was no sign of a police presence in the entrance hall now although more crime-scene tape still drooped forlornly around the entrance to the basement. Her natural curiosity made her wonder what was down there, although she had no inclination to venture down herself.

When she'd last talked to Beverley the woman had twittered on about contacting somebody from the cathedral who dealt with exorcisms – that friend of Joe's she'd met in the café. If it had happened, no doubt she'd hear all about it in due course. Beverley always liked to talk, which was hardly surprising. Looking after her bedridden mother must be a lonely and stressful existence.

She quickened her steps as she passed Alan Proud's door. Since her break-in she'd experienced a feeling of trepidation each time she arrived home, even after the culprit had been caught, so when she opened her front door she stood in the hallway, listening for any telltale sounds of intrusion, anything that might tell her she wasn't alone in there.

There were muffled sounds all right, but she soon realized

they were coming from Proud's flat. Not the usual footsteps, cooking and TV but the sounds of somebody conducting some sort of search – opening drawers and cupboards and walking from room to room. She told herself that Proud was most likely looking for something he'd lost. It probably meant nothing. But she knew in her heart it sounded wrong. Somebody was in there searching the place.

And she didn't know what to do.

TWENTY-SIX

Christopher Torridge sat in the interview room, his head in his hands, a picture of despair and defeat. Joe began to feel a little sorry for him. Emily, in contrast, was giving the man a hard stare that would freeze the fires of hell. Nice cop, nasty cop. A classic combination.

'Where's Daisy?'

Torridge looked up. 'She's fine. She's having a good time.'

'Even with her mum dead?' Emily leaned forward, accusing.

Torridge held his hands up in a gesture of self-defence. 'She doesn't know. We didn't know how to tell her. And since it happened we thought it'd be best for her to stay with Paul and Una because she can't stand Jack. Una reckons he's not fit to look after a kid . . . especially with Melanie dead.'

Emily shifted in her seat. 'So let me get this straight . . . what's your connection to Una and Paul?'

'I'm Una's brother. When her and Paul thought this up they asked me to help. They knew Melanie had been helping me with this stuff about our aunty and Una said if I followed her into the park and distracted her with some questions, her and Paul could take Daisy off. They told Daisy it was a game . . . like hide and seek. They were worried about the kid – Melanie was working all hours and Jack . . .' He hesitated.

'What about him?'

Torridge looked away. 'He wasn't interested in Daisy. Treated her like she was a nuisance. Like I said, she doesn't like him. Paul reckoned that now he's settled with Una he can be a proper dad to her but Melanie wasn't having any of it.'

'So he snatched her?'

'He felt he had no choice.' He sounded defensive and slightly self-righteous.

'You knew they were asking for money?' said Joe.

'Paul reckoned Hawkes wouldn't miss ten grand. He could have asked for more but he didn't want to be greedy. He's had some financial problems recently and he thought it would be a way of solving them. And giving Daisy a decent life. As soon as they'd got the cash they were going to take her to Spain and call Melanie as soon as they got there to let her know Daisy was safe and that she could come over and see her whenever she wanted. Paul thinks it'll be good for the kid to grow up in the sunshine.'

'Where's Daisy now?'

'She's being well taken care of and as far as she's concerned she's just having a little holiday with her dad and her Aunty Una.' He suddenly looked serious. 'But it's been awkward since we heard about Melanie. Sometimes Daisy asks when she's going to see her mummy and we've had to keep fobbing her off. But she never asks about Jack. Una reckons she's scared of him so once Melanie died there was no way we were going to let her go back.' He looked at Emily. 'Look, Paul loves that kid and so does Una – she's great with kids and can't have any of her own. Well, what would you have done?'

'I'd have gone through the proper channels . . . and I wouldn't have worried her mother sick and tried to extort ten grand from her stepfather.' She sighed with exasperation. If there was any truth in Torridge's dark hints about Jack Hawkes, then, following Melanie's death, her biological father and his partner might well have had a chance of getting custody of the child. But as things stood, they'd messed up the situation big time.

'So all that talk about your aunt, Dorothy Watts, was just a way of getting to Melanie Hawkes?' Joe asked.

Torridge shook his head so vigorously that Joe was afraid he might be about to do himself an injury. 'You've talked to my mum so you should know I was telling the truth. She's desperate to find out what had happened to Dot before she . . . passes away. Una didn't want to see Melanie because of . . . because of her connection with Paul. It would have been embarrassing for her so we decided that I'd do it.'

'We'll ask Una about that . . . when we find her,' said Emily. 'Where is she, Chris? And where's Paul?'

'I can't tell you.'

'Can't or won't?'

Torridge pressed his lips together in a stubborn line. He wasn't going to betray his sister and her partner. And, in his opinion, Daisy was better off with them now her mother was dead. In some ways, Joe sympathized. But he kept telling himself that the trio had broken the law and he was a policeman, not a priest. It wasn't his job to give absolution and tell them to go away forgiven and not sin again.

Emily nudged him. They both knew they were unlikely to get any more out of Torridge that night and it was time for a break.

Emily switched off the tape machine and nodded to the constable on duty by the door, a signal for him to return their prisoner to the cells.

When they got back to the CID office it was still buzzing with activity in spite of the late hour. Joe saw that Jamilla was still engrossed in Dr Pennell's notebook. He walked over to her desk.

'Anything new?'

When she looked up he thought she looked like a woman who'd just witnessed something unpleasant, an accident, perhaps, or a disturbing scene on film.

'Have a look at this.' She handed him a sheet of paper as if she could hardly bear to be contaminated by its contents. 'I haven't finished transcribing it all yet but . . .'

Joe took it from her and as he absorbed the words he felt numb.

It was a list. Horribly methodical. Cold and clinical. Dorothy Watts' name was there with the comments: 'Ice bath. Three teeth extracted. Burns to abdomen. Cuts to right thigh resulting in profuse bleeding.' Then there was a series of clinical readings: blood pressure, temperature, heart rate.

Jamilla spoke softly. 'I think he tortured them. Experimented on them.' She swallowed. 'Some of the entries have the initials PB beside them. In fact, most of them do. Do you think it's Peter Brockmeister? Do you think he and Dr Pennell were in it together?'

Joe bowed his head. 'It's possible that they fed each other's violent fantasies – doctor and patient. Only I get the feeling

Brockmeister was in charge. Any luck with the relatives of the other people named?'

'I've traced a couple and it's the same pattern. Unexplained death. And the interesting thing is that the patients in question were all comparatively wealthy and their money went to their next of kin . . . but after that the money gradually disappeared. Most of the people I talked to were the younger generation but there was one person who put the phone down on me. Might be worth a look?' She pointed at the notebook. 'And there's this name – Jane Hawkes – any relation, do you think?'

'Possibly.' Joe smiled. 'You've done a good job, Jamilla. Why don't you get home? Can you do more digging on the Hawkes entry tomorrow?'

Jamilla stood up and shot him a grateful look. She'd had a harrowing day.

'I hear you've got the kidnappers,' she said. 'Is the kid all right?'

'She's fine. Turns out she was with her father. He'd hit on it as a way of getting some cash. They were planning to go to Spain.' Before he could say any more his mobile rang and the caller display told him it was George Merryweather. He answered the call, glad of the distraction.

'Are you at home?' It was clear that George had hoped he'd be free for a chat. But he had to disappoint him.

'I'm still at work. Is something the matter?'

'I visited Boothgate House today. I just wanted to tell you about it.'

'Go on. What happened?'

George hesitated. 'Beverley Newson asked me to go there because she sensed a hostile atmosphere in the building. And with the late Karl Dremmer's findings . . . Well, let's put it this way, I couldn't resist the challenge. There was definitely something in that basement, Joe. You know I have to be sceptical if I'm to keep my credibility but I sensed real evil down there. I can't be specific at this stage but . . . I said some prayers but I think it might take more than that.'

Joe could tell by George's voice that he'd experienced something disturbing in that basement. And with Jamilla's new findings, things were starting to add together. But he knew there were many who'd scoff, Emily included. But he always kept an open mind.

'Beverley's quite insistent that I spend the night there tonight. She's frightened, Joe.'

'I wouldn't advise it, George.'

'Well, I have a committee meeting tonight at the cathedral so it's quite impossible. I told Beverley and she began to cry. I assured her that . . .'

Joe was surprised at how relieved he felt. 'Good. Promise you won't be tempted to go there after the meeting?'

'I'm tempted by lots of things, Joe, but the prospect of being in that basement after dark isn't one of them. I'll call Beverley in the morning to see how she is.'

'Good idea,' he said, hoping George wasn't just saying it to stop him worrying. If George thought Beverley needed his help it would be just like him to abandon caution to come to her aid. But he'd said his bit – the rest was up to George.

He told him he'd be in touch and ended the call just as the phone on his desk began to ring. When he picked up the receiver he heard a male voice on the other end of the land line. A constable who'd been on patrol in his car had been flagged down by a young man in the Museum Gardens area. The lad had been incoherent, half drunk and in shock and it had taken a few minutes to find out what had happened.

He'd been in the Museum Gardens, messing around with his mates and drinking cider, and when he went off to relieve himself among the abbey ruins he saw a man a few yards away, lying half hidden next to a low stone wall.

When the man didn't move he went over to have a look and realized that he was dead.

The constable who went to investigate found credit cards in the corpse's wallet. All in the name of Alan Proud.

'This is all we bloody need,' Emily muttered to nobody in particular as she stood in the abbey ruins watching Sally Sharpe do her bit underneath the newly erected floodlights. 'How long has he been dead, Sal?' she called to the pathologist.

'No more than two hours,' Sally answered. 'It must have

been dusk when he was killed. The killer took a risk in a public place like this.'

'The ruined walls are high in places,' said Emily. 'And if nobody was around at the time . . . I presume that's the cause of death?' She pointed to the wound in Proud's abdomen. A patch of blood, half dried to a rusty brown, had spread over his pale shirt and there was a dribble of dried blood around his mouth. 'What kind of weapon would you say?'

Sally sat back on her heels. 'A sharp blade – something fairly thin. I'll be able to tell you more after the post-mortem.'

Joe was standing beside Emily and when he leaned towards her and whispered in her ear that he had to make a call, she gave him an enquiring look and told him not to be long. He could see the strain was beginning to tell on her face. She hadn't touched up her lipstick like she usually did and there was a stain on her white shirt, evidence of a Chinese takeaway eaten hastily at her desk at six.

Joe walked away, stopping once he was outside the taped off area. He speed dialled Lydia's number and waited, holding his breath. When he heard her voice he felt relieved.

'Alan Proud's dead. He's been murdered.' He hadn't time to dress the news up in tactful words.

After a short, shocked silence, she spoke. 'I saw him earlier in the Museum Gardens. He was hanging around as if he was waiting for someone. Then I heard someone in his flat about an hour ago. It sounded as though they were searching for something . . . opening drawers and . . . I wondered whether to call you but then everything went quiet so . . .'

'You should have told me.'

'I thought it was probably him . . . Proud. Besides, I didn't want to bother you.'

Joe stood for a few moments, watching all the activity around the corpse. Suddenly the needs of the living seemed more important to him than those of the dead so he told Lydia he'd be with her soon and ended the call. Then he retraced his steps and told Emily where he was going.

'His flat needs to be sealed off and searched,' she said. 'And we have to find out whether any of the neighbours saw anyone go in there . . . or noticed anybody hanging round the building.'

Joe began to hurry away, anxious to ensure Lydia's safety, but Emily called him back. 'We'll need to check all the CCTV footage from this area to see whether Proud makes an appearance . . . hopefully with his murderer in tow. Get Sunny to organize that before you go?'

Joe nodded. It was a delay but it wouldn't take long. He left Emily watching Sally conduct her initial examination and made his way down the drive to the main gate, now closed to keep the public out. He found Sunny near the abbey's undercroft, leaning against a patrol car with a cigarette in his mouth, talking to a burley middle-aged uniformed sergeant, chatting like two men in a pub putting the world to rights. As he saw Joe approach he hid the cigarette behind his back and made an attempt to look alert.

'What's the verdict?' he asked as soon as Joe was in earshot.

'Stabbing.'

'Mugging gone wrong?'

'The killer left his wallet.'

Sunny threw the cigarette to the ground and stamped it out before slinking off like a reluctant schoolboy to do his duty. Joe exchanged a half-hearted greeting with the sergeant before hurrying back to his car. He suddenly felt responsible for Lydia. He needed to make sure she was safe.

Alan Proud was dead and whoever had been in his flat might have been his murderer.

The noises had stopped a while ago so, presumably, the intruder had gone. Besides, she needed to know whether Beverley had seen or heard anything too.

She undid the latch on her front door and peeped out, relieved to find that everything looked quite normal. Just a carpeted corridor, wide, light and airy with a large window at one end and expensive-looking art deco wall lights. She normally left her door on the latch when she went across the corridor to see Beverley, but this time the thought of someone creeping into her flat while she was out made her step inside again to pick up her keys from the hall table and put them in the pocket of her jeans.

She shut the door behind her, checking that it was locked, and knocked on Beverley's door, all the time keeping an eye on Proud's flat.

When there was no answer she knocked again, wondering whether Beverley had nipped to the convenience store nearby as she sometimes did when she ran out of essentials. But she had a niggling feeling that something wasn't right so she gave Beverley's door a tentative push and, to her surprise it swung open slowly. She stared into the dimly lit hall with a sense of foreboding. What if Proud's intruder had turned his attentions to Beverley's flat? Could Beverley and her mother be there cowering at his mercy?

She clenched her fists and walked into the flat calling Beverley's name, and when there was no answer she made her way down the hallway pushing open each door in turn. She'd never actually been further than Beverley's living room before and most of their conversations had been held in the hall. But she knew the place was considerably larger than her own with at least three bedrooms and as she tiptoed from room to room she took in the old-fashioned decor which reminded her of her grandparents' house while she was growing up. Much of the furniture was large, dark and dated from the Victorian period, and there were fussy touches everywhere: ornaments and plants that gave the spacious rooms a cluttered feel.

She peeped into a bedroom that she assumed was Beverley's own. It was neat with a peach candlewick bedspread on the single bed and embroidered mats on the dressing table and, unlike Lydia's own room, there wasn't a thing out of place. She shut the door, suddenly guilty about prying uninvited into her neighbour's life.

When she reached the far door she knocked and when there was no answer, she pushed it open gently. If this was her mother's room, she didn't want to frighten the old lady.

Saying a soft hello, she stepped across the threshold and her eyes rested on the small shape in the bed. The old lady didn't move which probably meant she was asleep, but Lydia felt she should make sure she was all right.

She crept to the bed and looked down on the wizened face

and the two stick-thin arms with mottled parchment skin that lay motionless on the coverlet. She stood for a few moments and listened for the old woman's breathing, watching for the rise and fall of her bird-like chest beneath the covers. And it was only when she was certain she was dead that she rushed from the room, out of the flat and down the corridor towards the entrance.

But before she could reach the front door she felt somebody grab her and hold her there, pinning her arms so that she couldn't move.

She struggled, twisting herself to see her assailant's face.

The last person she'd expected to see was Patrick Creeny.

TWENTY-SEVEN

Joe sat beside Lydia on her sofa, his head bowed close to hers as though he was hearing her confession.

'Thank God you turned up when you did,' she said quietly, her voice still shaking a little with the shock. 'I don't know what would have happened if . . .'

'Creeny claims you ran into him. He said he was just trying to find out what was wrong.'

She shook her head. 'He was here all the time. He must have been.'

'He's the developer so that's not surprising.' He hesitated. 'Let's talk about Mrs Newson. You say you couldn't get an answer and the door was ajar so you went in to check she was OK?'

'That's right. Has anyone found Beverley yet?'

'We've got people out looking for her. Don't worry.'

'I can't help worrying,' she snapped at him as though his questions were starting to annoy her. 'Her mother's dead and she's gone off . . . disappeared.'

'She might be upset . . . in shock. She might be wandering around somewhere.'

'Why didn't she call someone?'

'People do strange things when they're in shock. If she'd found her mother like that . . .'

'Was it . . .' She paused as though she was gathering courage to ask the question. 'Did her mother die of natural causes or . . .? Only I was thinking if it was Proud's murderer who was searching his flat and he went across to Beverley's . . .'

This was something that had crossed Joe's mind – but he had no evidence yet so he didn't want to make Lydia panic. 'There's no reason to believe it wasn't natural causes. Our doctor's due here any minute so she'll probably be able to tell us for sure.'

'Do you think Proud's killer's got Beverley? Do you think she's in danger?'

Joe said nothing. It was a question he couldn't answer. He had a sudden vision of Beverley, floating in water with flowers bursting from her mouth. An overweight Ophelia festooned with grim garlands.

When he heard Sally Sharpe's voice outside in the corridor. He gave Lydia's hand a squeeze and went out to greet her.

Killing is easy. Once done, it is so simple to kill again. But the murder of Alan Proud, that swift thrust of metal into flesh, didn't satisfy like the others. It was always best when he took his time. When he took them to his private place where he could bind their wrists and ankles and watch them suffer before he slowly squeezed the life from their earthly bodies.

He enjoyed watching for that elusive point between life and death. He had always thought that killing was the ultimate thrill but it wasn't until Pennell had introduced him to the real pleasure of suffering that it had become an addiction. And that addiction had never left him.

Proud had been dangerous, as obsessives often are. Dangerous to him and dangerous to those close to him. He'd known too much. That's why he'd had to die.

Now that Proud was out of the way there were others he had to deal with. And he knew they'd never catch him. They hadn't a clue.

'I can't keep up with all this.' Emily stood in the centre of Alan Proud's living room with her arms folded like some Northern soap-opera harridan. 'You've been in here, Joe. Can you remember what was in those frames?'

'They were letters Peter Brockmeister wrote to a man called Darren Carter. He'd shared a cell with him in prison before he was transferred to Havenby Hall. Carter died in a prison brawl and one of the prison officers nicked the letters and sold them on the Internet to the highest bidder. They ended up with Proud.'

'And he could have been killed for them?'

Joe shrugged. 'Well they're not here now and they weren't on his body so . . . I managed to read a couple of them but they didn't contain anything earth shattering as far as I could see. Carter had written to Brockmeister to beg him to take the blame for the murder he was inside for so he could appeal his conviction. But in the letters he wrote back Brockmeister told him he wasn't going to accept responsibility. Brockmeister didn't deny he was guilty but he didn't admit it either. I think he was playing with Carter.'

'Could he have committed the murder the lad was inside for?'

'It didn't bear any of his hallmarks . . . and Brockmeister was a sadist so he probably enjoyed keeping his former cell-mate dangling.

Emily shook her head, frowning, lost for words for once. Her blonde curls flopped over her eyes. 'That notebook you found . . . you really think Brockmeister tortured people while he was a patient here?'

'It was him and Dr Pennell as far as I can tell.'

'Do you think it happened in that basement?'

Joe said nothing. He was thinking of what Dennis Younger had told him about the screams he'd heard and about what George had said about the place. At least it seemed that his friend had had the good sense to stay away tonight. He'd been worried that he'd be tempted to follow Karl Dremmer's example and put himself in danger. And that was something Joe didn't like to contemplate.

After a while he spoke, quietly. 'I think Brockmeister and Pennell were probably kindred spirits, although Pennell might not have realized it until they met.'

'Is Brockmeister still alive? Is he carrying out these killings?' Joe had never heard Emily sound so unsure of herself before.

'I don't know,' he said with honesty. 'But I'm wondering why Patrick Creeny turned up when he did. He's already admitted that he'd had Dremmer beaten up and intimidated in order to warn him off. It obviously didn't work so what if he decided to take things a step further?'

'Well he's not Brockmeister. He's the wrong age for a start.'

'Did Brockmeister have any relatives? Children?'

'There's no record of it. You think Creeny might be . . .?'

'I'm clutching at any possibility here, Emily. We don't even know if Brockmeister's alive or dead.'

'We know what he looked like forty years ago from old

photographs. Although I can't think of anyone we've met in the course of this investigation who bears even the slightest resemblance to him. Can you?'

Joe began to picture the men he'd questioned who'd be around the right age: Cecil Bentham; the Rev Rattenbury; and Dennis Younger, the former patient. None of them fitted the bill and, in Rattenbury's case, he had George Merryweather to vouch for his good character. 'No. Which makes me think that if he is around we haven't met him yet.'

Joe looked round the room and his eyes focused on the empty desk in the corner. 'Proud's laptop's missing.'

Emily rolled her eyes. 'Surprise, surprise. I'll get this place searched thoroughly and you'd better make sure what's-her-name's OK.'

'Her name's Lydia. I don't think she should stay here tonight.'

'She must have a friend who can put her up.'

'I'll see to it,' Joe said before leaving the room and making for Lydia's flat. He knocked on the door and she opened it cautiously. When he stepped inside and suggested she call Amy, she looked disappointed. She hesitated. 'Last time I stayed there I got the impression her boyfriend wasn't exactly delighted. I'd feel safer staying at yours.'

'No problem,' he said, hoping she couldn't sense his reluctance. After that first impulsive night, the misgivings had been crowding in and Kaitlin was increasingly haunting his thoughts and his heart. He couldn't help feeling that things were moving too fast, out of his control.

But the situation was urgent so he gave Lydia a lift to his flat and told her to make herself at home. He hadn't had a chance to clean the place that week so the bins were overflowing and the bathroom was verging on unsanitary but Lydia didn't seem to notice as she undressed and curled up in his bed. He had to go back to Boothgate House so he left her there, content that at least she was safe.

'You will find Beverley, won't you?' were her last anxious words before he left.

He didn't answer. He'd never liked making promises he couldn't keep.

* * *

When Joe had returned in the early hours Lydia had still been awake and he lay beside her, their bodies hardly touching. She'd whispered in the darkness that she thought she was cursed. Perhaps he shouldn't have anything to do with her. Even her beloved grandfather – that gentle, harmless doctor – had died violently in a hit-and-run accident. Perhaps she was unlucky for all who came into contact with her.

Joe had murmured words of comfort into her ear. It was nonsense, he said. None of what happened had been her fault. She was just going through a bad patch in her life; everyone had them at some time. But he knew his assurances hadn't convinced her. And a small, nagging inner voice told him that he wasn't altogether convinced himself.

She'd dropped off to sleep but had awoken a couple of hours later, shaking with tears coursing down her face. It was the nightmare again. The clock. At that moment Joe felt tempted to march to Cecil Bentham's shop and take an axe to the ugly thing. But he was a police officer, a responsible member of society, so vandalism wasn't an option.

The following morning she went to work because she reckoned it was better than sitting in Joe's empty flat brooding on recent events. Before she left at eight thirty Joe called the police station to ask whether there was any word of Beverley, careful not to mention that Lydia had spent the night at his flat – he'd never hear the end of it from Emily if she found out. But Beverley hadn't turned up. He'd broken the news to Lydia as gently as he could but she'd said nothing, almost as though she was resigned to the worst happening.

After all that time in the slightly unreal atmosphere of Boothgate House he needed a dose of normality so he decided to walk to the station through the city centre. The sky was pale grey as he reached Gallowgate with its pubs, cafés and charity shops. Most of the people he passed were heading for work, bored yet purposeful as though their surroundings were so familiar that they no longer saw the quaint, medieval city the tourists came to gawp at in their thousands.

Turning right at the National Trust café he walked through Vicars Green and on past the cathedral. The great church dwarfed the surrounding shops and houses and the sight of it lifted his spirits. He was tempted to go in and have a word with George but he knew it was too early for him to be at his post in his chaotic office near the chapter house. In George's line of business, he didn't keep the same antisocial hours as the police. Joe was still uneasy about his friend's involvement with Boothgate House but he was thankful that he'd heeded his advice and hadn't visited the basement after dark.

Joe walked underneath Boothgate Bar and emerged from the pedestrianized quiet on to a street of flowing traffic. As soon as he crossed at the pedestrian lights near the Museum Gardens, now festooned with police tape, it began to spot with half-hearted rain but the drizzle stopped as soon as he'd crossed the river at Wendover Bridge. The police station lay behind the railway station and when he arrived he climbed the stairs to the CID office, impatient for news.

Jamilla was already at her desk and when she spotted him she gave him a little wave, looking rather pleased with herself. 'There's a CCTV camera on the front of the museum and it shows Proud walking past carrying a briefcase. There was no briefcase with him when he was found, was there?'

'His killer must have taken it. But he left his wallet so he wasn't interested in money. And if it was him who searched Proud's flat he must have taken his keys too. Anyone suspicious on the tape?'

Jamilla shook her head, disappointed. 'The killer could have come into the gardens another way.' She searched on her desk for a piece of paper and when she found it she handed it to Joe. 'This is that information you asked for . . . Jane Hawkes.'

Joe thanked her and when he read it he raised his eyebrows. But it was something he'd have to deal with later.

'There's still no sign of Beverley Newson, by the way,' Jamilla said as he prepared to make for Emily's office.

Joe saw that she was frowning, as though she didn't reckon much to Beverley's chances. And, unfortunately, neither did he. But all patrols were on the lookout for her . . . for all the good it would do if the killer had her imprisoned somewhere out of sight . . . or if she was already dead. He knew Lydia was fond of Beverley so it seemed personal now. If Peter Brockmeister was alive and killing, he wanted to find him and put him away somewhere where he'd never be able to harm anybody again.

Emily had poked her head out of her office door. 'Joe. A word.'

He hurried into her office and sat down. 'How's Lydia this morning?' was the first question she asked.

The question took him aback. Somehow she knew that he hadn't dropped her off at a friend's house. She could read him so well. 'She's gone to work.'

'It might be best if she stayed with you for a couple of days. Is that a problem?' She looked at him, a smile playing on her lips.

'No problem.'

'That Boothgate House place is bad news. And I know your friend has been hunting ghosts down in that cellar . . .'

'Not hunting ghosts,' Joe said, realizing his tone was too sharp. But sometimes he got sick of people misunderstanding George's work. 'Karl Dremmer was the one hunting ghosts.'

She frowned. 'I still can't understand why Dremmer was murdered. He was an eccentric academic without an enemy in the world, as far as we can tell.'

'Creeny didn't like him. He had him beaten up – warned off.'

'True. But he denies having anything to do with his murder . . . unless the thug he got to beat him up got carried away and went back for more when he found the warning hadn't worked.'

'Anything's possible. Do we know who carried out the attack?'

'One of Creeny's labourers. He got paid fifty quid for his trouble and he swears he only gave Dremmer a light beating, just to make a point. He's been arrested and charged so we know where to find him if necessary. Was there anything dodgy in Dremmer's private life? Any other reason why someone might pick on him?'

'Nothing's come up.'

The thoughts that had been forming in Joe's head over the past few days had been nebulous until now. But now he was ready to voice them. 'Remember the mortar dust that was found on the floor, as if Dremmer or somebody had tried to scrape it away from between the bricks? I'm still wondering if Dremmer was trying to break through that wall.'

'Come on, Joe, you know we've already checked out that possibility. It would have been pointless because the basement doesn't extend any further.'

'According to Jack Hawkes' plans – we only have his word for it. I want that wall broken down.'

Emily's eyes widened. 'What if it's structural? What if the whole building collapses? Think of the damages? The Chief Constable would wet himself. And there's no sign of any other entrance so . . . Look, I'll order a thorough search if it makes you feel better.'

'It would.'

Emily suddenly looked serious. He could see lines around her eyes that seemed to have deepened over the past few days, as if the burden of the investigation was ageing her as he watched. 'Think we're too late to save Beverley Newson?' she asked, her voice hushed.

Joe didn't answer. It wasn't in his nature to be so pessimistic but he had a terrible feeling that Beverley would turn up dead like the others.

Emily's phone rang. After a short conversation she replaced the receiver and looked up, triumphant. This was good news.

'Paul Scorer and Una Waites have been picked up in Scarborough. Daisy's with them. Her and Una were staying in a caravan there . . . having a wonderful time apparently. They're being brought in.' She paused, suddenly serious. 'They've called Social Services to take care of Daisy.'

Joe was unsure whether the news was good after all. Scorer and Una clearly loved Daisy more than Jack Hawkes did, but sometimes the law didn't take the heart into account when someone's done something really stupid. He suddenly felt sad. 'I suppose we should let Jack Hawkes know.'

Emily picked up the phone again. 'I'll ring Janet Craig. She's still at Hawkes' place so she can pass on the good news.' The last two words sounded unconvincing and Joe knew her thoughts matched his.

'What do you think of Hawkes?' he asked.

Emily took a few seconds to answer. 'I can't say I like the man.' She gave him a quick, businesslike smile and moved on to other things. 'Beverley's mum's post-mortem is in half an hour but my money's on natural causes. She was elderly and it doesn't look as if her health was good.'

'Do we have to attend?' Joe asked, hoping the answer would be no.

Emily pulled a face. 'I suppose we should, seeing that there might be a link to Beverley's disappearance.

They left the police station like a pair of reluctant school-children and drove to the hospital mortuary where Sally greeted them, favouring Joe with a big smile. She sounded remarkably cheerful for a woman who was about to conduct an autopsy. He noticed the engagement ring on her finger, a large solitaire diamond.

Once everything had been prepared and Sally had donned her gloves and gown, he and Emily stood behind the glass screen and watched as she went about her work, quietly and efficiently as she always did. At one point she stopped and began to work more delicately, a frown of concentration on her face as if she'd found something that worried her.

'What is it, Sal?' Emily said into the microphone.

Sally stepped back and stared at the wizened old woman on the table. She didn't answer for a while but when she did, her voice was quiet, as though she was shocked by what she was about to say.

'I've found a tiny feather caught in the airways and there are signs of pressure on the face.' She looked up at the screen. 'I'm as sure as I can be that this woman was smothered.'

TWENTY-EIGHT

Joe's mobile phone rang just as they got back to the CID office. As his thoughts were on Sally's verdict and his desire to see what, if anything, was behind that basement wall, he answered it absent-mindedly. He was hoping for news of Beverley but when he saw the caller was George Merryweather, he experienced a sudden desire to speak to him, to ask his advice about Lydia. George never judged and Joe valued his wisdom. But he knew there was no time to talk.

'Joe, I don't know if this is important but—'

'Sorry, George. Can it wait? I've got to get straight down to Boothgate House.'

'I'll meet you there.' George rang off. He'd sounded anxious, which wasn't like him, and Joe wondered why.

Emily entered the office, her huge handbag slung over her shoulder. 'You ready?'

Joe followed her out. She'd just been upstairs to bring the Superintendent up to date with the latest development and she looked peeved at the delay. She'd already given orders that Beverley's mother's room should be sealed off as a crime scene but Joe suspected it was a futile gesture after all those policemen, paramedics and undertakers had trampled all over the place.

Emily drove in silence, a look of fierce determination on her face. The killer had evaded them for too long. He was playing games with them, abducting and killing under their noses. And they had to put a stop to him.

When they arrived Joe was surprised to see that George was waiting by the entrance, passing the time of day with the uniformed constable who'd been posted at the front door because Emily wasn't taking any more chances. He must have made the journey swiftly which meant that his information was so urgent that it had made him break his habit of doing everything at a measured thoughtful pace. He stepped forward as soon as he saw Joe get out of the car.

'George. What's wrong?'

George waited for Emily to join them as though this was something they should both hear.

'Have you found Beverley yet?'

Joe shook his head.

'I've remembered something that might be important. Beverley mentioned it in passing yesterday but it didn't really register until I'd heard she'd disappeared and I started thinking over everything she'd said. She told me that her mother had worked here when it was a hospital. She said she'd been a nurse and that she'd been in charge here.'

Joe looked at Emily and saw her mouth fall open. 'In charge,' she said. 'How do you mean?'

'That's all she said. She worked here and she was in charge. This is important, isn't it?'

'It could be very important, George. We've been looking for the former matron, a Mrs Chambers, but we've found no trace of her. If that was Beverley's mother . . .'

'Before you get carried away we need to be sure,' said Emily. She walked away and took out her phone. Joe knew she'd be asking someone in the CID office to check out Mrs Newson's official history – her birth and marriage certificate, census and tax records. It might take time but if, according to the authorities, Mrs Newson didn't officially exist, it would mean she'd changed her identity at some point. But, if that was the case, what were the implications for Beverley?'

'I'm going up to the Newsons' flat,' Joe said. 'There might be some photographs of the mother up there that I can show to some people who met Mrs Chambers. I can start with the Reverend Rattenbury.'

George nodded. 'Yes. I'd like to catch up with Kenneth. I believe he went to live down south somewhere. I didn't know he was back. Nice little chap.'

Joe was about to make for the door when he swung round. 'What did you just say?'

George looked puzzled. 'Just that Ken Rattenbury was a nice chap.'

'You said "nice little chap". The Kenneth Rattenbury I met wasn't little. He was fairly tall.'

George shook his head, as though he was exasperated with himself. 'I've come across so many clergymen over the years; I'm probably thinking of the wrong person.' He gave Joe a rueful smile. 'Old age. Comes to us all. I'd better get back to the cathedral.' He began to walk away but when he'd gone a few feet he turned back. 'If I can help in any way . . .'

'Thanks,' said Emily. 'We'll bear that in mind.'

Without another word she led the way into the building, briefly acknowledging the constable who was holding the door open for them to pass through. 'Let's take the Newsons' flat to bits. If Beverley's mum was really Mrs Chambers I want to know.'

Joe followed her, making a call to the CID office. There was something else he wanted checking out. Something that might confirm his worst suspicions. But he knew it was likely to take a bit of time.

When he reached the Newsons' flat Alan Proud's door was standing open and he could hear the voices of the detectives who'd been assigned to carry out the search. He followed Emily into the Newsons' flat and began to search through the sideboard and bureau in the living room while Emily examined the bedrooms. Fortunately everything seemed to be neatly filed, which was to be expected as mother and daughter had only recently moved in. As they were packing they'd probably have discarded all those old papers and souvenirs that everyone builds up over the course of their lives. But there was a chance that Mrs Chambers – if she was Mrs Chambers – might have kept things to remind her of the time when she had ruled in this place . . . of the time when she had probably colluded with Dr Pennell's basest actions.

Joe found a birth certificate for a Katharine Johnson and a certificate of her marriage to a John Newson – both fairly recent copies by the look of it – but no birth certificate for Beverley and nothing to link Mrs Newson with Mrs Chambers. When he entered the bedroom where the old woman had died he found that Emily had drawn a similar blank. Perhaps George had got it wrong. Or perhaps she had worked here before Mrs Chambers' time or exaggerated her position of authority to her daughter. There were any number of possibilities so maybe they were reading too much into Beverley's chance remark.

'I've had a look in all the usual places,' Emily said. 'And there's nothing taped behind mirrors or at the back of drawers. I think we've drawn a blank.'

Joe nodded. He too had looked in all the hidden places known mainly to the police or to professional burglars and found nothing. No suggestion that Mrs Newson wasn't who she'd claimed to be and no clue to Beverley's whereabouts.

He heard a knock on the open door. 'Sir, ma'am. We've come across something hidden under a loose floorboard in Proud's living room. He must have used it as his hidey-hole.'

Joe hurried out into the hall and Emily followed. The young DC from Proud's flat was standing there, holding an evidence bag containing a sheaf of papers triumphantly.

He handed the bag to Joe who took the contents out carefully, scanned them and passed them to Emily. They were more letters from Brockmeister, this time addressed to someone called Jason, and it wasn't surprising that Proud hadn't wanted to display them on his wall because they contained detailed descriptions of his crimes. They'd been posted from various places abroad and they were all dated after his supposed death.

A brief perusal gave Joe the gist of their contents. He knew he'd have to read them in detail sooner or later and the prospect made him feel a little sick. The detail was vivid but it was the way he wrote with such relish that Joe found hard to bear. As Emily handed them back to the DC a couple of photographs fell out of the bag. And when Joe picked them up he saw that they were grainy and blurred, as if they'd been taken with a mobile phone. But the person in them was clear enough to recognize.

'George wasn't mistaken,' he said quietly. 'We've got to get over to Hilton.'

They pounded on the Rev Kenneth Rattenbury's front door but there was no answer. Emily tried to peer through the thick lace curtains but, having been made for privacy, they fulfilled their purpose well.

'Round the back?'

Joe nodded. They'd taken the precaution of bringing a search team with them and they were now hanging around their cars, attracting the attention of the neighbours.

As Joe stepped back from the front door one of the neighbours emerged, full of curiosity. 'Is something the matter?'

Joe saw Emily's eyes light up at the prospect of gossip. She hurried over to the neighbour – a woman of battleaxe proportions with cropped grey hair and a floral frock.

'Do you know him well?' Emily asked.

The woman shook her head. 'He keeps himself to himself. Doesn't even say hello. I heard he used to be a vicar or something but I've never had much Christian charity from him, and that's the truth.'

'What can you tell us about him?'

'When he first moved in I took him a cup of tea round – trying to be neighbourly, like. I asked him where he were from but he were right cagey.'

'Have you seen any visitors coming to the house?'

She shook her head again. 'I don't reckon he's the type to be entertaining friends.' She raised her hand as though she'd just remembered something. 'I tell a lie. I did see a young man go into his house. He had tattoos on his arms like a lot of them do nowadays and very short fair hair. Mind you, this was late last year. I haven't seen anyone since.'

Joe caught Emily's eye. The tattooed young man could well have been Sebastian Bentham and he'd already admitted that he'd interviewed Rattenbury while he was researching his play. This wasn't helping.

'Mind you, a few days ago I could have sworn I heard a woman's voice. In the back yard it was but the walls are too high to see over.' She sounded disappointed.

'Did you hear what they were saying?'

'Afraid not.'

'What did this woman sound like . . . young or old? Local?'

She suddenly seemed unsure of herself. 'I couldn't hear very well. I just knew it was a woman.'

'Thanks,' said Joe, suspecting she'd done her best to listen in and been disappointed with her failure. 'If you think of anything else . . .'

'What's he done?' The woman folded her arms, hoping for a dramatic revelation.

But Joe had to disappoint her. 'We don't know yet. We just think he might be able to help us with our enquiries. Thanks for your time.'

He walked away and Emily followed, leaving the neighbour facing another disappointment.

'I want to take a look inside,' Emily whispered as they reached the front door.

Joe knew at once what she was thinking. 'We should check the doors and windows . . . just to make sure the place is secure.' He lowered his voice. 'We can get a warrant later if we need it.'

'Well, he might have Beverley in there so we'd be neglecting our duty if we didn't check, wouldn't we?' She nodded to him and he hurried round to the back alley, counting the back gates until he was sure he'd got the right one. The black-painted wooden gate was locked but Emily caught up with him and pointed at the brick wall. 'Go on then. Up you go.'

Joe knew he was out of practice but he managed to scale the wall without sacrificing too much dignity. He unbolted the gate to let Emily into the back yard which was neat but lacking flowers or any other personal touches. He tried the back door but it was locked. But the kitchen window was open half an inch. Just enough.

Joe had learned the fine art of burglary through observation over the years and his examples had been amongst the finest in the profession. He knew just how to edge the window open and lean in to open the lower window to gain access. He clambered into the kitchen easily, landing on the worktop near the sink and jumping down. He opened the back door for Emily, wondering whether they should summon the team waiting round the front. But Emily decided to wait until they found the evidence they needed. If they were wrong they might be making fools of themselves. They might even be in trouble.

The kitchen was clean and tidy, as though the occupant of

the house hardly cooked there, or was obsessively neat. The spacious back room was gloomy with barely any natural light coming in through the small sash window and Joe resisted an urge to switch the light on as he looked around. There was a small pine dining table with two chairs standing beside it and a big oak sideboard.

Joe began to search through the sideboard and, in the left-hand cupboard, behind the utility bills, the balls of string and the manuals for long-forgotten electrical appliances, he found a cardboard box.

When he took it out and placed it on the table to examine it, Emily stood behind him expectantly. He prised the lid off and when he saw photographs inside he began to sort through them, looking for familiar faces.

And one face was very familiar indeed. They'd seen it in newspaper reports and on police records. Peter Brockmeister smirked out at them from the faded coloured rectangles of glossy paper. Peter on his own. Peter in the grounds of a large building that Joe recognized as Boothgate House, then Havenby Hall. Then there was Peter with a woman. She was wearing a dark nurse's uniform and a frilly cap, and they were standing close to each other, almost touching.

But now he had Brockmeister's image in front of him he saw that he bore little resemblance to the Reverend Rattenbury he'd spoken to. The height and the eyes were similar but the nose was much smaller, as was the chin. He said as much to Emily and she stared at the photographs, asking if he was sure.

'He told me he'd been living abroad. He might have had cosmetic surgery . . . changed his appearance,' Joe said.

'Wanted to start a new life with a new face and a new identity,' said Emily. 'It's possible. And if he'd been in on some scam killing off unwanted relatives with Dr Pennell, he'd probably be able to afford it and all.'

Joe pointed to the picture. 'You can change a lot but you can't change the ears. I noticed that Rattenbury had unusually small ear lobes and Brockmeister's are identical.'

'OK, Joe, I can accept that the man who lives here is Peter Brockmeister. But what happened to the real Rattenbury?'

'That's what we need to find out. And look at the woman with him in this picture. Does she look familiar to you?'

Emily stared at the picture and after a few seconds she nodded slowly. 'Well, I've only seen her dead but it could be a much younger Mrs Newson.' She turned the photograph over. There was writing on the other side and Joe cursed himself that he hadn't thought to look there himself. 'Me with Christabel. Wasn't that Mrs Chambers' name?'

Joe stood there, considering the implications. 'But if Mrs Newson is really Mrs Chambers, where does Beverley come into all this?' he asked after a long silence.

'Is she Mrs Chambers' daughter? Or could she be the child of one of the inmates and Chambers adopted her? There was no birth certificate back at the flat. And the certificates we had for the old woman were all in the name of Newson.'

'But they were recent copies. It's simple to get a new identity,' said Joe. 'What's the betting that if we look hard enough we'll find that John Newson's widow, Katharine, died some time ago. Or . . .' A possibility had just occurred to him. 'We have to find out if Katharine Newson was a patient at Havenby Hall.'

He took out his mobile and put in a call to Jamilla. She was still working on Pennell's records and she sounded a little relieved at the distraction. He asked her if the name Katharine Newson appeared on Pennell's list of patients and the answer was yes. It was in a section Jamilla had just deciphered and there was a note beside Katharine's name to say that she'd given birth to a baby girl while she was in Havenby Hall and she was suffering from post-partum psychosis. But there was no record of what had become of the baby. The last entry concerning Katharine Newson merely stated the cold fact that she had died from a cerebral haemorrhage six week after the baby's birth.

When he passed the information on to Emily she shook her head sadly. 'I don't suppose it was so well understood in those days. I had a spot of post-natal depression when I had our Matthew so . . . There but for the grace of God . . .' she said quietly.

Joe looked at her. This was something he'd never heard

before and he felt touched that she'd confide something so personal to him. 'Katharine must have been pregnant while she was in there,' he said. 'And if so, she could be Beverley's real mother. Maybe they killed Katharine Newson but they couldn't bring themselves to kill her baby.'

'And Chambers took Katharine's identity when she needed to disappear? How many did they kill there, Joe?'

Joe didn't reply. He didn't know the answer. But he was beginning to fear that when the truth came out it would reveal horrors beyond their imaginings. Horrors hidden over the years.

'Let's have a look upstairs. I want all patrols to be on the lookout for Rattenbury. When we find him, I think we'll find Beverley . . . if it's not too late already.'

TWENTY-NINE

The shop door opened and Sebastian Bentham looked up. He'd just begun to sketch out his next play and he resented the intrusion a customer would bring. But business was business and he'd promised his uncle that he'd keep things ticking over until he could take over the reins again.

He pushed his notepad to one side and stood up, preparing to fix a smile of greeting to his face. Shopkeeping, he kept telling himself, was almost a branch of show business. Give the punters what they wanted and make them leave satisfied and smiling.

'Hello,' he said, recognizing the newcomer. 'Looking for anything in particular? Thanks for helping me out, by the way. Did you get to see the play?'

The man he knew as the Reverend Rattenbury didn't reply. He was scanning the shop and his eyes rested on the clock. 'I'm interested in your clock. How much is it?'

'I think my uncle wants five hundred for it. But I'm sure that's open to negotiation,' he added, eager to make a sale. And keen to get the thing out of the shop.

'Have you had a look inside it?'

Seb nodded. 'A detective came to look at it because he found out it came from a house connected with a murder they're investigating. He found some kind of notebook inside and took it away. There's nothing in there now.'

The clergyman said nothing and stared at the clock. Then he turned to Sebastian. 'Thank you but I think I've changed my mind now I've seen it close up.'

'I've heard it originally came from Havenby Hall. Did you recognize it or . . .?'

'Yes. I recognized it,' the man said. 'How is your uncle?'

'On the mend,' Sebastian answered.

'Give him my regards.'

'I didn't know you knew him.'

But before Rattenbury could say anything more the shop door opened.

There was no doubt now that Peter Brockmeister hadn't died in the sea all those years ago. He had changed his identity and now he'd returned to Eborby to continue what he'd started.

Emily had received a call from Sunny to say that the police in Cape Town, South Africa had dealt with a number of similar deaths around fifteen years ago but they had stopped suddenly. There had been several cases in Germany after that and the police in the Burgundy region of France had a few unsolved murders that bore a strong resemblance, the last of which had been a couple of years ago. Perhaps Brockmeister, under assumed identities, had moved from country to country, killing as he went. But for the past two years there had been nothing . . . until now.

The most chilling thing of all, in Joe's opinion, was a photograph of Beverley, obviously taken without her knowledge, standing propped up in pride of place next to the others on the dressing table. If he wanted confirmation that she was the next victim, they had it now.

He made a call to Lydia, just to make sure she was all right. The last thing he wanted was for her to become Brockmeister's prey as well.

The shop was busier than it had been for days, Seb thought, as Lydia walked in and shut the door behind her. She was in her working clothes with a large bag slung over her shoulder.

'I'm on my lunch hour,' she said. 'I thought I'd have a look at those prints you mentioned. I see you haven't got rid of that thing yet.' She nodded towards the clock.

'This gentleman's been asking about it. He used to be chaplain at Havenby Hall where it came from. He helped me with the research for my play.'

Lydia gave Rattenbury a shy smile. 'My grandfather worked there as a locum for a few weeks, covering when Dr Pennell was in hospital. Maybe you remember him. Dr Reginald Speed.'

'I'm sorry. I don't recall the name.'

Lydia's phone began to ring.

Rattenbury left the shop without another word.

'I can't get through to Lydia,' Joe said. 'Her phone's engaged.'

'So?' Emily sounded uninterested, as though she thought he was fussing about nothing.

Joe shrugged. Emily was probably right. It was her lunch hour so perhaps she was talking to one of her friends. But he still felt he needed to warn her. Without knowing who the enemy was, she was vulnerable.

All patrols were on the lookout for Rattenbury. His description and the grainy photograph found in Proud's flat had been circulated widely. In all likelihood he had killed Melanie Hawkes, Judith Dodds, Karl Dremmer and Alan Proud. And if they found Beverley dead, that would make five – exceeding his previous score.

He tried to call Lydia again but all he got was her voice mail. He left a message telling her that if anybody answering Rattenbury's description tried to make contact she should call him at once. He left Rattenbury's house to the search team and climbed into the car beside Emily. There were things to arrange back at the police station . . . a manhunt to coordinate.

But he'd keep trying Lydia's number.

When Lydia's phone rang she found herself hoping it was Joe. But when she answered it she heard a female voice, speaking softly, almost in a whisper; it took her a few moments to realize who it was.

'Beverley. Where are you? They've been looking for you.'

Beverley didn't answer the question. She carried on as though she hadn't much time – as though she was dreading the return of someone or something. She had a message to convey and she hadn't time for small talk.

'Meet me at Boothgate House. Go past the graveyard to the back of the building – the part they haven't started work on yet. I'll meet you there. I'll explain everything when I see you.'

'Shall I call the police?'

'No. Don't call them whatever you do. I've got myself into a bit of a scrape and I really don't want to involve them. I've got to go.'

'Look, I'm afraid your mother . . .' But before she could continue, the line went dead and she was left standing there, wondering what to do. In spite of what Beverley said, all her instincts told her to call Joe. She saw he'd been trying to get hold of her so she tried his number but it was engaged so she left a message on his voicemail, saying she was going to Boothgate House to meet Beverley. She'd be in touch later.

She walked to Boothgate House through the busy streets, hoping Beverley wouldn't keep her long. She had to be back at work in half an hour.

When she reached her destination the silence made her uneasy; she'd almost preferred it when the building had been buzzing with builders and policemen. She realized she'd never ventured round the back beyond the graveyard. The side wall of the yet-to-be-developed wing was sadly neglected and weeds trespassed right up to the brickwork. Her sandals were hardly suitable for tramping through the undergrowth but Beverley's instructions had been quite clear. She tried Joe's number again but when she couldn't get a signal she carried on.

The clinging weeds slowed her pace as she walked round to the back of the building. There was no sign of Beverley so she called her name, quietly at first, then louder. But there was no reply. She took out her phone. Still no signal and she was reluctant to go any further without at least telling Joe where she was.

The weeds and overgrown grass tickled her legs as she started to retrace her steps to the front of the building, the phone held in front of her. The grimy gravestones stuck out of the undergrowth to her right. All those sad souls sleeping beneath the earth, the ordeal of their final years over. There had been times in her life, times of pain and loss, when she would almost have envied them . . . but recently everything had changed.

The tiny bars on the phone screen that would tell her she had a signal still hadn't appeared so she walked on. Until she heard a noise somewhere behind her, a footstep muffled by grass. Then, before she could turn round, everything went black.

And the last thing she felt was the cold damp vegetation on her bare flesh as she fell to her knees and oblivion came.

THIRTY

'Beverley's called. I'm meeting her back at Boothgate House. Just thought you'd like to know she's OK.' The message was terse, as most voicemail messages are, but Joe felt a wave of relief as he listened to it. He tried Lydia's number but he couldn't get through, which meant that either she was somewhere with no signal or she'd switched the thing off.

When he told Emily about this new development she ordered him to get round there and see what Beverley had to say for herself – and to break the news about her mother's death . . . if she didn't already know. There was always the possibility that Beverley had ended the old woman's life herself as an act of mercy or frustration. Perhaps that was why she'd fled.

Emily also wanted to know about any dealings Beverley may have had with Brockmeister. But Joe pointed out that she might not even have known Brockmeister had her in his sights. The only important thing now was that Beverley was safe.

His phone rang and when he answered it he heard Jamilla's voice on the other end of the line. The man calling himself the Reverend Rattenbury had been spotted near Cecil Bentham's house.

Emily took the phone off him and, after a quick conversation, she announced she was going back to the station to supervise the hunt for Brockmeister, leaving Joe to look after things at Boothgate House.

Joe drove there, exceeding the speed limit as he hurtled down the old, straight Roman road into the city. He parked in front of the building and slammed the car door loudly before dashing to the entrance and pressing the key beside Lydia's name. When there was no answer he tried Beverley's but again he heard no disembodied voice coming from the grille beside the row of metal buttons.

There was no police presence at the building now; just some remnants of tattered blue-and-white tape around the graveyard signalled the fact that there had been a crime here. But Joe felt that the place should have been swathed in the stuff. This was the epicentre. Everything stemmed from the days when Boothgate House was home to the disturbed and vulnerable and, in Peter Brockmeister's case, the evil.

He tried all the other occupied flats but there was no answer. There was no sign of Creeny's builders either so Joe began to dial his number. At least Creeny would have a master key.

Creeny sounded remarkably cooperative and promised to be there in fifteen minutes. Joe just hoped that was soon enough. Standing at the entrance to the silent building, he had a bad feeling. Something was very wrong.

Lydia's head was pounding and when she tried to put her hand up to see what was causing the pain, she found she couldn't move. Something was restraining her arms and it took her befuddled brain several moments to realize that there were straps around her wrists and her ankles. Everything hurt: her brain, her limbs, her stomach. And a brilliant light filtered through her closed eyelids.

Through half-opened eyes she could see that the light was huge and round like the sun. It was focused on her face, blinding her to her surroundings, and she guessed that it was the kind she'd seen before in operating theatres. She was lying on some sort of couch and when she shifted the leather creaked under her weight. And she sensed that she was naked and that she wasn't alone.

'What do you want? Who are you? Where's Beverley?' The words came out slurred and incoherent, probably the effect of whatever had been done to her. She feared that whatever was happening to her had already happened to her neighbour. Beverley might have been forced to make that call to lure her there. Wherever *there* was. And if that was the case, Beverley might already be dead.

Somebody was moving beyond the light. Why didn't they speak? What were they waiting for?

* * *

Sunny and a couple of uniformed officers broke down Cecil Bentham's door and, once inside the house, they discovered him cowering in a corner of his small kitchen like a terrified animal, huddled in fear, his emaciated limbs drawn up to his chest. When they tried to help him up he babbled incoherently, his eyes staring in terror as if they had witnessed the horrors of hell. Sunny was lost for words for once but, after summoning an ambulance, he raised the old man up gently and sat him in a chair.

Bentham grasped his arm so tightly that he winced, surprised at the strength in the bird-like limbs. 'Don't let him in,' he hissed in Sunny's ear. He's outside but don't let him in. He said he's coming for me . . .'

Sunny frowned. 'When did he tell you that?'

His eyes suddenly widened and met Sunny's. 'I need to confess. I don't want him to have power over me any more.'

'Who are you talking about?' Sunny asked, suspecting what the answer would be.

'Peter Brockmeister. Mrs Chambers made the arrangements but he was in charge. He was the one who did it.'

'Did what?' Sunny asked.

'Killed my wife of course,' the old man replied before bowing his head in exhaustion.

Whoever it was had moved again, shifted a little, all the time watching. And waiting.

'Who are you? Where's Beverley?'

There was a sound that sounded like a sigh. Then a shadowy figure stepped forward.

THIRTY-ONE

Patrick Creeny emerged from his BMW, casually, as if he had all the time in the world. 'You realize you've dragged me out of a meeting,' he said. He sounded annoyed as he shut the car door slowly, making a point. 'This had better be important.'

Joe suddenly felt unsure of himself. He might be panicking for nothing. Lydia and Beverley might have walked into Eborby for a coffee. Beverley might have been upset about her mother and decided to go off on her own for a couple of days. People do.

'I want to check that someone's OK,' he said with confidence. 'I've got reason to believe they could be in danger.'

Creeny didn't look impressed but he took his key from his pocket, opened the front door and stood in the hallway while Joe rushed down the corridor and pounded on Lydia's door before trying Beverley's.

He shouted over to Creeny. 'Do you have pass keys to all the flats?'

Creeny followed him slowly, like an old man panting with the effort. He took out a bunch of keys, sorted through them and handed one to Joe who felt his hand tingling with nerves as he opened Lydia's door, dreading what he'd find inside. But there was no sign of Lydia . . . and no sign of Beverley either when he entered the Newsons' flat which looked as though nothing had changed there since the night of Katharine Newson's death. Or had she really been Christabel Chambers? Maybe they would never know for sure.

He felt rather sheepish as he returned the keys to Creeny who wore an expression of martyred patience.

'I'm going to have a look down in the basement,' he said, hurrying towards the door.

'Be my guest,' Creeny mumbled, following behind.

Joe opened the door to the basement and took out the

small torch he usually kept in his pocket, shining it around. The room looked the same as when he'd last seen it, right down to Karl Dremmer's sleeping bag and equipment. He walked over to the far wall and shone the beam at the place where the mortar had been scraped away. Again, nothing had changed since his last visit. He felt disappointed. And frustrated. There was nothing here. He took out his phone but there was no signal. So much for the wonders of technology.

'Seen enough?'

Joe turned and saw Creeny watching him from the top of the steps. 'If we could have a quick search through the rest of the building . . .'

Creeny gave a mock salute, resigned to the delay to his schedule. 'No problem.'

They walked round the building; round the empty flats and then through the veil of plastic sheeting into the unmodernized wing with its dark green walls and its institutional corridors. The old asylum hadn't been a huge establishment so the search didn't take long. Joe asked about the old staff quarters – the flats where Mrs Chambers and Dr Pennell had lived. The reply surprised him – the matron's flat was now Beverley's and the Medical Superintendent's was Alan Proud's. Lydia's had been occupied by another, more junior, member of staff.

'Is that all?' Joe asked as their tour ended. 'Is there anywhere else we haven't looked?'

Creeny shook his head and looked at his watch.

'What about round the back?'

'We've just checked that wing . . . there's nothing there. Remember?' He sounded exasperated but Joe wasn't going to be put off.

'Can I see the plans?'

'They're back at the office. Besides, there's nothing on them you haven't seen.'

Joe suddenly wanted to see those plans, to check for himself that he'd seen everything. He wasn't sure he trusted Creeny. But, on the other hand, why should he be lying? 'Can you get them for me?'

'I suppose so.'

Joe could tell he was annoyed, as if this request was a step too far.

'Leave the keys with me,' said Joe.

Reluctantly Creeny slouched out of the building and when he'd gone Joe decided to have one more look down in the basement. Dremmer had sensed something there, as had George Merryweather, and Joe wondered whether, once he was alone, he'd be able to sense it too. An atmosphere. A presence. He realized he could be wasting precious time but something made him open the basement door and venture down there again, torch in hand.

He reached the foot of the steps and shone the beam around, standing quite still and holding his breath. He could feel something in there, something unpleasant, a cold, clammy feeling of dread. But he told himself it was probably his imagination. There was no sound in that place. Just a thick, impenetrable silence. He could sense the suffering that had gone on in that room like a physical ache in his heart. What terrible things had those patients endured at Dr Pennell's hands – if it had been Dr Pennell? Maybe Brockmeister had supervised proceedings himself. Maybe he had had them all in his power. Maybe he still did.

He was about to climb the steps again when he heard something. A muffled, high pitched sound like a scream of pain. Then a female voice. He couldn't make out what it said but he heard the desperation, like a plea for mercy. Then another cry, distant and muffled as if it came from somewhere behind thick walls. He used his torch beam to make another search but the place was empty. Hawkes had assured them that the basement didn't extend beneath the whole building. But what if he'd been wrong . . . or lying?

He ran back up the steps and made for the front entrance. He stood there for a while, wondering whether to begin his own search or to wait for Creeny's return. He decided to wait. With the correct knowledge, it might be quicker in the long run.

It seemed a long time before he saw Creeny's BMW sweep into the drive, its tyres crunching on the gravel. He rushed over and opened the driver's door, hand outstretched. 'Have you got the plans? I think the basement extends further and I think there's someone down there. I need to find out if there's another entrance.'

Creeny said nothing as he got out of the car and spread the plans out on the bonnet. Joe looked over his shoulder as he studied them and shook his head.

'The only place we haven't covered is the roof space,' Creeny said.

'It's definitely not the roof. It's the basement.'

Again Creeny shook his head. 'According to these plans, that's the full extent of the cellar area.'

This was getting them nowhere. He left Creeny standing there and began to run round the side of the building, his eyes focused on the base of the wall. He was aware of the sad little graveyard to his left as he carried on, increasingly desperate. There was nothing that resembled an entrance inside the building so this was his last desperate attempt to find a way in. But as he searched he began to wonder whether the sound he'd heard had been in his head. The atmosphere in that basement had been likely to conjure all sorts of strange imaginings.

But in spite of these growing doubts he carried on. Just one more check. He had to be certain.

'Bloody hell.' Joe swung round and saw that Creeny was a few feet behind him. He looked a little embarrassed, like a man who'd tripped up on a pavement, and was brushing down his beige trousers.

'What's the matter?' Joe asked, more out of politeness than anything else.

Creeny didn't answer for a few moments. Instead he studied the ground, tapping his foot. Just a drain cover, that's all.'

Joe retraced his steps and stood beside him. At his feet was a rectangle of rusty metal which looked like a drain cover. But there was a ring let into its centre. When he squatted down and grabbed the ring the cover came up smoothly and he heard Creeny gasp.

When he saw the lights and the stone steps he knew he'd found what he was looking for. He turned to Creeny. 'Did you know about this?'

'No. I bloody didn't.' He sounded indignant that Joe should think otherwise.

'But Hawkes is the architect. He would have done.'

'He never mentioned it and it's not on the plans,' said Creeny as though he was trying to defend his colleague. But Joe knew that Hawkes must have examined every inch of the place. Unless he was lazy or incompetent he must have known.

'Stay there,' Joe ordered, staring down at the steps. This was a cellar. And the lights told him it was in use. He hesitated and took out his phone. He couldn't get a signal at first so he rushed to the front of the building and made a call to Emily. He needed backup. And he needed someone to make sure Daisy was all right. She had been returned to Hawkes when Paul Scorer and his partner, Una, were arrested. And now Joe had an ominous feeling that the child might be in danger.

He gave Emily the bare facts then dashed back to the cellar entrance where Creeny was standing, shifting from foot to foot, unsure what to do.

'I'm going down to have a look.' Joe didn't wait for a reply. He walked down the stairs slowly and found himself in a corridor lit by a row of dusty metal lights that hung from the ceiling. He held his breath, listening for any sound that would tell him who or what was down there. Then he heard a faint moan, like an animal close to death, and carried on towards the source of the noise.

'Is someone down here? What's going on?' Creeny asked. Joe had forgotten that he was following behind. He knew he shouldn't allow him to be there but he was comforted by the presence of another human being.

'Stay back and keep quiet,' he hissed as they came to a wooden door. It was closed but Joe put his hand on the rusty handle and pushed. He could smell cigarette smoke from somewhere. Somehow he hadn't imagined the killer as a smoker.

When the door opened the first thing he saw was Lydia. She was lying on an operating table underneath a brilliant surgical light that left everything else in the room in gloomy shadows. Her arms and ankles were restrained by leather straps and her eyes were closed. She shifted her head a little which told Joe she was alive. Instinctively he rushed over to her and tried to unbuckle the restraints with clumsy fingers. Then he heard a shocked cry of pain behind him and when he twisted round he saw that Patrick Creeny had collapsed to the floor, a small circle of blood spreading out on his white shirt, just above his heart.

A figure was standing over Creeny's prone body. And the thing in its hand looked like a scalpel, sharpened and lethal.

'Put it down,' he said softly. 'You're under arrest.'

The killer looked him in the eye and laughed.

THIRTY-TWO

Beverley stood over Creeny's body like some triumphant tribal queen, and her large form, clad in a loose, blood-spattered white dress, seemed to dwarf everything else in that room. She still held the bloodstained weapon and Joe knew that if he approached her she would use it again. And he knew that if he made a wrong move she would kill Lydia too.

'Let me help Patrick,' he said reasonably. 'Please.'

Beverley shook her head.

'There's backup coming. They know where I am.'

'Liar,' she hissed, rearing up in front of him, suddenly monstrous with her pitiless eyes and mouth set in a grimace of hatred.

'Why are you doing this? What harm had Melanie Hawkes and Judith Dodds ever done you?'

She lowered the weapon and Joe could see that his first impression had been correct: it was a scalpel, horribly clinical, and probably the instrument that had cut deep into Melanie Hawkes' and Judith Dodds' flesh.

'They were poking their noses into things that didn't concern them.'

'What do you mean?'

He saw her hesitate.

'If you're going to kill me what's the harm in telling me?'

The smile she gave was smug and knowing. 'The Hawkes woman was going round asking questions and I couldn't allow her to put my parents in danger. I had to protect them. They're elderly.'

'Your parents?'

'My mother was matron here . . . and my father was famous once.'

'Peter Brockmeister is your father?'

'He recently came back to us from abroad because he

wanted to spend his final years near his family. We'd been down in the Midlands but Mother had wanted to move back up here . . . to her roots. I knew all about Father of course because Mother had an interesting line in bedtime stories. She told me what he'd done . . . and what they did together here. I had to protect their secret.'

'Your father stole the chaplain's identity?'

'Mother saw him in Eborby one day and when Father came back we thought it would be rather fun if he took over his blameless life. Rattenbury had just come back to Eborby from somewhere in Wales and I found out his wife had died and he had no family. It was perfect . . . as though it was meant. Father moved everything out of his rented flat and bought a nice little house with Rattenbury's life savings so it worked out very well.'

'Did you kill him?'

'It was my first time. Mother was so proud of me.' Her eyes glowed with the memory.

'Where is the Reverend Rattenbury now?'

'In the graveyard here. Where else would he be?'

'You do know your mother's dead?'

The smile disappeared and was replaced by a look of anguish. 'Father said she was suffering and it was the kindest thing. He said it would just be the two of us and we had to depend on each other. He told me to do it so I took the pillow and . . . I gave her an easy death,' she added softly.

'Where is your father now?'

She frowned. 'He's on his way here. He likes watching them die. Dr Pennell was conducting research into pain thresholds and he used the patients who were . . .' She hesitated. 'Who were on the death list. They were going to die anyway so why not make some use of them, he said.' She seemed to shrink before Joe's eyes and she suddenly looked frightened, as though the memory of Dr Pennell disturbed her.

'Tell me about Dr Pennell,' he said.

She pouted like a petulant child. 'I think even Mother was a little afraid of him. But Father wasn't. Father wasn't scared of anyone. People were scared of him,' she added proudly.

He glanced at Lydia. She was lying quite still now and he

fought the temptation to rush over and undo her bonds. He could see the patch of blood on Creeny's shirt was widening a little which gave him the hope that he was still alive. But it was impossible to help him while Beverley was standing there between them, alert and murderous. He knew Emily was on her way and he prayed that she wouldn't waste time.

His best hope was to keep Beverley talking.

'Did you kill Karl Dremmer?'

'He was scraping away at the wall. He must have known there was something here and I couldn't allow him to find this room, could I? I came to the basement door and beckoned him upstairs. I knew I couldn't speak because he had recording equipment down there.' She grinned at her own cleverness. 'Once he was in the hall I told him I'd seen something outside in the graveyard. He was such a gullible man.'

Joe knew that this was the last epitaph the academic would have wanted. But he said nothing. 'Did you intend to kill George Merryweather? He knew Rattenbury so there was a chance he might have given the game away.'

'I tried to get him to stay the night like Dr Dremmer but he wouldn't.' She looked disappointed. 'If he'd cooperated . . .'

Her words made Joe shudder. 'Does Jack Hawkes have anything to do with all this? He didn't put this part of the basement on the plans and, as an experienced architect, I can't see how he could have missed it.'

Beverley's expression became secretive. She knew something all right.

'His father worked on your father's case. He must have known him.'

'Maybe he did.'

'A woman called Jane Hawkes died here – she was on Dr Pennell's death list. We've discovered that she was Jack's mother and when she died his father married again soon after. Did Jack's father, Sergeant Hawkes, pay Dr Pennell to dispose of his first wife?'

'My parents and Dr Pennell got rid of a lot of unwanted relatives.' She gave a little giggle.

'Is that what you meant by the death list?' She nodded. 'What was in it for them?'

'A cut of the profits. They used to ask for ten per cent . . . then when the deed was done they'd up it to ninety per cent – nobody argued.'

Joe suddenly recalled how the heirs of those who'd died unexpectedly in Havenby Hall had become inexplicably poor.

'They told them it was a contribution to the work of Havenby Hall.'

'And if the heirs said anything they would have been incriminating themselves. Clever.'

Another small giggle. Suddenly she looked like an overgrown and unpredictable schoolgirl with her smooth, puffy flesh and long hair hanging lank around her shoulders.

'Did your father have some sort of hold over Jack Hawkes' father?'

No answer.

'Did Hawkes' father find out what was going on and write it down? Did Jack Hawkes find out and pay you to kill his wife too? Like father like son? How did he get in touch with you . . . or did you get in touch with him?'

'You'll never prove anything.'

'You'll be amazed what we can do, Miss Newson.'

She straightened her back. 'I'm taking my father's name from now on.' She straightened her back. 'Beverley Brockmeister.'

She took a step towards Joe, the scalpel pointing straight at his heart. He could hear the blood pumping in his head. If the backup didn't arrive soon, he was in trouble. And so were Lydia and Creeny . . . if they were still alive.

'Why did you kill Judith Dodds? She was Dr Pennell's daughter.'

'Her mother had brought her up to disapprove of everything Pennell stood for. When Mother realized that when he died she must have inherited his records, she knew it was a time bomb. Pennell was a meticulous man, a scientist, so he wrote everything down, you see. Mother said we needed to find his notebook. When we . . . when we questioned the daughter before she died she admitted that she'd sold his clock and Father remembered that he sometimes hid things in there.'

'You tortured her to find out what she knew?'

'Why not?'

'And you killed her and Melanie Hawkes in the same way your father killed his victims.'

'Nobody knew Father was alive so it served to muddy the waters. Besides, I enjoy killing. It's almost an art form, isn't it? Certainly more of an art form than the terrible play that boy wrote. If he'd got any closer to the truth I would have had to kill him too of course but he was way off the mark.' She waved the scalpel at him. 'I like to see the look on their faces when they realize it's me. Harmless Beverley, the overweight spinster. Homely, they used to call women like me. I hate attractive women. I hate the pitying way they look at me.' She almost spat the words with venom.

'If you brought Melanie Hawkes and Judith Dodds here, how did you move them?' He was curious to know but he also needed to keep her talking.

'I knocked them out and brought them here in my little car. I used Mother's wheelchair to move them so it was easy really. Then Father and I conducted a few experiments in pain before we killed them and disposed of their bodies – running water confuses your scientific people and we used Father's idea of the flowers. That was rather fun.' The words made Joe shudder.

'It's over, Beverley. Let me have the weapon.'

Beverley lunged forward like a swordsman and made a slashing movement. Joe managed to dodge the blade but he knew that if he hadn't been so quick he might have joined Creeny on the floor. Beverley was between him and the door which stood open, allowing the sunlight to trickle in. Lydia was quite still now and he wondered what had been done to her. He could see small dark circles on her arms and he remembered the smell of cigarette smoke that had hit him when he'd first arrived down there. Beverley wasn't a smoker: she had used burning cigarettes to inflict pain. He had to stay alert to survive.

He heard a noise in the passageway and he looked at the doorway hoping that Emily had arrived with the back up. But when he saw who was standing there he was hit by a wave of despair.

Peter Brockmeister was only in his mid sixties, hardly an

old man, and now he had abandoned his retired clergyman role he looked strong and dangerous. Joe wondered in passing how he had become involved with Beverley's mother, the matron who must have been at least ten years his senior. They might have been kindred spirits . . . or she might have been convenient. It was unlikely he'd ever find out.

'What are you waiting for, Beverley? Just finish him.' He glanced at Lydia. 'We've got to go.'

As Beverley began to descend on Joe he instinctively put up his arms to defend himself. There were two of them now so the odds were against him. He felt something cold and hard pierce his flesh but it was a few moments before he experienced the pain and collapsed to the hard stone ground, grasping at the air.

Then he heard voices . . . and he wondered if they were angels.

THIRTY-THREE

Joe only stayed in hospital overnight. Unlike Patrick Creeny who was in there a fortnight. Lydia was suffering from burns and concussion but Joe knew she was lucky. A few more minutes and she would have been strangled like Melanie Hawkes and Mrs Dodds, only to be discovered in some river or stream, gagged with flowers. The thought made Joe feel sick.

Beverley had been disarmed by a six-foot constable from the Armed Response Unit and now she was in custody, awaiting trial, along with her father, who had yielded quietly. The press would be in a frenzy when the case came to court. A serial killer resurrected from the dead and his mad daughter. It would make an irresistible story.

Lydia was determined to sell her flat. The market, she told Joe optimistically, was picking up and she couldn't face returning to Boothgate House. She was staying with Amy in the interim, her boyfriend, Steve, being a thing of the past. In the first flush of relief at her survival, Joe had suggested that she move in with him but she'd said no. It wouldn't be wise. She was bad luck, she said. Cursed. He'd felt as if a burden had been lifted when she'd refused his invitation . . . then he'd felt guilty about his relief. He couldn't win. Emily kept asking after her but he hadn't felt inclined to feed his boss's insatiable curiosity. There were times when he liked to keep his private life to himself.

Joe had arranged to meet Lydia for a drink that evening. As he walked to meet her at the Star he had a feeling of reluctance, like a schoolboy dragging his feet towards a dreaded exam. And when he saw her sitting there in the corner waiting for him, sipping at her beer, she looked serious. But then he hadn't seen her smile since that night down in that basement . . . as if she now regarded the world as a hostile place with no chance of any future joy.

'How are you?' he asked, aware that he asked the same question every time he saw her. But he couldn't think of anything more original.

She didn't answer.

'Want another drink?'

'No thanks.'

'Something the matter?'

She shook her head and he waited for her to speak. 'I've got something to tell you, Joe.'

'What's that?'

'I don't think it's working between us.'

'Maybe it all happened too quickly. We were both lonely and . . .'

She put a finger on his lips. 'I like you, Joe. I hope . . . well, I hope you find what you're looking for.'

'Whatever that is.' He felt lighter, hopeful for the first time in ages. He hadn't wanted to hurt her – he knew pain only too well. But now she'd handed him the perfect get out.

'I saw Seb Bentham the other day . . . the playwright. He, er . . . asked me out for a drink.'

Joe's first feeling of relief was replaced by a pang of jealousy. But he told himself it was probably hurt pride.

'I went to his shop because of that clock,' she continued. 'I want to buy it.'

'Why?'

'I thought if I lived with it every day it would lose its power. Can you understand that?'

Joe didn't know whether he could. He said nothing.

'Seb said I could have it for nothing because he can't stand looking at it. His uncle passed away last week, you know. He left Seb his house and he's moving in there.'

'But that clock belonged to Dr Pennell . . .'

'I'm not superstitious.' She looked away, as though the memory was painful. 'When I was down in that basement I remembered why the thing scared me so much.'

Joe waited for her to continue. Her gaze was focused on a hunting print to her left, as though she didn't dare make eye contact. When she eventually spoke, it was in a whisper, as if the very words hurt her.

'When I was staying with my grandfather I woke up and started wandering round. I must have only been tiny at the time – probably as young as three – and I got lost. Somehow I must have found my way down to the basement and I saw things down there, Joe. Terrible things I didn't understand. The whole cellar was one room in those days – the wall must have been blocked up later. I saw somebody strapped to a bed and she was screaming and some people were bending over her. Then a man saw me – it must have been Brockmeister. He took me by the hand and led me back to grandad's flat. I remember grandad coming out into the hall. I remember the terrified look on his face. He grabbed me and pushed me behind him as if he was afraid the man might harm me. He was defending me, Joe. If it hadn't been for him I might not have survived. And that clock was watching me. It used to stand in the hallway of the flat.'

Joe saw tears appear in her eyes. 'The man bent down and whispered in my ear. He said that if I told anybody what I'd seen he'd come for me. But if I'd told my grandad what I'd seen he might have alerted the authorities and all those people wouldn't have died. And Grandad might not have died. I could have stopped them, Joe.'

He gave her hand a comforting squeeze. 'You were a small child. How could you have known? And who would have believed you?'

She shook her head as though his words didn't convince her. In her mind she was still guilty of a sin of omission. Young as she'd been, she should have told. She should have ended the terror.

'I'm sorry,' she said.

She stood up and he watched her weave her way through the crowds of tourists and regulars, making for the door.

And he felt unexpectedly empty.

THIRTY-FOUR

Jack Hawkes had put the house he'd shared with Melanie up for sale. He had no firm plans, except to take life as it came. And since Paul Scorer and his partner had gained custody of Daisy things were much easier.

Scorer had been given a suspended sentence and had convinced the authorities that Daisy would be better off with her natural father. Scorer's sincerity and obvious love for his daughter had seemed to work wonders, but perhaps it had been Jack's casual indifference to Daisy in front of the social workers that had clinched it. The child had clung to Scorer and Una during the meetings, not even making eye contact with Jack. Kids were unpredictable, but Daisy's behaviour couldn't have fitted in with his plans better even if he'd bribed her with sweets and coached her for hours.

He'd negotiated with Patrick, who seemed to have developed a more generous streak since his close encounter with death, and landed himself one of the new phase of flats in Boothgate House. First floor. Four large bedrooms, all en suite. Spacious lounge, study and huge kitchen as well as a private roof terrace. He was a single man again so things had worked out rather well really.

Joe looked up from his paperwork and saw that Emily was watching him through the open door of her office. Ever since the arrest of Peter Brockmeister and his daughter she'd been subdued, as though she hadn't been entirely satisfied with the outcome, which was unusual as she was normally the first to suggest a celebration after such a major case was concluded. But there'd been no trip to the pub in high spirits. She'd just gone home to her family.

He caught her eye and she stood up. 'Joe, can I have a word?'

He walked into her office and shut the door. Her face was

serious and something told him that what she had to say was for his ears only. Since Brockmeister and Beverley had been remanded in custody they'd not had much chance to talk about anything other than work and the preparations for the trial. Joe found he missed their conversations more than he expected.

'I heard about you and Lydia,' she said as he sat down. 'I'm sorry.'

Joe shrugged. 'These things happen.'

Emily gave him a sympathetic look, as though she thought he was only making light of the situation to convince others – and maybe himself – that he didn't care.

'The big news is they've just found Rattenbury's body,' she said. 'Exactly where Beverley said it was, in the graveyard by Boothgate House.'

'Where else would you find a body?' Joe said with a smile.

'We also found another corpse that shouldn't have been there – buried with her handbag so identification was easy. Her name was Jean Smith and she was reported missing in 1979. She was a nurse at Havenby Hall.'

'Betty Morcroft mentioned her. From what she said, it's my guess that Jean knew too much. But I really wanted to talk to you about Jack Hawkes. You still think he was involved in his wife's death?'

'We searched his house for evidence but there was nothing there. Our only hope is if Brockmeister or Beverley says something at the trial . . . but I wouldn't bet on that. Of course there was Creeny's evidence that he gave him thirty thousand pounds when Scorer was only demanding ten. Hawkes said it was for his children from his first marriage – paying for a holiday – but his ex was pretty cagey. Twenty thousand pounds. And Melanie was insured for a quarter of a million. Trouble is, can we prove anything?'

'Twenty grand in cash was paid into an account in the name of the Rev Kenneth Rattenbury soon after Creeny gave him the money but there's no paper trail to connect it with Hawkes. We know it's him but unless we have solid proof . . .'

'We've done our best. So unless something new comes to light or Brockmeister decides to talk . . . He can't benefit from any blackmail money where he's going anyway.' Emily looked at her watch. 'Why don't you get home, Joe?'

Joe returned to his desk and sat down. At that moment he couldn't face returning to his empty, silent flat.

As the architect who'd designed the place, Jack Hawkes knew he had the best flat in the building. And since he'd moved in, Boothgate House was filling up nicely now that the work was on track again. He'd managed to pump more money into the project and everything was going well. There was even a chance that Creeny's PA, Yolanda, would move in with him. Patrick Creeny had called him a lucky dog – he'd always suspected that he'd fancied Yolanda himself but had never had the courage to do anything about it – and it certainly seemed that his fortunes were on the rise.

Yolanda was away this weekend at a health spa – a friend's hen do – so he was on his own. After a few scotches, drunk from the new lead crystal glasses he'd bought when he moved in, he decided to have an early night. He had watched a film that evening rather than listening to the news which was all about the trial of Peter Brockmeister and his crazy daughter. He wanted to forget all about Brockmeister. He'd soon be put away for life and he'd never have to think of him again.

The scotch had taken effect as he climbed into the cool Egyptian cotton sheets and switched off the bedside light. Then, just as he began to drift off into a vague and satisfied oblivion, something brought him back to consciousness; a sudden chill, as though some unseen hand had seized the bedclothes and tugged them with some force off his sleeping body. But he could feel that the duvet was still in place. He had probably drunk too much, he thought. The effects of alcohol were often unpredictable these days. He was no longer a young man who could sink a couple of bottles of wine with no ill effects.

He opened his eyes slowly and saw the woman standing there. She looked middle aged but she might have been younger, with brown bedraggled hair liberally peppered with grey. Her flesh was as white as the long nightdress she wore and her eyes were sunken pools of darkness. There were marks on her exposed pallid arms, little dots of redness, and what looked like blood crusted around her lips. He caught his breath and his heart began to pound.

He tried to say something, to ask what the hell she was doing there and how she got in, but no words came. As he watched her he realized that he knew her. He had seen pictures of his mother, even though his father's second wife had tried to destroy them all. And now she was here . . . accusing him.

She lifted one emaciated arm to point in his direction and he closed his eyes tight, trying to block out the unbearable. And when he opened them again, she had vanished.

He wasn't normally prone to bad dreams and he was surprised at how much it had shaken him. But he knew that in the morning the terror would have vanished like dew.

He fell into a fitful sleep but the nightmare didn't return. Then at dawn he was awoken by a loud hammering on the door. It took him a few moments to come round and in his confusion he thought he saw the figure of his nightmare again, standing in a far, shadowy corner of his room, with a smirk on her bloody lips. But when he looked again he saw nothing. His mind was playing tricks.

He stumbled out of bed, pulling on his dressing gown, and when he opened the door he found DCI Thwaite and DI Plantagenet standing there. He could see a couple of uniformed constables behind them. And he knew what they'd come for.

'Peter Brockmeister called in his lawyer last night. He said he tried to contact your late father but he ended up speaking to you. Said you'd built up quite a relationship. He's decided to make another statement concerning the death of your wife, Melanie,' Plantagenet said before reciting the words of the formal caution.

Jack Hawkes bowed his head. His fortunes had suddenly dived.